GHOST
AT THE
LOOM

MP PUBLISHING
12 Strathallan Crescent, Douglas, Isle of Man
IM2 4NR, British Isles
mppublishingusa.com

Printed in the United States
First Trade Paperback Original Edition

Publisher's Cataloging-in-Publication data

Cotler, T. Zachary, 1981-
     Ghost at the Loom / T. Zachary Cotler.
     p. cm.
     ISBN 978-1-84982-245-9

1. Brothers and sisters ~Fiction. 2. Epistolary fiction. 3. Dysfunctional
families ~Fiction. 4. California ~Fiction. 5. Rome ~Fiction. 6. Travel
~Fiction. 7. Poets~Fiction. I. Title.

PS3603.O86833 G46 2013
815.6 ~dc23

ISBN: 9781849822459
10 9 8 7 6 5 4 3 2 1

For my sister

Also by T. Zachary Cotler

House with a Dark Sky Roof

Sonnets to the Humans

GHOST
AT THE
LOOM

a novel by

T. Zachary Cotler

Leya,

I walked today in hemlock
woods, following

a creek. Some books
with me, some work

to do. Books you would like,
I think. I found a ruin

of a homestead. The cottage had
a waterwheel, broken, and

a window broken. I began
a longer letter there. Instead,

I sent you this.

—your brother in New York, Oct. 1999

Leya,

This isn't a letter I finish and send. It's more like you're watching me write, but watching from someplace far removed. Just take with you the parts you understand, the truer letter in the letter. Maybe the rest can be, at least, a "defense of poetry."

For you to understand, my words must be enough like you, removed, the tip of my pen like the pinhole in a camera obscura, with what I might too painfully tell you (if you were a standard-hearted woman, if your blood were red) forever outside the box.

In October, I walked in a national park, wrote you a few lines you maybe received, rode back to Manhattan. I'd been calling Mama once a month, calling drunk, so she made sense. She never tried to put you on the phone. She rarely mentioned you. I rarely drink. I was near to believing you gone—not dead, just somehow simply gone.

But I would think of you at some point in most hours: often standing by a window in your birth-black hair not cut since birth, never older than eight, quite still, but charged with weird potential, posed, as if to have your picture taken or be taken yourself, away from me.

A book of my poems had been recently published. Whenever I wanted a hundred dollars, I played my Pakistani drums all day in a subway station. I kept my eyes closed. John paid my rent: a room with a sliver of view of that un-American diaphaneity, Saint Patrick's Cathedral, built of pigeon bones.

If I tell you about John Minus, you must listen only to what I say back to him. He's as far from you as anyone is in a world too untidy for binary opposites. I wouldn't write his side at all, except he asks me to, or makes me. Some of his opinions have become my own. Or some of my long-held opinions now seem reconfigured in his idiom. Is he so much more intelligent than I?

I BECAME AWARE OF MINUS at a lecture at an uptown university, a lecture I'd been tricked into attending titled "Literature is the Question." A man jerked up from his seat, twirled two fingers in a gesture of dismissal, and exited the theatre. He was not-quite-lurking just outside the foyer when the lecture ended. He had an immense and imperative nose.

"I've got the fuck-it sensibility," he said where I was briefly employed. "What are you doing?"

"Tending bar."

He raised his cup and dripped his coffee on that bar. "If you ever write about me, don't tell them how I 'take my coffee,' you know. It's a kneejerk hack habit that characterizes nothing."

"I'm Anxiety incarnate," he said where I was living. "I'm going to write about Israel. It's fucked up largely. Two perspectives, two main characters, an old Jew-American tourist and a Palestinian shit urchin. He's fifteen, you learn to love the kid, you really feel it in your hernia, the brainwashing on both sides, the reward systems. I'll fleece a Qur—" he breathes "—an, read it, read it, get it, sell it on the Internet. In the end you really *identify* with the little fundamental plagueratfuck because he's in love with a Sephardic girl, can you feel that? Because he feels the things you do, I mean, not *you* do, but, you know, he likes puppies, nipples, nibbly chocolates, honey almond cakes; he's got a cummerbund of dynamite, he bombs something, a bistro, a station, the old Jew's there, and they both die. What a story."

"Go to Israel."

He grinned or grimaced. He kicked off one of his flip-flops. It left a fuck-it footprint on my wall. We hunched, side by side, on the edge of my bed, regarding this development.

"We're living in a time of great turmoil. At least...I am." He nodded at my desk. "You?"

"Poems, lines, notes, what happens, nothing with a bomb."

"What happens?"

I tried to be mime still.

"You're dull, a dullard. Disagree?" He produced a bent sandwich from a jacket pocket. "It's time for your lesson on *la condition humaine*. Not your self-pity—I mean the moral, mortal, intestinal story."

"I know about conditions."

Minus nodded. "But you aren't fascinating me."

He nipped a scrap of hanging ham. Even if he acted out a careful plan, he felt that he was improvising. I, too, felt he was. From his backpack, he removed a bottle of Bordeaux, positioning it on my table. He adjusted it.

Ghost at the Loom

He moved his head next to my head, then tapped the bottle sideways—"What am I doing? What am I compassionately doing for you now?"—so that, of the label's large letters, only "eau" was visible from where I sat.

I reached and touched his hair.

"The Miracle at Cana in reverse!" he squealed. "In French!"

"Are you balding, what's this?"

"Widow's peak." He slapped my hand. "Widow's peak, idiot. Look at yourself."

"I think you need one of these vitamins...that I have somewhere."

"Look at *you*, you flapper!"

"Someone left vitamins here." I reached again.

He slapped my hand. "What kind of rabbithole pellety food did your mother feed you when you were tiny? Mine sent me to *Hebrew* school!"

"Yes, I know."

"Take me, for example, me. It's not my effortless ideas, it's me, my *personality* that's too derivative. The old love generation keeps professing so behind my back, and they might be on to me." There was dribble on his chin, but this in no way marred his essential dignity. "The only difference between us and them is that we've got an even fouler mess down here, with all their sewage in the pot as well. And they had better drugs. But they aren't *on* to me. The over-forty-fives are unaware our type still in America *exists*. We're hydrocarbon hyperboreans.

We don't type with one finger our diaries onto the Internet. We aren't geneticists or programmers. We aren't the pagans for whom Hollywood is Olympus. We talk whole sentences, whoa. The state this country's education's in, with China swooping in, breathing fire, my civic duty's to be holy-fucking erudite—if I'm the last of the uncompromisers, last of what was strong about this country—and the Chinese *love it* that we're too concerned about elitism to seriously educate our portly babes. I mean, you're educated, too, though not to the degree I am."

"That's true," I said.

"Too many proper nouns are floating near the surface. Floaters. I found myself yelling 'Too late!' while abusing myself at my desk last night. I've got Churchill's radio broadcasts invading the fantasies I try about this sort of dark psychotic queen figure I've...wait—"

He held both index fingers up a foot apart, seeing me between them.

"You can't see? He's saying—why do you—Church says to John, 'Sir John, it's absolutely true that talking sentences, admitting that you masturbate, et cetera, these are among the most lamentable crimes in the human catalogue, but then aren't you, sir, your paltry generation's covert answer to what those leftists had in Paris in the 1920s? Yet you love lucre. What is your aim?!' demanded Church. 'Escape,' I said. So help me or yourself to my predicament. Escape, you inverse cowboy. You, I'm saying this to you, Mr. Sonnenreich, Mr. Sonnenreich."

Ghost at the Loom

If not profound, at least this typified the misery and generosity of Minus in his great struggle to enchant himself and anyone else he deemed cosmopolite and/or liable to sleep with him. During his soliloquy, he had launched off the bed to vigorously move about the room.

I said, "You'd like to be famous. I would not."

He considered this, bit, chewed, and carefully placed his sandwich on my desk.

"But what I hate is *inspiration*, bad breath. Dance!" He shimmied, mocking Cupid, loosing phantom arrows at me, at his sandwich, out the glass balcony doors into the banks and residential towers.

But beyond the sensibility, written on each of his arrowshafts was the mythical taxon *John Minus*, in which I did believe, though he believed so fervently in nothing that the nothing shifted somethingward to please him. He did not believe in nihilism. I reached again, and he let me touch his head, which was hot, full of entropy, reorganization, new entropy, salts, dark gaps.

He remains for me, a sign in the road:

> *Dear friend, don't*
> *watch me closely.*

O NE NIGHT, I CAME up from underground with my drums and pockets full of coins and bills and rode the elevator to my room, and my emails were these:

Rider,

Your mother's upset about L again. I thought we were all past this a long time ago, but as always with your mother, I am wrong. I don't see her of course, I keep an eye on her, mostly for your sake.

Eli Sonnenreich
1648 Octavia St.
San Francisco, CA
94109
www.sonnenreichtech.com

Jesus, did you email my lawyer? I can get you into the Fraternity of New England Sons of State Senators, FNESSS, if you would just behave yourself, just wear a linen shirt and make some jokes about your old bad habits. Don't be glum.

In hoc signo vinces,
Sir John "Prester" M.

You should know that things became a problem here but don't worry about Eyeball she is fine but Leya's gone. I think that you'll take care of this if I don't have the energy. Leya's more important than my projects and they are not coming in a good way right now. Can you tell Leya to come back.

Love, Mama

Eyeball has some trouble with her eyes. Someday please come home, you too.

———————————————

I set up a few things in the back garden to hold flowers. You didn't call so I will tell you if you aren't in southern Europe Rider when I find out where she is it is too late. She told me she's in southern Europe. She wants me to tell you and no one else. I know you are busy with new york things, but if you aren't in southern Europe I think you know something very bad would happen. Do you have some money? Because if you don't find her as soon as we find where she is I think well there is a thing we can't fix. I want you not to worry. You can call the house phone tonight. Sometimes I imagine where everything is going, what it is called in its own language, but you see what I mean.

Love your Mama

———————————————

MAMA'S HOUSE IS A house you can exit? In my deadened, medicated state, I reread Mama's messages. I drummed my desk. A heartlike beat, then fives and sevens. In the streetlight through the window, the glass on a print on the wall reflected my weaving hands. That print (some anti-referential blear of brown) belonged to John. The sheets and blankets on the bed behind me also did.

This was no epiphanic moment in which the sensory poverty of my commonworld life was exposed. I did not reel. Music was on; it did shoot the mood through with elegiac color, but even when I'm folding pants or washing out a cup, whatever's playing in my room is tintinnabulist and minor key. My poverty I comprehended utterly and had for years, since the night or day I lost the glimmer and you.

You understand? I lack a better term than "glimmer." What else could I mean? We didn't call it anything.

For Mama to write to me about you was uncommon. For you to have left home at all imbued me with a fine disjointedness, a fives and sevens emotion. For you to be in "southern Europe" was too many sigmas out on the curve.

Who—how old—were you? Seven? Twenty-five? Who but you could know the kind of clarity-within-irrationality I craved? Maybe there are people, many long dead and a few alive, remote in houses full of books, clandestine children in adult lives, maybe this letter could be as much to them as to you, but I only knew you, or had known, years ago.

I drank some rum and spoke to Mama for an hour. She said nothing more or less than what she'd written. I

Ghost at the Loom

had never thought to look for you or anything at home: Mama's house, the glimmer having died in me in it, had been, in a sense, anti-consecrated, zoned as a site of loss. That you could be in Europe (I perceived and rapidly put out of mind the possibility that Mama was mistaken, lying to me, to herself) meant I might find you in an untainted place, a place alien yet therefore intimate with us, and because I was foolish, nostalgic, not just for Horse Hill and you, but foolish in a way I did not understand was potently American, I thought I'd heard a quiet call, a knight errant's summons. I thought, if America bombs me with noise, maybe Europe, Rome, the silence of statues, whatever is left of the broken sublime, bring no medication, wait until a mind in me arrives with which I am admissible to where you are.

A brown mood, calm. I'd been ready for years. I had tried to maturely exist in the commonworld. Bombs were falling somewhere. The commonworld is full of pain, but in America, it hurt me how unhurt the humans seemed. Lack of sense of the brutality implicit in the images and slogans hurt my head and ears. Even children, on the subways singing pop songs softly to themselves—a fury focused me on them, then an ache to protect them; their parents had failed. In a daydream, I pied-piped the children after me, away into the hills.

I called John Minus. "What are you doing?"

"Ice cream. High yolk content."

"Will you do something for me?"

"Would you like to come over?"

"Maybe——"

"When I want it, ice cream, I put on my sweatshop sweatshirt and I jog down to the cream shop. On my way, I pass my friend Alí Araque, who sells nuts, you know, and looks not unentirely like your girlfriend. He's there selling nuts, and I exchange a greeting with him, because, you know, I'm a fellow man, I'm just like him, except on my way to the cream shop. Jesus, I could have friends who are farmers. Araque looks a bit like me as well."

"I'd like to go to Rome."

"Exactly. You're just like my aunt, except there is this physical audaciousness to her. She's aging into, more and more, a kind of Roman——Agrippina, civil you know, civil twilight, murderous."

"Or Southern France or Athens."

"You have never met my aunt. She wouldn't tolerate your bleak self-centeredness. She'd want you to ask me to tell you more about her."

"I would like to go to Athens."

"Jesus was from Athens." I could hear him opening a can. "South France is Paro's bailiwick, or else you call our social-network-savvy comrade Willy T. He thinks you're 'really interesting.' Doesn't say so, but he likes your tan. He's——what is he? Handholding, a backpatting——a kind of Providence-nosed, angelfood-faced fuck. Everyone he meets he compliments, especially idiots. Cake. It's whore."

"It's whore?"

"It's whore."

Ghost at the Loom

"I don't want to be whore. You ask him for me."

"You ask Paro first. I know only quant fund guys
in Europe, and you shouldn't travel by yourself, and
Europe's gotten old, you know, old, and fuck airplanes!
We can take my father's boat. You've never been alone
with a Minus mid-Pacific. There's a France-sized sargasso
of pulverized—of particles of garbage out there.
Nowadays, garbage is everybody."

In Manhattan, I felt not disdain or alarm but awe.
Around each woman or man on the sidewalks, I nearly
visually perceived an aura of complex power, of rapid
transaction and consequent faraway violence. Awe at
these bodies in fine clothes, these bipedal neurons of a
Mind so densely interlaced it must become, with a few
more connections, something not unlike a god.

I walked through this to Paro's loft and told her I'd
be exiting the country. She was unconcerned or acting
so. "Before men invented laws," she said (or not exactly,
but she said things like this frequently), "it *was* men—
women wanted men who hunted lots of meat," implying
she was whimsical or maybe decadent to sleep with me.
Hazardous guesses. What do I understand about Paro?
Why is she in my letter to you?

She represents my difficulty with all women
who aren't you. Anything unfeeling or cynical I say
about her is your faultless fault. You are no easier,
but touching you, the difficulty moves beyond my
power to describe, its point of exit something like

a humming, too reticulated, braided-strands-of-difficulty sense, whereas with Paro, women in the commonworld, one can explain my disconnection simply, one is pressured to: I am, in commonworldly terms, disturbed, and this must have something to do with my mother.

Paro and I talked about music for about thirty seconds. I put on some eerie, tape-looped jazz.

On her balcony, she took a lighter and a small joint from her purse. "Do this with me."

"No." It makes me witless, colorless. "You, if you want." I hoped she would not.

The CD scratched and restarted. "Do this with me."

"You don't want me to," I said.

"No, I encourage you to go." Her accent was from Jaipur through Los Angeles. She didn't use contractions. "Sravanthi, you know her father died last year."

"Do I know that?"

"Yes. I have to sneeze." She waited and did not sneeze. "I told you he owned weird cheap houses, some in India, in Europe, little towns. He was not nice."

"Not nice," I said.

"I can ask her to let you stay in one. I might join you at some point. She is far too busy to begin the chore of selling all of them. It will take years. There was a house in Germany, one in the Balkans somewhere."

"No need. I have something."

Paro laughed. "Are you lying?"

"No."

"Floppy socks." She laughed again, this time with venom in it, one part in a thousand, still—"Are you not cold? Your sock toe has a hole in it."

"I just don't feel like laughing at myself. Little children don't mock themselves."

"Oh no? Well...well, you are just a giant head. You go around bonking into things." She laughed at this discovery.

She was revolting, lovely, someone's daughter, someone many loved. I touched her hip and visualized the bone there: bone, then polished wood under skin, then aluminum, plastic. I imagined, for a few seconds, a metallic plastic pelvis scribbled with numbers and signatures, until she flicked the remnant firefly of her joint into the dark.

"I have to sneeze." She did.

Maybe last year, maybe this one, I told her there was something snakelike to her face. Her eyes would thin to white slits when we kissed and mine stay open. She had come into a bar I tended.

A thin gold cobra locket with a crystal head half full of mercury. She dangled it near my chest.

I began to mix her a cocktail with a plastic umbrella. "That's a Paro-snake?"

"I bought it for you yesterday," she said.

Roaring, silent noise, a kind of anti-Leya, common as the noise of cars in the city, poured off this purple umbrella, the top of which told me the name of a vodka company. I said, "I think I don't want any jewelry."

"Oh my god, you frustrate people, not me, but you do."

"If you want to buy me something, why not—"

"Wear it. Wear it." She was giggling now.

I understood she was, in the commonworld, a serious person, and I was not. Her narrow body was, in the light through a wall of bottles, a sly bribe, which I accepted and returned—at least, I felt she also felt it (something strong, a reproductive urge? anyway, not courtly love), not as thinking words, but a two-way rhythm, a pattern of cobra-as-pendulum, breathing, and pupils dilating and shrinking with eye contact and looking away. In this guesswork, half second by half second, a sense of being made as if of chessboard blocks of corrupted and honest glass, of balanced yes and no.

This was in winter. A fixation had been with me for a few weeks. Thin ice over dark material. Ice like the skin of a glass being. I'd be walking and encounter it, a sudden patch on the sidewalk, a high-up hint of it on Saint Patrick's bones. This ice did not reflect like other ice—not my face, the city towers, or even the violent video light of a sci-fi-themed ad on the building opposite mine.

◇◇◇◇◇◇◇◇◇◇◇◇◇

O N THE PLANE, I am writing to you:
In the yard, on a branch of the dogwood we called
No No Name, there was a good stick, which I got. I
didn't climb the dogwood. Those are fragile trees.

Sticks of the right length and flex brought the
glimmer. I needed light, preferably from the sky, and
space enough to run when the glimmer got strong. You
didn't need me or a stick or light. You glimmered at will
(or in response to shocks from the commonworld—
that's what I call the one that does not glimmer, that
I'm in, a kind of postscript world, composed of money,
noise, and isolated shards of beauty) to be One'Bandy,
who looked after me. Sometimes you glimmered so hard
I had to shake you by the head to get you back.

My glimmers came from patterns in the air drawn
by the tips of sticks into a rhythm. It was architectless
architecture, arcade rhythms of the spaces tree to tree or
cloud to cloud. We spoke, and when words and patterns
twisted, our minds twisted together. Then we'd go out
on Horse Hill.

A barbed-wire fence stood between our yard and the
hill, and next to it, an old violin-colored tree called Bad
Worm, who was "good" in our cloudy moral system.

There were no houses on Horse Hill. Someone must have owned the horses, but we glimmered them wild.

You had gone to the kitchen for lemon juice. You liked to sip and squint. Soon, you would come through the yard door and be One'Bandy, indigo-skinned, with willowish limbs that caused strange changes: dust to light, or fingerprints on walls to hand-shaped windows, wind to wanderers who whispered where to go, then left. The story was, One'Bandy had lost two brothers in the Tug Foot Hills, which we believed to be beyond the hills beyond Horse Hill. Only Bandy'For, the tiny one, was left, and I was he.

I climbed the live oak Up Crow and slid along a branch until it bent, my ankles linked around it. Over yards and houses, I could see a small span of the commonworld. We did not go to school.

Reaching down to where the dogwood met the oak, I snapped the good stick off. You had returned, looking up at me dangling by an arm and two feet, the stick in my teeth. You held a plastic lemon in one hand, brown sugar in the other, licking with a small, sharp tongue, alternating juice and sugar.

"Me?" I said.

"You can," you lilted can, two notes, high-low, "have, if you want, but in the mirror, I forgot, which one she she?"

"Me?" I said. I was on the ground.

"First suck lemon, Rider'finder." You held out your palm.

Ghost at the Loom

Rider'finder, Rider'sneak, never just my name. I took the lemon, shot juice in my mouth and, without swallowing, licked your hand. In your other hand, you held out a sixteen-penny nail.

You spoke of the man who lived with Mama: "See, I took it from him. He is building he is building it looks like spiders." Around the corner of our home, the sound of sawteeth eating wood.

"What's that spot?" I said. A fleck of ruby paint was on the nail's head.

"A *seeing* spots."

"You painted it."

"You painted it?" Your lips had sugar on them.

"I *said* you're not supposed to take his thingitings." I knocked the nail into the needlegrass that looked like grain and covered the yard and hills and hooked in our clothes and couldn't be eaten. After Eyeball tried, she hacked up green-gold barbs and bits of rawhide bones.

"Good Eyeball...'s never mad, she's never bad. Bad dog? But sometimes scared, sometimes if——"

"Listen to *meee*." I softly stepped onto your toes. "A horse is not like Eyeball. They are mad."

No Eyeball on the hill was Mama's rule.

"She she...'s never sometimes," you explained.

You licked your hand and held my arm. I touched the good stick to your head. The colors in my vision's outer ring sharpened, and the ring thickened inward like an iris hit by light.

Bad Worm bent a many-elbowed arm above the barbed-wire fence. I have collapsed too many memories into this one, or else Mama, in her bedroom window, did wear the white dress this day, not the one she wore when she married our natural father. That had not been white. They signed papers at the city hall in Passaic, New Jersey. Mama's white dress came one night with Uncle Connor, who rolled cigarettes and dressed in clothes that looked like clothes in paintings in books, and Mama said he said it was someday for you.

Bad Worm dropped us at the foot of Horse Hill. You sucked your plastic lemon. With the good stick, I drew rapid, asymmetric lemniscates. Mama watched us running up the trail until we were a dot.

•

ONE'BANDY SNIFFED THE WIND, which carried dust and ash from Road, the land where bad crow-talkers and their families burned whole hills of piled pulled weeds. Crows land on scraps of paper wrapped around the talkers' wrists—One'Bandy leaned back in the cart that led her caravan and told her brother this. Dust blowing by caught bits of light, lightening the shadow of the cart.

One'Bandy's last brother rode at her side, holding reins to a yoke of cloth-and-metal dogs, which were only occasionally "bad" and then had to be fed batteries shaped like eggs, which they broke with their teeth. The Bandy carried crates of food from settlement to settlement, from these hills to the airport city, someday

to further cities with names like the hitting of drums—
this is what One'Bandy told old headless wanderers or
mentioned aloud if a spy crow perched nearby.

In truth, the Bandy were searching for threads. Two
threads, the hardest two to find, would lead them to...
her brother was too small to understand.

She put three fingers on his round, dark skull. "We
haven't heard the music since the question-trees. We
should have stayed and looked in sides."

The tiny one chewed a hook of question-root. "No
no. Dere be'd oddhead birds in doze trees," said he. "Dis
robber bird."

"We should have poked in every knothole."

"Me say back dis. Knothole not hole. Anklebite!"

"You are the tiny one."

He flailed the reins.

"You forgot," One'Bandy said, "to learn your
numbers, little toe. Here are your numbers: one, two,
two, two, two."

He shook his head. The cart pitched. Axles creaked.
The Bandy rolled from hill to hill. A pale green oasis
glistened into view at the convergence of three trails in
a valley. On the valley's far wall, under a lone cloud and
a swirl of vultures, stately, long-legged creatures stood,
scanning the land, or gnawing jets of weed.

•

HUNDREDS OF THESE SCRAPS drift out the windows in my
broken-open memory, the scraps I don't write down.

Do you remember them? We had one mental life. This
letter's my attempt to return my half of a life to you now,
at least to make my thoughts your thoughts again, as
nearly as words on paper can. If I had a letter like this
from you.

Horse Hill was not one but a line of hills, the end of
which I never found. The first three abutted the highway.
I went out alone once with a dogwood stick. There was
an electric tower on the sixteenth hill, and a tree named
Six Ten grew beneath it. Children died near power lines.
I had been told this, but I touched the metal. Eli (I think
you know he's our natural father) had taught me about
conduction. Sometimes he came and taught me things
like metals, math, and etymologies.

    I swung from Six Ten's shoulder to the tower's
lower crossbeams and began to climb, the weathered
metal delivering dozens of miniscule cuts to my hands. I
pulled my hands into my sleeves. I looked up into wires
and sky and sniffed the metal that had made me bleed.
We'd named the dogwood nameless, but that this tower
had no name was built out of its being foreign—it was
no tree, and you weren't with me. It was outside our
influence. Builders, men with gloves, had erected it here
as an indefinite warning.

    Then there was a diligence in me, to be higher than
trees, to be potent in a tall place that did not think,
look out across San Pablo Bay. Near the apex, webbed
in wires, for minutes with the feel and weight of hours, I

monitored the highway. It was dusk, and the cars made two threads, white and red, pulled against each other's way. If I had brought you there, and somehow got you to the top, you would have seen four threads of light.

Mama stopped reading aloud to us when you were four. She believed she had run out of books that would not hurt her children. You saw two of everything unless you closed your eyes. You closed your eyes in glimmers. When we ran, I held your hand.

The sound of hooves caused you to break the glimmer. As we came into the first valley, four horses crested the second hill.

Mares were safe. I fed them crabapples. The man who lived with Mama said stallions were mad because they weren't gelded. I had once ambushed Cloudy Leg, the huge white stallion. I hit him in the testicles with a crabapple.

"Don't listen," I said. Unsure of their sex, I pointed. "See, you see them, don't listen."

You had the warning look, like thin, tan cloth wrapped tight across your cheekbones. Sometimes, just before a seizure, you covered your mouth with your hand.

I tried to calm you with a glimmer. "Dis our dogs too quick," said Bandy'For or I between our teeth, but it had no face: we wondered if this shape to which we spoke was One'Bandy or an image we had miscreated in her image.

"Doze stick legs no ketch us," pleaded Bandy'For less so than I now. "Soon be hid in di ode koppur mine."

The glimmer fell away. Your breath skipped, and the sky was vulgar purple, colder with the sun behind the hills. I grabbed your wrist. "Quick us. Into di mine. Be safe dere."

We ran across the tiny valley, past a clawfoot tub of pale green horsewater, to the Copper Mine, a five-foot diameter metal tube that jutted from the needlegrass, a storm sewer entry with a dirt trail cut into the hill above it. We had hidden here before. Inside, there was a mound of crushed cement and mica-speckled earth we'd glimmered into copper ore.

You ducked when I tried to hold your head. You covered your ears—you're six or seven, beakish nose like no relative's, tips of your crowfeather hair on the dirt and your rubber sandals—squatting on a solid landslide, rocking and ready to exit Earth. I scrambled from the inner mound back to the tube's lip. Two horses galloped down the grade toward us, outdistancing a dog. It wasn't Eyeball and it yipped once on the hilltop, ran a few more yards, then sat.

I pulled you to the lip and hugged your arms and back. You had shut off your senses. In these solo semi-seizures you had no eyes, ears, or voice. Over your shoulder, framed in the circular view of the valley still visible, the plastic lemon shone in the weeds, a lost yellow gem. The sound, as horses crossed the trail above the mine, was semi-rhythmic and industrial.

There's never been a time I couldn't carry you, but at the fence, I couldn't climb Bad Worm without my arms, so

I laid you gently in the weeds on the Horse Hill side and went across to get the man who lived with Mama.

He had Eyeball on her back. He rubbed her belly and told her over and over that she was good. He returned to his work. I came out from behind the corner of the house and spoke. Carefully putting down a foam wedge dipped in varnish for a table he had built, he followed silently, and I kept looking back. He twitched his beard.

"You left her in the dirt."

I'd laid you with your head propped up, but you must have convulsed while I was in the yard because now you were face down, with blood and sugar on your mouth. I jumped and grabbed the climbing limb, and the back of my shirt bunched in his hand. My palms and fingers ripped. I was on my back, windknocked near his carpenter's boots. A woodenness formed in my airless back, behind the slow, decaying-out-of-world remainder of a Bandy heart in me. I was again then, briefly, smaller than you, as I'd been on the hill, and the wood expanded—now it was a small tree exiting my back, rooting in the ground, ripping free as I rolled to my stomach, the branches strained by a cluster of greenish, coppery, droplet-shaped fruit.

He was not vivid, not an enemy exactly. It was wrong, his massive body climbing Bad Worm.

You slept until midnight, then woke and sang to yourself, while I read with a flashlight in my room, and the song, through the vent between our walls, though the notes of it are missing, slant-symmetrically fits in my memory as music from the question-trees.

One night, you had a seizure of unprecedented magnitude. Mama doesn't go to doctors. Eli got you doctors, and they diagnosed you variously and confidently. Two agreed on one thing, my memory of which seems suspect now: some overstimulation of the optic nerve or blocking or unblocking of a vessel had been triggered in the seizure, undoing your double vision.

I'd not glimmered in nine years when I left California. It's been nine more since. These are all things you should know if you don't.

I asked Mama, maybe a year ago, on the phone: what does she do, how does she look? You play piano with eight fingers and your thumbs point up, Mama said. Hair to your waist, blacker, eyes now not green, gone gold somewhere in your late teens. Mama says it is her life to guard you.

IN ROME, I SLEPT alone three nights in a two-room
hotel with some woman's permanent footprint in the
shower. I took notes, followed strangers. Schoolchildren
ran away from me. I stalked a pack of prepubescent
gypsies stalking tourists near the trains. They knocked
a woman's glasses off and rifled her pockets. She cursed
them in Hebrew, then Italian. I met nobody and soon
craved northern, pointed, English sounds: *compass
needles, frost.*

Twice, I pulled from my wallet a card Will Trelidori
had given me and put it back without calling. I mentioned
him, or John did...not important. I had thought to exit
my generation for a while.

Writing in this little mostly blank book: obelisks,
wires, and the shadows of both extending and cutting
up the Gothic moment, the Fascist split second, late
twentieth-century billboards, *contrapposti* in the haute
couture display windows, I leaning on a corner, imitating
the displays against my will, leaning on the wallstones
in *archaic sun*—red cracks, mosaic skin beneath the
shadows in the delicately shattered noise on walls and
on Italic and African faces foreshortened like faraway
houses atop human necks passing into and out of my late

shadow halfway down the block in this long handwriting of mine.

Your brother on foot on the Via Minerva, thinking *compass rose, archaic sun, mosaic Rome.* I bought a long bread and ate one end. Along the blocks of affluent decay, of sprezzatura. I hadn't sensed (or if I had, I had not known they were) directions toward you yet. There was, in the sun and wires and split seconds and stones, the suggestion that all Rome (even if it was not all at all, this thread-thin, waxing crescent Rome of my experience) suspected me of ardor, but that, in such cases, a city-in-mind must be careful not to encourage too strongly too soon. Or, to put it in epistolary terms, I idled at the place one writes: *What have I been doing? I don't really know. I miss you.*

I N THE PAST PRESENT, approaching a line of egg-shaped payphones at the Termini, I'm pulling a card from my wallet, the card of a poet I've never met, nor could I refer to her by name, one Irish syllable, so I rename her "Celt" out of lexical fetishism: easy to fixate on a sound like that, like an ax falling out of a hand onto stone. Lost peoples—Hittite, Karuk, Celt. Leya, I think you would like these words. Pelasgian, Urnfield, Scythian, Shang. I'll make a list for you, a gift for if I find you. You can use them in your songs, on your piano, if I bring you home.

"I like this place's wine," says Celt. "Occhi di lupo, wine, fish, penne, fixed menu."

Forgive me, I have to include her. She's going to give me some books, important books.

I say, "Fish, okay..." We'll meet at Largo Argentina, twenty-one o'clock.

It is the hour of cats. They sleep on slabs of stone and columns in the sunken ruins. Across the tram tracks to the west, she's in a black suit and a cloud of dyed red hair. I know her from a dust jacket photo. In the photo, she is younger. I am introducing myself to a woman in a dust jacket photo.

We're in the zigzag alleys. Diamond cobbles, patterned in arcs. Romans in denim colorfades of military green and amber. Many of the women feather their hair like yours naturally grows.

Celt points across a promenade. "That blue door? That's an expat watering hole. The younger courtiers go there. Heh! Don't go there. Go find a nice Italian girl to marry. You look like the actor from—"

I write what I and people say in the commonworld and try to make it not opaque to you, not too offensive, not too loud. I make us all a bit archaic in our diction, sacrificing slangs and slogans on your altar when I can.

"So courtier's a term for an expatriate?"

"What *has* Will told you?"

"Nothing," I say. "He told me you'd tell me what to do."

"So no agenda? None?"

"He said you'd tell me."

She laughs, a manly grunt with *heh* inside it, jerking her jaw to the right.

A half block later, she says, "Will sent me a copy of your book."

"I know."

"Well, I adore it. Do you mind me saying that?"

To properly respond or even look at her is hopeless. Possible replies attack each other like starved dogs.

Ghost at the Loom

"Are you embarrassed?"

"No," I say.

We're in a restaurant.

"Do you need a place to sleep?" Indifferently as if she's asked for salt or the time.

I'm nodding slowly at her. Without any means of measurement, of detailed comprehension, still, I feel I *feel* her sexual history as what, an abstract weight, velocity? Velocity of pouring wine, of writing with a dark pen, pausing, weighing this pause or me, pouring a little more. I scan her face and neck, the loose black suitcloth in search of breasts. I won't attempt to justify testosterone's effects on thoughts and actions of a man, not to you, if I am one.

I say, "Tonight?"

"A slew of nights, if you like."

"What is a courtier?"

"Who's Jan, you mean? He's Belgian, but he bought a little palace from the church, a little palace, very small. It belonged to a bishop who died. He's a person with money, but not like you're used to, not like when Americans are."

"So he 'holds court'?"

"No. He sponsors artists, mostly wishful tinkerers, that's what I call them."

"What kind of money am I used to?"

She's looking at a nearby table full of brightly dressed Italian men, engaged in what appears a humorously stimulating argument. "He's not Flamand, but very rich. His last name is Gigot."

"He sponsors you."

"Well, that's complex." She taps her plate's edge with the tiny tines of her prosciutto fork.

"Complex," I say, not as a question.

"I live in the palazzo with him, in my own rooms, my own rooms. It sounds perverse, but really, I have more dignity here than in the States."

"Sort of a belated commune?"

"Commune implies Marxy angles," winding meat around a melon cube. "Ours is a monarchy, benevolent, absolute, and divine. Heh!" She drinks her glass and pours us both another from a prism-shaped carafe. "Tell me about your long life."

Though it's difficult to listen to her speak, something compels me for a few weeks.

"I'm not done," I say as a man attempts to take my food.

Celt: "Of course, I'd rather die young, too."

"What?"

"Die young. Too late," finishing her glass. "Have you heard——" She mentions something banal and for sale.

"Sorry, no."

"Heh! Tell me more. Tell me your one great ambition. William says you're a strange fellow."

Probably I'm not supposed to understand her literally. Nevertheless, I warily attempt a Confession to a Stranger. "I wouldn't mind becoming sharper, crazy I

Ghost at the Loom

mean, not weak-minded crazy. Subtle disconnections,"
gesturing with my own tiny fork. "Redeemed?"

"Well, that's not strange, that's typical in younger
people, no?"

"No. I don't think so."

"Oh, I think it is."

I say, "Okay."

"Okay?"

"I don't know what to say."

"That's fine. So did you notice all the waiters here
are male. That's what goes on in Rome. That, and also
no one pays for bus or trams. Tram polizia get on, watch
everybody run. It's latent socialist mentality." She's
looking at a waiter. She selects a black vanilla cigarette
from a metal case she carries in her suit. "You have a
light?" as if we're in a poor film.

I frown—I tilt the long candle on our table.

Out of a taxi into the triangular Piazza dell'Oro, bounded
by a church ("Heh! That's a Borromini, if you couldn't
tell"), a one-way street, and a cracked residential façade
with one small door. Celt clicks across the cobbles to the
doorbell. I am looking at a scrape on my brown shoe.

This is the patron's palace? Cracking walls
compute—Romans accept the aesthetics of ruin—but
the windows don't, plain glass, dirty wood trim, not
windows of a grand ecclesiastical estate, because I've seen
one in a book of architecture in a library in America. I
tilt and shake my head as if to shake out water from my

ear. Maybe there has been a little water in my ear for several weeks.

Up stone stairs to a doorway and a man. "Xabier," says Celt. "This is Xabier. This is Rider. May he stay with you?"

Black-bearded, short and broad, in skintight Euro-garb, his squint bestows a sense of distance, not like squints from you—this one is calculated, not your unselfconscious isolation. Squints and stares from you were like searchlights not searching. One of my drunken minds flies to the hotel where I've left some books and clothes.

I say to Celt, "He lives with you?"

"I live in the palazzo."

He says something in Italian, then to me, "This is dell'Oro," then to Celt, "He doesn't speak it?"

"No," she says.

I've missed some data here. His accent is not Roman, not Italian.

"Doesn't what," I say, "Italian?" Yes, a little wine is in my ear. I shake my head. "Or do you mean the windows? I don't know how long I'll be in Rome."

He lowers one eyebrow at me and goes inside. I follow, and the hall curves faintly to the west, or I am drunker than I think. Red curtains hang in doorless archways. Painted mirrors on the walls: hyperbolic Kama Sutra diagrams, blue fire on surfaces of bowls of water, tasteless female figures eating fruit. Paintless areas add shards of my reflection. Art, I guess, can unintentionally insult the viewer by presuming to include him.

Ghost at the Loom

A commonroom with bedrooms to each side. The grandly named dell'Oro is no more than an apartment. My lower back—it aches if I walk far in a day. This Xabier leans at a table: snifters, papers, spilled cosmetics from a leather purse. He claps thick hands to the stereo's drum, guitar, and tambourine.

"She brought a guest. *Vai, vai,* dance to this," he says to a woman in jeans and black braids.

Another woman plucks, with matte black fingernails, quite long, a tooled guitar, just out of rhythm with the music. She's Romani, but not like in the streets and stations. I think she owns six kinds of salon shampoo and the purse on the table.

"*You* dance," says the one he's asked to dance, and she gets a remote from the table and turns on a soccer game on a small television on top of a crate marked FIORI in block letters, and this detail fixates me: there is something irreal, I can't quite say...

Celt: "This is Gigot's annex. They do lots of nothing every night. Do you like it?"

No—it's in her voice when she drip-drops "Gigot." She's close to him and can influence, possibly abuse, the lower castes. Because I can't afford hotel rooms, this will be my limbo until you tell Mama where you are. So be kind to me, maybe you don't know, but there are few games I am worse at than the courtly convivial ones played by adults: their actions and emotions seem not their own, my reactions to them not my own; they scream at me with closed mouths; if I were a little boy,

I'd squat in the corner and cover my ears.

By the room's one window, a knock-kneed blond man pours a glass of gin. I lean in from the hall. I'd like a glass of gin. The archway crowds my head. I attempt to convey with my height and stance a signal I don't wholly understand, something unthreatening, impervious, but more so something else, a white-blue mood full of presence and absence and hoping for silence; you understand this. Xabier is clapping. Only the gin man regards me. A nod and a mustachioed smile.

I would like to propose a metaphysical organ (if it has a size, no larger than a quarter of a cortex) called an image drum, inside and on the surface of which words are truly things, and "truly" is a word with uncontested meaning. Now in mine, my hand extends away from me, in California, offering a shred of turkey to Eyeball, who tensely sits and doesn't bark, because I trained her (you helped) when she was young with us, and now she's blind, and now we're called adults. Adults, but speechless animals remain for us less difficult to know than humans. In an image drum, the weather changes suddenly: a corpse of a white dog turns to an eye that sees in four or five dimensions, socketless, eye-white whipped by arterial lightning, sees lightning-forking histories of Earth from birth to burnout. But an image drum is not nearly a substitute for glimmering. I guess a child's dog lives at most as long as the child, then there's a dead dog and an adult.

"Annex," I repeat.

Ghost at the Loom

The one with the remote turns down the stereo. She has the deliberate face of a pretty ox. I like the shapes her lips make very much.

Xabier grips her hips. "It's the worst Spanish music, no? No?"

He tries to dance with her. She pushes him. The gypsy stands. *Thanks, thank you all for having your burlesque in English while I'm here tonight thanks that's hospitable.* The women cross trajectories. The gypsy takes a glass of gin off a moisture-ringed magazine on the table, drinks half, speaks to Xabier in strange, opaque Spanish, causing him to slap the air in front of her in a gesture I can't read, and then he takes the glass and finishes it.

"No," he says to her and rubs his eyes.

The knock-kneed man observes. The one with the remote is backing toward me.

"What accent is that?" I point my chin at Xabier.

Celt's mouth is very near my ear: "This little pig is Basque, and he's pretending that he's angry at his girlfriend."

One is called pretentious when one is pretending something. What am I pretending? But I can't think about that, because Celt's pointing at them, saying, "Xabier paints mirrors. Tahnee plays guitars. She's from Romania. And this one is Garcia, that's her mother's surname, and what one is awkwardly encouraged to refer to her as. This is Victor Sperry, who flunked out of the London School of Economics just to waste his time at court. Heh," jabbing her cigarette too near my face, "and Rider's from New York."

Xabier says something loud, in Basque I think. The

gypsy, too, pretends she's angry, dropping at his feet her empty glass, which does not break. He makes a rude or maybe appealing gesture involving his pelvis, she backs toward Celt, and I step entirely into the room.

"Oh, hello," says the gin man, whose legs are now straight.

The rest of this night repeats in permutations of the pattern I have just described. Tell me where you are if you don't want to hear about courtiers.

TUESDAY MORNING OF MY second week at dell'Oro. Celt picks me up in taxis. Trouts, steaks, pastas, vodkas, wines. Her appetite's extraordinary.

No information yet from you or Mama. Though my sleeping pad is in the commonroom, I try not to be often seen. Even if they all live free and were invited and arrived as I did, I am last and so an interloper here. An altercation will occur, if not tomorrow, soon.

The vaguely human-face-shaped intercom box chirps. Garcia passes me a glass of water and a shot of sugared tea. She pats my head. Invisibly, involuntarily, I shrink, despite her torpid prettiness. Garcia, Sperry, Xabier: it pains me every time I write the name of anyone for whom you mean nothing, nor could ever, into this letter— interlopers crossing, tangling my approach—to you.

"You could have come down when I yelled." Celt's head, above a bulky grocery bag: "I saw your long back in the window." Sweat gleams on her upper lip. "I brought your food."

She drops the bag, which spills hardbacks, onto my sleeping pad.

"There are some Shelleys, Byron, Keats, the best biographies, Trelawny. Percy Shelley was a feminist, then drowned, as you may have read in some undergraduate bombshelter," and she continues, but I can't put what she's saying in this letter, until: "then Mary saved his heart, the organ, you didn't know that, in a jar, with some of his poems, in a drawer."

I say, "Thanks."

"Don't be standoffish. Kiss my feet."

I go and stand over the books.

"Well," she says, "I thought about you last night. My conclusion," pointing sagely-bossily, Jewishly almost, at the books, "is that you share the good intentions of these men, and yes, I know you have already, but *read* these before you're presented at court?"

Not to be rude but fuck your court... "Okay."

"Shelley, Byron, Keats. Three men in a tub. I can't eat out with you tonight."

Tahnee shouts from the hall. "Make eggs with us."

Cuckoo. I'm a cuckoo's egg. "Come in here," I tell Tahnee.

"Minute!" she shouts from the bathroom.

Celt: "You will *read* these?"

"I've read them. Yes, I will."

It isn't that I'm lying, but it's difficult: I've read them, Shelley, Byron, Keats, at least, I feel like one who has. I couldn't tell you anything about them. Certain medications make it difficult to recall text especially. I rub my head, I'm not sure why, but not because I'm thinking about difficulty thinking.

Ghost at the Loom

T. Zachary Cotler

She says, "There are people on the Internet who still make videos and post them of themselves reciting Byron. You don't have to just read magnets on the fridge, right?"

"Thanks," I say. "Thanks for these books."

◇◇◇◇◇◇◇◇◇◇◇◇◇

I SLEEP BENEATH THE WINDOW. My head lies on its side, a silo full of cells.

It's silver oil.

A nocturne spins out of the night's consistency, its threads collected by a statue of Minerva, but she wasn't Roman when we glimmered, and she isn't Mama, not exactly, doesn't stand for long for anyone: Minerva-for-a-moment, picking at her loom, spinning shadows as they rise through stacks of stone from the wreckage of Christian fires that burned her father's empire down. She's indiscernible from shadows of empty bottles and a guitar case.

Keep'itsecret, building some'ting, rigging ting.

A motorino knifes the street. Its blast and echo riddle in the circuitry of threads.

Don't go down dere.

A faceless image of a woman rides the blast. Her hair is long and carbon black. It beats behind her as her wheels blow scraps of paper trash toward the edges of the alleys. She's looking for something, a pattern in the weft of the path of my revolving head...or nothing but an echo in a motor's wake, a warp in the fabric, and I am only looking for her.

Bandy voices: *Heard you little someone crying.*

Not make noise.

Be careful little no one taught you to talk. You keep it in your roundy brain.

Quick us, no tell.

She pulls in the sound of doves and the Tiber. Submerged in the river sound, the creak of churchstones. These sounds are external and imaginary.

In dell'Oro, sound is less a songuary. Walls and floor emit a din of pipes. Behind the wall, every night, one of these young women, Tahnee, makes sounds not unlike the scavenger doves, but with a less instinctual cadence.

Who's that?

Little no one?

Drumonesomeone.

World of violent and gentle people who believe in that world and each other...but there is at least a kind of peace in the commonworld's indifference to you and a second kind of sight in some way tied to sound awake in me beneath the window where I am asleep.

◇◇◇◇◇◇◇◇◇◇◇◇◇

I THOUGHT I SAW YOU yesterday. Cloudy red west light. Windows opaque with glare, panes of solid, unintelligible prayer. Returning to dell'Oro on a back street, I walked behind a young woman many blocks. She had your balance, her weight on her toes, and long black hair. Look back at me. I didn't want to scare you so I didn't run. If you can understand, something about her being so unquestionably not you had begun to stretch toward its opposite, as if a ring had formed where only a line should have been: the strange continuum from Absolutely You to Someone Else. She did not turn, but the line did and joined its ends, and so I had to see her face.

I now was not more than ten strides behind her, but she moved onto a smaller street, and I slowed and debated whether it would not be predatory-seeming to follow her into a place where we would be alone, a darker street between three-story residential buildings, vines on walls, orange berries on the vines, with openwork grates on the doors and the first-story windows.

You stopped, but your profile was distant and shadowy, and I don't really know what you look like grown up. Mama sends me photographs, but photographs of objects, not of you. The living subjects of her photographs are insects, flowers. You stepped into a building. The gate you opened locked behind you.

I waited, and the texture of my apprehension thinned and snapped, and I went and memorized the number of your gate and the name of this street. I'll come back soon. Maybe you walk at the same time every evening.

◇◇◇◇◇◇◇◇◇◇◇◇◇

CELT PRODS ME OUT of Shelley's *Adonais* with her shoe. She's here to take me to some churches, and there hasn't been a day she hasn't given me a meal, a museum tour, a book, and why? And yet these books come uncannily close to you in me at times. I mean there are familiarly alien moods and environments. Words, two or three in a row sometimes, from these poems could fit, if my memories aren't too crooked, into your songs I fell asleep to through the vent between our rooms. If you were here, I'd read you scattered lines I have been finding in these old dead English books. *Lines to what?* That's hard to answer, but I sense it just beyond the edge of sense. Maybe lines of a riddle that, folded across the right axis of mind, becomes its own answer.

I say, "I think I don't like churches."

Celt kneels beside me on my bedding on the floor. "I'd like to point out something to you." This tone is a warning, far from the tone she's used with me before. This one is laced with subtle righteousness, conviction from the world of those who have become adults. I don't know what she'll say, but it will be a violation, a request that I betray you in some minor way.

"What?"

What can I stuff my ears with? Fingers. Bits of paper ripped from *Adonais* mixed with anti-siren wax already in my ears. I try to be as still as I have learned to be when Minus says upsetting things.

"Well, have you ever asked me anything about myself?"

Thanks for these books, important books. She's asking me to like her? Could there be, in her, if nothing but a dust-grain in a book she'll lend but has not read for years, a trace of a child on a hill?

"Have I not?" I say. "I'm bad at certain kinds of conversation."

"You're not trying to be rude."

"No."

"This doesn't have to be uncomfortable." She's waiting for me to respond. "We've been to dinner many times."

Then, not your brother for a moment, I say, "Where did you grow up?"

"Detroit."

"Okay."

"You're terrified of me."

"I promise you I'm not. Let me get up and get some pants on and we'll go."

Her look is one that commonworldly people use that says *I am larger than you, but generous, too, and your errors are easy to fix with my help.* "Then I'll give you some time. How long do you think you'll stay?"

Last night, in the bottom of my backpack, I found a note rubberbanded around my carbamazepine and twenty hundred-dollar bills.

Sir,

See that you spend this all on self-improvement. Possibly you think you once had some obscure birthright, some property waiting for you in the Holy Land, but that you've been disinherited because your mother is a scalp-collecting savage.

Yours, Johannes

"Not too long," I say. "I'm waiting for some news."

"What's the news?"

"My family."

"Don't want to tell me?"

"Something with my sister."

"That's fine." She stands. "I'm going to give Xabier some tickets to a show. Be ready in five minutes, go put on your pants."

Relief, a papery blankness. She exits. I go through the curtain to Sperry's room, obtain jeans and a white shirt from the extra dresser there, a long tomato and a sphere of mozzarella from the kitchen, and run downstairs to a taxi.

Celt chats with the driver in Italian. Crossing the Ponte Vittorio—I am, for now, marooned in the limbo of inexperienced travelers, that mental zone in which all foreignness remains behind an overlay of where one comes from: so, I'm in a taxi in a Roman San Francisco, driving north. In a mood for facts, Mama's house is a physical place in the hills north of San Francisco. But in far more frequent, softly startled as if always having just been sleeping moods, I see it as a house-and-hill-shaped planetoid, a minor falling world, farther and farther from the sun. I'm not the sun; the harsh, factual light of the commonworld is. Such falling-away worlds are akin to places in the last dream in a sleep: the smallest, most subjective, most important-seeming, irrecoverable worlds. You see how frangible my logic turns when not just bits of memory, the faint transmissions, voices, images escape the plummeting, but you, the central figure in the dream, emerge impossibly after almost two decades falling. So you see how this determines me to take no medication. Medication only ever blocked the half of what we have that is a common diagnosis...sometimes I worry I am that half.

Here where it takes a more-than-automatic effort to read signs and billboards, and the television has been moved into Garcia's room and is unintelligible through the wall, if I barrage my mind with old rhymes and older churches, maybe then a retrogression will begin in me, and then you will appear and show me how to reexit the commonworld. To glimmer is to be an other-self, an unself-conscious self-containing other.

Celt walks along a wall of tombs at a chapel of the Jesuits. Saints' likenesses man the buttresses, like dummy defenders designed to look real from a distance and scare off the enemy, but I keep saying peace to myself since I've been in Italy, I don't know why, breaking the word into pieces, dead letters, cold coals. I do wish I knew what this is, what promise more alluring than common heaven. Or is heavensoon the only thought that makes an old man on his knees beside me rock and hold his smiling head?

A choir from speakers hidden in the saints. Arrows, light from candles and arrowslit windows. Bells, but not from this church. There's a clock on the wall and a watch on Celt's wrist that breaks a shaft of stained light from above into prismatic milliseconds.

Shelley, especially. I think he knew, *knew*, you know what knowing I mean. I think he had a little sister.

Cornaro Chapel. Cast bronze rays surround Bernini's Saint Teresa in her cloth-of-stone.

"What do you think of her?" Celt pokes my shoulder with a fingernail. An angel stabs Teresa's stomach with a gold bolt.

I am studying her: the near-erotic mask, the mouth half open. Optical tricks from high windows move

Ghost at the Loom

her eyelids. A delicate beakish nose. She kneeled in a
flowering
>orchard at night.
>A symmetry of
>pains and colored
>sounds: feathered shards,
>gold-blooded pipes,
>and cloven
>apple-black horizons.
>>Hooves,
>in syncopation
>with the wings
>buffeting her
>arms and head,
>and with the wings
>inside her, ripped
>>the red eggs
>inside her—

Celt slides closer, and I put away my writing book.

"Come here, I feel like whispering in church. I was
telling a really good friend yesterday, I have a lot of energy,
compared to men my age, and I smoke. You don't, do you?"

"Stains your fingers."

"Heh. Go back to New York. Rome will eat you.
You're not a nice boy. You'll taste horrendous."

"Okay."

"Think about the opposite of eugenics. Think
about before Voltaire, all of our most brilliant, educated
men—what an idea, all married to Jesus, forbidden to

impregnate us, like all the men you want, at least the ones who read and write, but you know what they want, and Europe got dimmer and dimmer, heh. I bet you've already been told Gigot has asked to meet you. That will be an interesting meet. He's with you on a few points, you'll see, but he really is a European, no neurosis about it."

"Neuropean," John somehow remotely makes me say. "Eurosis."

"Right. Are you enjoying this?"

"Hm."

"All this." She waves her arms.

"It's beautiful enough. It's grandiose, a bit victorious."

"It *was* victorious, but try not to use the word 'beautiful.' It's fallen out of favor in the last few decades. Interesting, though. The better word is 'interesting.'"

If I were writing not to you, but to People, like Shelley thought he was, I guess I'd try to understand Celt's postures, compass her compassionately. Luckily, there is no need. She's written books about herself. She's no less decadent than I. I don't work in a mine. I do not grow my food. Leya, writing to you makes me safe. I've tried, but it is so presumptuous to write to People.

I won't write down what Celt says anymore.

◇◇◇◇◇◇◇◇◇◇◇◇◇

MOMENTS OF DOUBT, COLD whitish moods like weather fronts, come and go—is there a reason I believe Mama knows you're in Europe? I understand I am, to make this all a bit too neat, in Rome because much of the Western hemisphere's nostalgia is, and all of my nostalgia is with you, but are you anywhere within a thousand miles? I'm on a corner waiting for you to arrive. You walk here every day.

On a corner in Rome with a pen and a book still mostly blank. It's irrational to believe Mama: very good, I'm here because to be here is irrational. That's my reason, and if "reason" can extend to such a sense, then I can see—you're here. I push off from the corner I've been anchored to and follow you, just as I did some days ago. Walking up this back street toward the alley with the gate I saw you go into, you are the same, same hair, same brittle gait. Your clothes are European, cheap and worn. Who's feeding you? Who makes sure you have proper bedding? But it's warm at night. I have to see her face. I should have waited at the corner of the alley, not where I first saw you days ago.

Wordlike sounds in my head today: *memnos, momnos.* Could be terms for ephemeral memories, gamma rays.

Moments of greenish scent in this city—organic, algae-like, like the green-furred rim of the horsewater tub on Horse Hill—interrupt me.

I am predatory, harmless, trying not to be afraid that I'm confused. I need to be confused to find you. Someone's dropped a man's hat in the street. A car has flattened it. You're stepping past a hat, I'm catching up, I'm moving to one side to pass, I'm going to see your face, but then the windy, whitish fear of seeming predatory comes in with a new intensity, and I fall back. I don't want to scare anyone.

She turns into the shadow of the buildings in the alley, and I trot to the corner and watch, but she doesn't look back and turns a key in the black iron gate with fleurs-de-lis, and I haven't eaten since noon. I'll buy some bread. I'll come back soon. I'm nearly certain that, if I can see her face, I'll remember something important.

I'M IN A TINY Internet café next to a monumental church, with twice as many people here as in the church.

Dagon Abroad,

My cargo can't be bought, so hoist your Jolly Roger. New York's empty. I am in Miami on the Yacht of Da. I have had a sexual intercourse with your girlfriend so do not be angry. You don't care for chauvinistic contracts, strictly resource-economic at bottom and top of the class struggle, very well veiled in the middle. Used to be useful, though, in pre-prophylactic centuries. You don't want to raise my babies? Oh, you do? Too bad, I used a rapier sheath. Ate bad pad thai four times this week. I have decided I will go to Europe, too, so please reply with info.

Newest is a fantasy involving women with six legs two arms, sometimes the other way around (important reference here, but I won't annotate), more hands on deck, more action, eh? I had an old boarding school acquaintance on board until last night, when he, emasculated by my banter, ran home to mother, or perhaps was forced to walk the plank by me, who expects he will attempt suicide.

Dixi,
John the Drinkard

Do you have creative thoughts in rome? I want to make sure both my children have the opportunity. The truth with me is I didn't travel everywhere. It isn't sad though if my children travel if I didn't Rider because I know how to live in a certain way. Sometimes people don't know how to keep from being too fast. My question I had is do you have enough money? You have to be ready to travel immediately. I hope you understand Leya's more important than certain things I think you do sometimes. I told you this before. You are important too and you can't always be in a city. Leya's not in one.

There are also some emails from Paro.

I'm in the Pantheon's piazza. Tourists, gypsies, Africans purveying drums and sunglasses. I settle on the Pantheon's outer wall, a mix of old brick, gray and jagged, laid by Latin-speaking men, and newer terracotta the color of Horse Hill soil.

Ghost at the Loom

South along the wall, a couple kisses vividly. Young Romans kiss in public. The woman's technique is mothlike, mouth on his neck, jaw, lips, a flurry of rapid, light contacts.

I am looking at my boots, at crooked brickwork, AA batteries at the bottom of the wall, from a tape recorder I imagine, from a man who needs to hear his voice once an hour to recall how to speak. Imagine finding this recorder, pressing PLAY: *Now for those of you who don't know what you're looking at, this is the funeral of the West. The coffins and fiori are right here. You'll find the hired mourners at the end of the procession in Las Vegas and Los Angeles.*

I'm no less out of focus here than in New York, where John keeps my motorcycle, Paro my drums. What else? Books, shirts, pants, defunct computer. I don't send money to Mama. A book of my poems sells for $12.99, and what is a bard: an extinct winged mammal. You alone are never self-conscious.

I buy a dumbek from an African and run a finger along its red rim. Flat, the goat-hide too thick, but it has volume for a small, cheap drum. A middle-aged Romani man plays mandolin on the wall today, most days. I listen for a while. His rhythm is immaculate. There is, in his mane and face, a not-quite-mockery of Christs I have been cautiously regarding in Celt's churches. Truly admirable rhythm, notes as if quantized, robotic. Imagine this man with a crown of briar-electrodes. Leya, how long will you let me ferment in Rome-Limbo?

So I pound the dumbek to the mandolinist's
time. The kissing couple drifts away. The mandolinist
knows I'm playing with him but won't look at me. A
soft cacophony of languages and shoes on stone, with
seabirds crowing on the Pantheon's dome. A mandolinist
is pretending I'm not here. My rhythm is immaculate.
Little children don't mock themselves, I told Paro. I saw
some Englishmen in waistcoats drinking from a public
fountain yesterday.

Sunday fifteen o'clock. The Vatican's most modern
venue: loud-colored stained glass like comic book panels
and a louder stereophonic system, the voice of God.
Behind the stage hangs a massive wooden carving of
Christ in flung-forward crucifixion, long chin pointed
at the dais, where scarcely stands Pope John Paul II,
leader of the world's smallest nation, winged by Swiss
halberdiers in orange-and-purple pantaloons.

Celt and I find seats amid a busload of Japanese,
who, twisting in their chairs, conversing frantically,
upset me. John Paul II has drawn a horde to what may
be his last Mass. He rolled in in a box on wheels.

Celt's talking, talking. You don't like her.

A volley of Texan lifts from the chatter: "John Paul
Two! We! Love! You!"

John Paul lifts a quaking hand in affirmation of
Lone Star ontology.

The Japanese, primarily men in dark blue suits, yell
past and over us, discussing I don't know: luminiferous

aether theories, money markets, possibly the planned assassination.

John Paul gurgles through the speaker system in Church Latin, a cheerless voice, full of teleological knowledge (the man may not know, but the voice knows), of sadness that the City of God's been abandoned by all but the easily led. He blesses in Italian, French. At each oration's end, a fraction of the horde stands and holds aloft rosaries, bibles, infants, statuettes of the Madonna, crucifixes, wedding rings.

He blesses in Spanish, in English now. It hurts him to talk. "Now...hold...any...objects...up...on which...you wish...the blessing...of God."

The Japanese respond to English. I stand and hold aloft this letter to you, this little clothbound book, into a cloud of beads and bibles, in an act so far beyond the end of organized religion that it finds itself right here—at post-post-metaphysics on the möbius—without disdain or admiration for the sheep or shepherds

D EAD-EYED QUEENS LIKE QUEENS on cards, the women
and girls who hung in the hall, in the quilts Mama
made—they were neutral when Mama screamed. She
screamed again and struck an eye-shaped hole through
my ear, my ear a tiny door unable to close, as I crouched
in my bedroom doorway, as the anger from the man who
lived with Mama scattered through the ripping sound
she made.

Far inside the wailing hole, an edge was dimly visible,
a cat's-eyelike horizon splitting black sky and water,
shadows of running people, black quilts ripped along
the seams. I could fall into Mama's screaming, scatter
anywhere—my smallest bones, glass chimes attacked
by high frequency. Inside the frequency, a horrified
encryption: Mama, who had been like you, had made
this sound before; the glimmer had been taken from her
in a story she would not tell.

"Bember-rember-nee," I chattered.

Eyeball slunk past my door, a nervous ridge of hair
along her back. A crash from Mama's bedroom—quiet.
The hallway air contained a resinous, familiar tang.

I went into the fire-and-piano room. The seat of
the piano bench was secretly a lid, beneath which was

a cache of good sticks, thinner than pens. I stood on the bench to pretend to be able to reach the decorative saber that was the man's, that hung on hooks above the mantelpiece. It had been given to him by his grandfather.

Beneath the quilted sisters, down the hall, my stomach a violent suspension, I followed the point of the pretended saber and stopped at your room, pushing the door with it, leaving a nick in the wood.

You lay there twitching in the waterglow of the aquarium Eli had given you.

The man's voice jabbed through Mama's, something like: "Fuck this house and your weird trip, fucking fairy princess."

At the hall's end, in diffuse smoke, I pushed the saberpoint into a crack of light and leveraged against the door—the dark was shot with orange from the row of ovoid bulbs on the wall above the bed. Mama faced me, and a slow second later, the man did.

"Neeb," I said.

His face had an animal blankness. Mama's lip was split. A slip of blood divided her chin. She wasn't making any noise. The scream was from her, but not coming from her—it swallowed its tail, closing the eye-shaped hole in my ear, her throat constricting visibly. Her throat skin, it was moving like when she would drink a whole glass of water, both of her children quiet, watching. *Where is Leya?*

Then his quiet voice. A lit joint. I don't remember what he's saying. Violins and drumming on the stereo, wrecking-hammers, houses made of buzzing string. His hand was flat and out to one side. Mama's throat was closed, but she restarted a remote scream inside me, intensifying over several seconds. At least seven violins fought to be loudest, and, as the scream spiked out of sound's range into eardrum pain, the joint dropped from the man's mouth, end over end, onto the carpet, and the ember broke off.

"Shit." He bent to get it.

Mama mouthed words, maybe instructions.

So I jabbed the saber at his crotch. I missed—the tip went in above his knee, not more than an inch, the scream pain in my head flickered then flicked off as the hit kicked back through the blade to my hands, and the man took up the screaming where my mind had left it, stretching from his throat: a storage tunnel full of webs and dead machines. I looked into his mouth at teeth. My head was tilted like a dog's.

The man, bent and leaning, blew at the blade as if it were too hot to put into his mouth. He lurched and slashed his arm into my side. I was on my side on the carpet and hadn't let the stick go.

Mama stood between me and the man. She was taller and stronger than I. Maybe she could kill him. He was swearing, saying Mama's name and mine. The two of them were in the hall, a howl harooed from Eyeball, hidden somewhere in the house, and then my head was in the hall, my body in the bedroom.

Ghost at the Loom

Mama chased him down the long hall to the front door to the street. I heard them talking loudly and then quietly out there.

Then I was in your room. I made a cradle of my free arm for your head. The front door slammed and opened, slammed.

"Where be you, One'Bandy?"

Mama ran by with the man's guitar. The whites of your eyes rotated. An acoustic guitar striking a street is a singular sound.

I swung the broken dogwood stick in crescents, pushing my head against yours. The guitar-sound extended a red, inflamed string—it was volumeless now, but it whipped through the house. I kept pushing. *Rider'hurting stop*, you said or I said. I pulled back, your eyes an inch away. Your pupils were barred portals, behind which sprawled vast arcadias lost to me.

This night's become infected in my memory, corrupted maybe, more and more Gothic each time I've tried to write it out.

◇◇◇◇◇◇◇◇◇◇◇◇◇

A PARTY AT GIGOT'S PALAZZO. Pop songs, cocktail waiters, walls and floors of pale orange stone. In a baggy suit and a man's arms, Celt drinks a highball of lurid blue liquid. Limbo is a place in which, no matter how long you stay, somebody or something screams, "Welcome to Limbo!" silently (yet with great force, enough to make you twitch) every few minutes.

This man called Mikhail, an American flown in by Celt for the party, seems to shout in my direction, but the music is too loud. He pulls Celt by the face for a full-mouthed kiss. She laughs into his mouth. I look away—at flowers in a leather-jacketed man's hair.

I meet the courtiers and guests. Names are spoken solemnly or quipped in witty spots. I do not know these names or why you've not told Mama where you are. I even start to think about returning to New York, but then three men about my age, arguing in English about the recent Congress of Vienna, are concerned the British have been too conservative, and whether Italy is more than "but a geographical expression" now. This interests me intensely, yet I can't seem to introduce myself into their conversation.

I drink and drink. I tap my foot against a pillar.
What's the tallest thing you've urinated off of?
Go, I'm busy.
I drink limoncello.
Mr. Sonnenreich, excuse me, this is the director.
A gold disco light hits my empty glass. The bass riff inverts—I'm dancing. The room spins opposite my spin.

Tahnee's hand is on my wrist. You don't remember her, but I've been living with her and the others. It's a tendony, guitarist's hand, a long-fingered masculine object, inanimate—animate now, feminine, pulling me out of the ballroom. "Come, come."

We're in an elevator like a phone booth. Phone booths were everywhere not long ago. There's a memory of you and Mama in one. I'm in the car. Someone is upset.

I say, "What's on the middle story?"

Tahnee's rich breath, licorice: "Killed girlfriends of everybody. I don't know."

"Grandfather I never met died in an elevator."

"It is sad," she says.

I fingercomb a shred of plastic from her hair, the gore of stillborn lyrics pooling in the back of my closed mouth, just rhythm, sound, no sense: *each shred of blank blank in its groove / a rosehip in a midwife's womb.* Or at dell'Oro, showering before the party: *blank water, blank if I lock / my rhythm to the cosm's clock.*

She says, "Don't touch," the elevator opens, and she sniffs into a dark hall, frowns, and walks and pulls my hand.

I sniff and only smell my burning lemon breath. She pulls me languidly along. Semicircular windows spy down on the courtyard, bougainvillea twined across the panes. At the end of the hall, a double door hangs one-side-open, spewing firelight and a jazz of horns.

"The other night you let me touch your hair," I say. "I like your hair, it's long and black. It's full of crows and midwives, plastic crows. I like your demimondaine face. You don't know what I'm saying."

"Yes okay, you have to go in there."

"In dere?"

"To see Gigot." She indicates the door.

"You're coming?"

"No. She said to bring you only."

"What's the next floor up? Let's ride the elevator up," I say. "Won't be in Rome much longer. Left a couple days ago."

"This is the top. Okay? I go."

"Okay, but bring me up a drink. I'm looking for my sister up here in this hallway in the top of a palazzo. Can't you see I'm sleeping here?"

Ghost at the Loom

"Too much for you." She taps my face, the softest
kind of slap. "I go."
"Then do it quietly," I say. "Don't wake me up."

Waiting, sleeping standing like a horse, drinking the last
of my cup. Waiting for nothing, for you, in this hall...

In through the double doors like an idiot film cowboy.
Figurines of bronze and wire on the walls. A strong
fire in a marble hearth. Chairs of carved wood are the
cupped hands of ogres. In the grip of one is Celt, her
visitor Mikhail in another, and who must be Gigot,
beside them on a black divan, holds up a black dish of
pills.
"These are the Pleiades." He has arranged the seven
pastel capsules accurately, mimicking the scatter of the
northern sky. "Who needs some love?"
To his left on the divan, a woman with a young
face—hair, shirt, and eyelids all silvery white. In another
ogre's hand, a buxom, tanned woman with maybe the
aftershadow of a black eye.
Leya, what is for this letter, what is not? It seems
every detail could be a crucial clue or else an insult to
you.
From a corridor, a bearded Arab or Sephard in a white
sport coat enters, court fool, improvising for his lord:
"I have no love, nor sisters, my brother,
but would, like any economic man
take either of another's
where they're given free (as in the Marshall Plan)."

He plucks a capsule from the dish. I've partly improvised his rhyme. I don't remember if his rhymed, but rhymes are in my head, and I've maintained his tone and sense.

Gigot: "Who's this?"

Fool: "Chardonnay, or must I take this dry?"

"—because he's recently discovered Florida, the whole scene on rollerskates there, the culture," continues the black-eyed woman, Spanish accent, jouncing as she leans and takes a pill.

Gigot, pushing his pug face at her: "You spoil the metaphor!"

"It's all biography, cult of the self," the fool speaks aloft, commiserating with the ceiling or some deity, then to the black-eyed woman: "Will you pour me one more glass of wine? I don't care what that little ass discovered. That whole situation is ridiculous, it's real estate. Elizabeth. Hello?"

Gigot to fool: "But, naturally, she spoils my metaphor."

The fool steps across Celt's legs and swipes one of two bottles from the table.

"Who's this?" Gigot's nodding at me, one hand organizing his courtesan's breasts, the other rattling the dish. He slams the dish onto the table. Cracks appear in the ceramic. Pills fly up and fall, all somehow back into the dish.

Elizabeth: "Don't rock the ark."

Gigot's sport coat is white. Mikhail's is nearly white. These people look like doctors.

Ghost at the Loom

"*Mes amis*," Mikhail, snapping bony fingers twice: "the war against Clichy."

Gigot: "Very good, good. I see your *mes amis* and raise you a *conquistadores* massacring the Huguenots in Florida. Out of the fountain, into the pants of the lion, no? But this isn't fair to us, is it? To play with so many Americans. No more Americans."

Celt grunt-laughs and introduces me. They're playing some kind of verbal game.

Fool: "My brothers!"

"Good evening," says Gigot. "I'm sorry that I cannot offer you a seat, you'll stand?"

I indicate the empty chair.

Courtesan: "I'm going down. He sits with you."

"No, Valentina! No! You stay. I am an *old* man."

"Lean upon a wall," the fool advises.

Gigot: "Have a quaalude."

Valentina: "Ludes are from the eighties."

Gigot: "Where did you come from?"

Someone says, "New York."

"North of San Francisco," I say.

"Ah." Gigot: "I spent a winter there in rain. That's a city of loafers and no goodness."

Fool: "We did have halibut for dinner."

"Charm of the next world. Vietnam..." Mikhail grimaces, thickening a forehead vein. "I'll be straightforward. In the bush you've got to pinch it off clean."

Fool: "Or prunes, or dates or figs between your meals."

"In Vietnam." Mikhail: "I'm talking about bacteria!"

John might enjoy these people. I attempt to speak—

Elizabeth: "So you were 'in the shit'!?"

Mikhail: "Nice. I was a journalist."

Valentina takes a pill with wine.

I tell Gigot, "You were a tourist."

"Yes," he says, "whereas I understand you are a social critic."

Celt explains she bought my book for him for $12.99 on the Internet.

Gigot: "He is a sentimental indignant, your narrator. I feel I know your mind in a delicate way. Must I worry a man with your politics might find our life here frightening? So I offered you a quaalude. Would you like some wine? You'll have to have a glass for sake of temperance at least, because, again, as your premier outré declared, 'All things in moderation.' I'm obsessed by them, Americans. Such porcine, tragic patriots, and such dissenters in your country. I was in Chicago, 1969. I poured imported beer on burning flags." He pulls his collar. "In moderation, sobriety even, yes?" He nods at nodding Valentina.

"No thanks," I say, "I'm drunk."

"I have no doubt."

Mikhail: "A journalist is only in the shit by accident. The Cong were——"

"There's a hundred-million-headed hydra in America," mutated by their jabber, I, not your brother for a moment, say, "and highly educated people, both of which it seems you missed. You read the news?"

Gigot grins at me, frowns at Celt, then to his courtesan: "The love is working. Valentina, a recess. This large American is full of hate, but I am full of love."

"I don't read news," I mumble.

Mikhail pulls his sleeve to show Elizabeth a scar.

"I have to go," I tell Gigot. "I didn't plan to come up here. Some people made me meet you. You were disappointing."

He speaks at me calmly in French. With the parting and rejoining of his lips, inarticulate anger builds in me and subsides and rebuilds and subsides, and then an instinct comes with great intensity to spin this into something gravid with symbolism, something about Europe and America, but I don't think it's here. My lemon-fire breath drifts from my mouth into my nose and eyes. This man and I, this place and I, have made too little impact on each other. The commonworld declines to foster urgency, symmetry, climax, a life with a plot. Unless one is perhaps a politician, soldier, or considers adultery dramatic.

And yet there is something, a ghost of sense or sense of ghost, a scrap with threads of Europe and America in it, something beyond the curtains of this decoy situation while I wait for you, I'm nearly sure there is, but I don't understand it.

Out of the throne room, into the hall, whispering to myself. *Please report to the left exit.* Riptide, riptide. At the windows, watching humans in the courtyard smoking, laughing, courting, calculating. Then the elevator stops. A harpstring somewhere snaps. The elevator gate clangs open, and I squint into the black but can't make out a human shape, though someone's definitely whistling down there, and the elevator shuts. I guess the whistler did not exit on this floor.

◇◇◇◇◇◇◇◇◇◇◇◇◇◇

A FTER THE NIGHT WITH the screaming comes a hole in your place. You were in your room for seven years with the door closed, you were with doctors, I can't remember. Then I was nineteen and leaving California. If I think of the years between twelve and nineteen, I don't think of young Americans or school, though Mama let me once a week go to a public independent study center. Mostly I think of Bronner. Could you not know who that is?

I was coming out into a nation of loud kitsch. We sometimes went to Bronner's nation to escape the noise. There was no glimmer in his house or on the reservation. Still, the lack of noise beguiled me into thinking being native was a privilege, a mark of grace, and that to think so was a native thought. The deception here is difficult to notice as a child: What could be louder and more deeply transatlantic than believing purity and mystery are to be found on reservations?

Deer blood and dark cologne were the scents in his truck the night the Fish and Game truck chased us on what Bronner called the "lava roads," near the Oregon border. Fish and Game won't cross the reservation line—is that true? Were they chasing us or merely on the road behind us? I required a father. Eagle wings were mounted on the dashboard of his truck, I'm sure bought at a powwow, but I did what he required in return, imagined him up in some aerie, thin clouds on his shoulders, bargaining, because it was an old raptor's last Earth hour: *your wings for a dance and a cigarette*, or *your wings for a sage smoke prayer*.

He was a religious leader for the Karuk. I met him through his daughter Root. That wasn't her name, and he called her that. We were twelve. I found her on a hydrant where the driveway met the road, a cruel-looking girl. What was she doing out there in the dark, I asked. She told me if I wanted to, come with her. You weren't there, so I did.

Down our street to a house built onto the hill, downstairs to a room that smelled like cologne. Through glass, I saw him outside, grilling beef. Antlers leaned against a propane tank. He wiped his hands and came in with a long steel fork with grease on it.

Pointing it at me: "Your mother's the one with ribbons in her braids."

I said so.

"I see her by the mailboxes. She's some Indian?"

I told him Mama's mother was a Blackfoot who had tried to burn a church. He liked that very much. It could be true. Uncle Connor says it is.

Bronner said, "I'll trade with you. I'll let you run around with Root if you get me invited to your mother's house to eat."

We were moving toward the river. At our camp atop the canyon ridge, Mama and his mother slept. Eyeball was with them. You weren't. Bronner called Eyeball *chish'ih.* Salmon blood was poisonous to dogs.

America was not a word in this place. The Ikxareeyav had been gods. They made people.

"One god, Eel-with-a-Swollen-Belly, lived at the downstream end of the world and swam the River-Earth and stopped to stack rocks here on the north side. Those were singing places for the people. He stacked rocks on both sides of the river. He had made the Center-of-the-World. Believe me? That's a story for children."

It was before dawn. Around us were huge toppled cairns.

"You'll die if you fall in," he said. "Even I would."

We crossed a field of halfsunk stones in the canyon, between great boulders and the rapids. Jeans, snake boots, a sand-colored leather vest, his hair pulled through a ring of desert jade not crafted by his tribe. His rifle pointed backward on his shoulder. On his other shoulder, he balanced the bowed wood fishing frame-and-netting he had told me weighed a hundred pounds.

He let me carry the sack, stained black, last used when he had fished with one of his natural sons. He let me carry the spear. Thin stainless steel. It had two tines. I turned the

Ghost at the Loom

shaft and saw the shadows on the metal as the hands of distant blood, long dead, the metal, for an instant, wood.

"Mama. Are you making food?"

"Not today. Make yourself."

"A man is coming. Can you make him something?"

"Who?"

"I think he's coming now. I forgot his name."

"You have a friend? Who is his mother?"

I lay under your piano, where she'd placed me. She had cut some locks from her abundant hair, arranging them around my head on the wood. She'd put the scissors in my hand.

"Maybe he has one," I said.

"Maybe. You love me but...you'll never be a mama." She took a picture. "You don't know how I feel. It would be better if you knew your own friend's name. Hold them near your head" —click— "but if he has one, then...she should make him something to eat."

"Can *you?*"

Click. Click.

"You, Mama."

Bronner knocked. I crawled across the room and stood and pulled the latch. He held a bloody plastic bag in one hand.

"Rider, you weren't making up." Then Mama said to Bronner, "Who are you?"

"I know your boy. I brought you the haunch of a deer."

This now seems unbelievable, but it is what he did. I think he understood his sexuality was tainted by, yet nonetheless dependent on, mass media iconography of the Sioux brave. Even Mama, who never watched screens, understood.

"He's funny and has his own food." Mama took a picture of him standing over me.

She introduced herself. I don't remember most of what they said.

"I buy and sell gold."

"Do you have a lot of gold?"

Now I was picking up the locks of hair—what did he know about us?—putting them out of sight in the piano bench compartment.

He said, "I saw you one time by the mailboxes."

A small, spheroid moment, like a thinking head but without that image, opened near me, and I was quiet, hoping it would not crowd him out of the house (he remained by the door), and he said to her, "You do eat game?"

She took the bag. It was heavy, and he took it back.

"You show me," she said—they were in the kitchen.

We crept stone to stone. America not a word, but he whispered about Vietnam, about hiding in mist when he was a Marine. Hopping a pool, he landed wrong. The net frame dragged him backward, and he yelled for me to get his rifle. I retrieved it from the pool. I held the rifle, sack, and spear, and waited as he pulled himself onto a boulder.

Ghost at the Loom

He took the rifle and cursed for a while. Then he said, "Hey. Don't laugh, this is a quiet place."

I hadn't laughed. The Vietnam mist hovered near the tops of taller rocks. He set the rifle, dripping from the barrel, on his shoulder, and I followed him across the last of the slow water. Sideways, he edged out across a chain of stones, into the Klamath, and turning, squatting, motioned, come.

He wedged his bulk into the net frame's V, dipping the open end in a pit. I crouched at the pit's rim. Little maelstroms. Maybe Mama was awake now on the ridge. I speared an image, scared the salmon toward the net. I helped. He reared, his great weight counterweight to the water, net and salmon, and I yipped, and he dropped the net between us, cursed approvingly, and let me club the salmon with the spearbutt.

Afterward, alone in the shallows, I scrubbed my hands with sand until not even the idea of blood remained. I didn't want Eyeball to die.

At camp, he split fish with a knife. I studied his hands, the blood on them, his rolled-up sleeves and wordless working sounds. His mother came out of the hunting shack built by her father. She moved with a hobble, knit shawl on her shoulders. She looked nothing like her son. He had no father.

"Get some sticks," he said.

I walked in the firs and heard him telling Mama she should know that eating hunted salmon makes a woman loyal.

"You're a paranoid delusional," she murmured something like.

I gathered sticks. He gathered logs. He made fire. I knew how to make fire.

We ate, sitting close to the fire, then his mother sang stories, her voice in her throat. It pulsed through the grooved skin there, bird in a hollow tree:

"Ninivássi vúra,

vitkiniyâac ta kóova,

tu'áxxaska,

tu'áxxaska."

Bronner in the needles, nodding his head, thumbing the bone of his knifehandle. I stood behind him, chin on his head. His mother was nearly blind. Her songs were repetitious and about extinction.

My back,

It has become like a mountain ridge,

so thin,

so thin.

"That's just a prayer for ending stories," Bronner said.

I slept in the hunting shack with his mother. He'd planned to sleep in the tent with Mama, but they argued, and he stayed out all night with his gun. Between the boards, where the shack's mossed wall had warped, I watched him run a cloth along his gun and plug his eye into the scope aimed into the zodiac. What kind of proof of there is no immortality was this? And yet he was the opposite of what at twelve I understood of death. Eagles don't have night vision. He tilted at the moon.

His hair became longer and thinner, his belly imposing. Always traveling: Santa Rosa powwows, a casino on the Modoc land (he had a stake), to see his mother on the reservation who had gone completely blind, to Hoopah Nation for his grown sons, who had families.

Mama didn't want him at the house. Maybe he used me to hear about Mama. I told her to take him back. No one talked about you.

"I prefer the grocery store," she said, aware, I think, of how much irony was there, and how much more was not.

The day she told him that, he took a crossbow he had ordered in the mail onto Horse Hill and west into the oak trees, where no one saw him kill a deer. That meat was better than the reservation deer.

Root and I were sixteen, and I watched her differently. She was not my sister—*beautiful, beautiful,* I said in my head. Long legs, lynx eyes. She put on makeup.

"Go with her," he said.

She didn't want me, but I had to see where she went at night with eyes like that.

She drove us in her older sister's car through rain, north on the highway past the electric tower I no longer climbed, into a neighborhood I didn't know. Gangs were drinking gin from a bottle in the street. I had a sip. A boy put his mouth on her neck. I pretended a gulp. It tasted like the smell of trees.

No one was talking. Somewhere out behind a blacked-out supermarket, generators made a cyclic sound of many parts, and with my head at the right tilt, I learned to isolate a part more percussive than the rest, as of a thin pipe striking a flagpole over and over.

Gangs were talking, but the talk was near rhythmless, and the pipe resurfaced. Then a truck arrived that filled the street with bass and lyrics about jewelry and cash.

Root pushed the boy. Makeup in the rain was calligraphic on her cheekbones. She drank gin. I watched her swallow. She danced to the bombing rhythm from the parked truck, slim hips swinging, arms over her head.

If they would turn the music off, I thought I could make the pipe-sound the cycle's salient end and beginning, and then I'd remember something important, much more important than Root, whom I imagined taking off her clothes, rapidly, without affect or grace or clumsiness.

Some girls got out of a car just arrived. Aztec girls hissing Spanish curses. One stood ahead of the others, spoke English, and when Root said nothing, spat in Root's face. So Root hit the girl, and the girl stepped back, then they flew at each other like hatchets.

Boys encircled them and chanted. I stood in the circle. Catching the girl by a twist of hair, Root wrenched up and down. Tendons in the girl's neck surfaced, out of place. Her fingernails cut Root beneath the eye.

Ghost at the Loom

They fell, and Root brought the girl's mouth, wailing down, onto the street. The girl went mostly limp, a few kicks—a scraped brown thigh and a denim skirt.

All Indians I've met, except for Mama, are completely of the commonworld. I, for years, suspected otherwise, and that was partly Bronner's fault: he didn't know what I was looking for, but, through some fatherly-unconscious impulse to provide, encouraged me to look in him. So the commonworld tricked us both. A poor farce, looking to one's native part for what in one is alien. Let me find it instead in dead Englishmen's rhymes.

Bronner said, "You are my son," when I was nineteen, leaving.

I think you were there. You didn't say anything. I said something unintentionally hurtful and flew east and became educated, which has been a great privilege.

Bronner stopped putting letters in with Mama's mail and moved his family back to Karuk Nation. In New York, a year or two ago, I began to suspect I knew where you'd been. I abolish this thought each time it returns.

◇◇◇◇◇◇◇◇◇◇◇◇◇◇

THE YOUNG WOMAN WHO is not you. I'm waiting at the corner of her street. You're not in a city, Mama says. Mama's confused. I need to be confused. A cricket-like noise emanates from a faucet that juts from a cornerstone by my knee, and I drop to that knee and put my ear to the faucet.

This close, it no longer sounds like a living thing. I watched you once watching an insect, some summer. You're seven or eight. I'm watching you, a long time. Mama sent me pictures last year she had taken with a macro lens: a katydid on a stem. A long time, I'm thinking of trivial things, then of you in a maybe false memory-fragment of summer, inching your hand's shadow onto and off of an insect at rest on a dogwood bract...thinking what the Coliseum might look like if it were full of horses, katydids, crows, tens of thousands, kicking, writhing, and flapping on top of each other, no people. Mama sent me pictures of the insect's legs, blown up to twenty times actual size and studded with droplets of silvery liquid. Dew, I guess it was.

Mama and her semi-mythic brothers grew up in Ohio. Here's what I've been told. All three "got lost." Matthew drank a cup of LSD and disappeared. Ethan went to prison somewhere in the South for breaking with his hands the necks of three flamingos and beating near to death the park ranger who tried to stop him. Connor, the youngest, is or was a fashion model in Los Angeles. Except for Connor, rarely, have you noticed Mama doesn't speak of them? One time she did, when I came home with a punched mouth. I was maybe fifteen. You weren't there.

One of Rome's many motorcycle-mounted mini trucks rolls by with a cargo of oranges and grapes. Grapes are Leya food. Someone's taken the hat that was here in the road a week ago. The light bends, white to red, the sky is clear, then cloudy, clear. A young woman walks toward me. Dozens have since I've been standing here.

I don't want to scare anyone. Certain instants, I fall into two, as if, almost, into "me" and "you," and then, with a cricket-like twitch and a buzz like under electric towers, the parts redeposit themselves into a singleness, a single vessel covered with my skin. I drum one hand behind me on the building. Real commonworld pedestrians of Rome—one's walking right into my zone, right where I'm twitching, buzzing, leaning on a cornerstone, a mostly blank book in my hand. Her hair is long, black, the black of Italians and Native American Jews. Her face is visible, but somehow not.

How terrible is it to truly look into another primate's face? I'd like to commit a terribly kind act. She's so near now, I could, if I had it, hand her a book in which is written the solution to a great sadness. But, Leya, this young woman, distinctly not you, has a void in her face, a deafening, silent zero in place of the side of her face as she turns and proceeds to her wrought iron gate. I'm confused or pretending? I truly looked for a half second. Maybe she can be some kind of new allegorical figure: the child-turned-adult with a hammer-struck face, but she's no longer scared, no longer aware that a trauma occurred, with so many flavors of forgetfulness for sale.

O R POSSIBLY IT WASN'T lost on a night with screaming and the man's guitar breaking outside. It could have happened quietly, in the windowed alcove half obscured by the bookcase too long for its section of wall. Dark windy light outside, Pacific northern sky colors, you humming to yourself on the alcove pillows, eating currants, grapes, or soybeans, any small, discrete, iterative food.

My back against the alcove's other side, our legs crossed in the center of the circle window. "O," you said and cupped your hands, as if to hold the little word, still hanging and spinning invisibly there.

"Is your jobby," I said, "to protect eggs with a little cup? Are you protecty eggs?"

"I found a baby rat." You put a soybean in your mouth.

"That was a hundred years ago."

"*You* are, Rider'raby."

There was something else invisible, outside, off to the left, and soon, more deeply, to the right, that dodged and decohered, a will-o-the-wisp that shepherded the floating pieces of Outside into a whole, a field of more-than-view, containing named and nameless trees, a fading road and, above the trees, Horse Hill, onto which we can't go—it's too windy to talk outside this day, and yelling cancels glimmer.

Then we were not talking, or not simply *not*, but *un*talking, and, in this sensual void, the wisp diminished, winked away into the closing world behind the grays and greens in the tunnel window view. Subtle violence, maybe of impending masculinity, pushing up (it was an imageless but bladelike thing, a dull but dangerous idea) from a submerged place, pricked the surface of what I would later call my image drum.

You were closing your eyes that stayed open. A little girl, not my sister, spitting a currant into her hand. You were untruly looking at me. What was I not quite seeing? Something lumbering, abyssal, in/behind her tunnel eyes. A thing had pricked the surface of your pupils from within: my imageless reflection?

◇◇◇◇◇◇◇◇◇◇◇◇◇

JOHN KEATS DIED IN this house on the Spanish Steps. Encased in glass: books, letters, surgeon's tools. On the wall hangs the sixth Lord Byron in profile, patron saint of noble sinners, posing with such affectation that the loop is closed, to call it affectation would be affectation (de-romanticizing a Romantic is no more instructive than removing someone's heart to see if they're alive). Solid lips, nose straight and large, with sneering nostrils open to the brain:

I have this morning seen a live pope and dead cardinal,
said the lord to Lady Liddell and her daughter
Maria on the rooftop of St. Peter's. What then
came over Lady Liddell she could not describe,
though had the lord been asked what he imagined
it to be, he'd have refused (it was this narcissism
that distracted him from too often crossing
the Phlegethon, the one dividing his cerebellum)
to stoop to say—if pressed, allowing it
might be described akin to the not quite fatal
awe one feels in the presence of a fallen angel,
who, though physically lovely, because he's an angel
does not strictly exist.

                      She would, a fortnight later,

having thought about it while digesting veal, write:
What came over me I cannot describe,
but I felt ready to sink, and stood
as if my feet were rooted to the ground,
looking at him, horror-struck.
                              The roots of St. Peter's
and stones of the rooftop released her feet
when the lord, half-responding to pleasantries,
said, *I'm debating whether or not to sit*
for a bust by Thorwaldsen the Dane,
whose studio is somewhere near about. It
can be tiresome. One begins to believe in nothing,
rather one begins to think as if one were a stone,
and though he'd never before been sculpted,
his opinion did not strike him strictly false, nor that
among 140 saints atop the colonnade, not one had not
lost wings to vandalism or mordant weather.
                              I think I'd rather
be anything but a stone, said Maria, not considering her words,
and Lady Liddell, disentangling her party from the lord's,
said to Maria, *Do not look at him*, with lowered eyes,
he's dangerous to look at.
                    With his hand on St. Macrina's thigh,
gazing across the Eternal City, he imagined strangling
his wife (who was in England) down in one of the necropoli,
in which he'd seen some cardinals' bones that morning.

                          —Rider Sonnenreich

Ghost at the Loom

I wrote this on the blank page in the back of a biography of Byron I've been carrying around. It's anxious, late, exhausted work. I feel I didn't write it. It is more like something from the mind of Minus. I am staring at the nostrils of a portrait in this tiny deathhouse museum. Humans near me here are far away. The mental space around me is the dark bronze inside of a bell.

Celt's writing in a tomelike guestbook with a pen chained to it. Opposite the Byron hangs an angel-colored P. Bysshe Shelley, painted softer-edged in darker light... staring at this portrait, too, for a long time. I have not physically desired a man or image of a man before.

As long as no one's watching me but you, I sense the way they felt and spoke. It's summer, 1816, and because of the volcano on Sumbawa, little daylight reaches Europe.

Sulfuric ooze-drops fell through floating ash.

Like eggs of plague toads, breaking on black glass.

•

"OR," MARY SAID, "ONE might liken this sky to a mirror too near to the stove, a sooty mirror."

"Yesterday, I mentioned this to Mary," Bysshe to Byron, who leaned on an antique flamberge in its scabbard, sidelit by the Gothic bay windows of the Shelleys' tea room in the Hotel d'Angleterre on Lake Geneva: "that Franklin, Yank ambassador to France, published an exposition linking vulcanism on the islands of Iceland and Japan in 1783 to the violent sky over Paris in the summer of 1784."

"There was a book about the science of the weather that we left, you left it in the coffer," Mary said. *What was that little sound?*

I don't know, has the messenger arrived?

"But before that, just after what you said about bones...what was I remembering," said Byron, "a moment ago?"

A harpsichord somewhere below, some fragment of a canon in minor from a lower story.

"William?" Mary said. She sat atop the footstool of a chair containing Polidori, Byron's doctor.

Rider'raby, did you hear a baby? William Shelley slept in the adjacent room, and the door was open.

Bysshe watched Mary's lips, pressing the "m" at the end of the name of his son. A yellow gem on Byron's cuff, *a minor lodestar*, led his eye away. The cufflink flickered from the candles, then resolved into the whole man, in whom Bysshe perceived a vulcanism, too, subtle as the music from the rooms below these rooms *for if his countenance is as the cold root of a mountain, not disdaining earthly matters, then the summit is a Mind above the alpine clouds, and would he say the same of me?* His eye returned to Mary *for Mary, my words upon my heart thy accents sweet of peace and pity fell like dew on flowers half dead, half dead...*

It pleased her, seeing Byron's widow's peak was aimed into the ash storm, *diabolical he's not.* Nor was he, she deemed, a "good fellow," and a gust broke on the windows, and the gaps beneath the lintels whined like reeds.

Ghost at the Loom

Byron said, "These men of science..." to the windows, then to Bysshe, "Few men can claim a hand both stained by ink and acid. But what of our neophyte playwright? There he lies, contemplative, and the storm will not abate. Awake! Indoctrinate us with the surgeon's lyric. Polidori!"

Polidori stiffened in the armchair with a sudden bowel pain. "You know nothing of my art," he quavered, "and you would be wise to quit your arrogance. After all, what is there you can do that I cannot?"

And with what seemed to Bysshe the slowness of people from earlier eras, whole centuries without a queen pulled by her hair from her carriage into the street, Mary curled atop her footstool, morning glory in the dusk, but Bysshe had forgotten——whence came dusk? No clock or compass in his rooms, and even at noon, the sky looked like far northern summer night. He touched her coiled hair, *for certain rarer intimacies two attain only where there are no clocks.* Vanity was in his touch, too: he was like any piece of art that sees, and therefore sees itself in other effigies.

"Since you force me to say," answered Byron, "I suggest three things I can do which you cannot."

"I defy you to name them."

"I can swim across that lake. I can snuff out that candle with a pistol shot at the distance of twenty paces. And I have written a poem of which fourteen thousand copies sold in one day."

I HAVE EMAILS FROM PARO about plans and money. Then, in ascending intensity, these:

Why are you ignoring me? If you don't tell me where to meet, that is the end of me as benefactor.

Best,
St. Gogarty

As you know, I don't like getting information through your mother. She says basically you're fine, but will be going very far away "to look for Leya." As usual, I can't imagine what that means, so I hope you have a calling card. I want to discuss the following things with you:

Health insurance.
Teeth.

I don't mind doing things for you, but it seems to me you will find it more pleasant in your approaching thirties not to rely on me. I would also feel better doing things for you if you were more open with me about what you are doing. For example, I'm assuming this trip has something to do with your career and you forgot or didn't think to tell me.

You've been doing fine for years and we can start a transition.

On a less exciting note, your mother called the police again, and I believe they reprimanded her. Make sure to call your mother. I am simply telling you what has been told to me.

Eli Sonnenreich
1648 Octavia St.
San Francisco, CA
94109
www.sonnenreichtech.com

You are on the lam. I understand this and will not be contacting you again. I'm in Miami. I have traded insecurities with a woman named Marie who was not a virgin, and my Watson fit her Crick so perfectly it must have been intelligent design. I feel betrayed: you see, my daddy sold the yacht and bought Israel bonds, but don't worry, we still get to go see the garbage sargasso, because Da says he's about to buy a new one, cabin cruiser with a solar panel, Jesus, I mean Jesus, and I love these Puritans who write on laptops, not even getting out of their Egyptian cotton 1500 thread-count beds, these articles condemning global commerce leviathan fuck. I can't believe the way I look. I am extremely getting bald. Please understand this pathos. It's the strands in my hands when I shampoo. I have this oatmeal raisin shampoo. I am all drunkbut, y'know, and I didn't drink anything I swear but near beer. I hope you get your feelings hurt in Europe.

I will be in Europe in a week. You let me know or I will strike you strike you smite smite. No more e-pistles.

John the Raptist.

You didn't write to me and this computer's trying to stop me from writing but what I was going to say is I'm a good Mama. I wanted a son and a daughter and I want you to come home, too. Find Leya now and also your dog is now very blind.

Dear Rider'will,

I wonder do you still? I don't know any words to talk to these children. I see them in the road here on the map. Even in another country children in the English that they learn in school they never say and if I ever wonder you I read some of the books you sent to Mama and the book of poems better than a small wind blows its name on my skin on a small patch. Are you a little speckled egg? Are you in Italy Mama said but then she saw a voice that you call it and I went like you and she did different a long time ago. Did you know that? I'm in Ljubljana on a map but I have never been here. Didn't know the things I know? I was in Italy and running out and tried to call you in New York and didn't pick up but someone helped me. Ljubljana is a black word but a light place I don't know if you have been to and the house is in a little town Jamnik. You could see me. The first house alone on the road before the town all summer over the valley with a church that no one so it's only with the sky. Want to see me? Maybe Rider'will you come?

◇◇◇◇◇◇◇◇◇◇◇◇◇

Bells in the Borromini. Courtiers snore behind the curtains to their rooms. The street is quiet, Sunday. Rome is in the churches or asleep. I told them all last night—one at a time, at different hours—I was leaving. I steady myself against the table, having stood too quickly, too little blood in my brain. The room implodes softly, fluorescent colors.

Purplish scents, organic, composted. Could be the crusts of wines in bottlebottoms on the table. Sunlight glares off Tahnee's makeup mirror. I pick up the mirror: straight lines, mutt-brown hair, thin eyes. My breath against the glass, deflected back on me, is still (because I did something last night you wouldn't understand) adulterated with a purple-brown, beached mermaid scent. Indeed, one of Xabier's paintings on the wall depicts a turbaned fisherwoman holding up an octopus with giant mirrored eyes, in which are men, each with my naked back, and each one holds a mirror, so I sneak into Sperry's room to the extra dresser and repack my backpack.

Empty glasses on the dresser; a rectangular bottle of gin, clockwork of moisture rings; footsteps in the commonroom where I just was. I'll travel light, having abandoned my American clothes and gained a suitable disguise. I don jeans, backpack, black Italian boots, a white, high-collared shirt.

Are you an adult? You use computers and travel alone? And why Slovenia? Most alarming of all: Who gave you money? *Are these honest questions?* I suppose I am, without my medication and America, becoming more adept at not ingesting painful commonworldly information. Any citizen of that world would be right to call this lying to myself, and yet they would be wrong on all the deeper layers. I am writing this to you, and if I don't believe me, how can you?

I need time to think about this, but the curtain flips aside, and a bolt of hominid fear fires, anus to brainstem: run, kill, or die. I need money. I don't know what happened to mine. Xabier advances, shirtless, dark around his eyes. I'm waiting for John, or else I'd have left three days ago when your message came. I should have gone to a hotel. What happens in this house is too predictable. I crash into the dresser. A glass spins off and does not break. One of my eyes goes dark.

Maybe I have twenty seconds. I fought a man at night once in a park in Brooklyn and won. Bronner taught me some when I was young. Young men say to each other it's not who is larger, but more often the berserker combatant, the brave, the stupid. Missing his face, catching his beard. He hits my chest again and again. I lose his beard. The gin on the dresser—I slap his jaw with it—one-quarter full, it does not break. Behind my eye, the one he has not punched, a pile-up of black waves. I swing the gin. He falls onto his side with low, surreal velocity. A second figure, not his shadow, dances in periphery.

•

A FUGUE OF STRINGS blows through a street of windowless and doorless structures. Time without partitions: if a clock were here, the hands would glide, not tick. Long words, embossed across the dark material of a manhole lid, are unintelligible. No source of light, no vector or consequent shadow, but a weird deficiency of blackness individuates each object, and although the fugue, diminishing, arrives at volumelessness, it continues informationally, transcribed as the spiral grooves on manhole lids, which slowly, phonographically turn.

Silence from the streetbed and the polygonal structures, but where does this greater silence come from, this arrow of vocative zeroes that glides in from nowhere you could be?

I'm here perhaps a minute, but the minute warps and dilates:

Something scrambling on the cobbles, spinning closer, sounding like the cooling fan inside an old computer, now resolves into an animal cocooned in fire. It thrashes tooth-at-tail in blue-orange halos, flops to one side kicking, and a wolfish echo, visible, a burning ghost, whelps out of its throat to fly at no moon.

Old dust of a gone glimmer merely? A fist knocks it loose? Too little dust, if so. This is a helplessness. Inside

Ghost at the Loom

a glimmer, I have will, a lucid dreamer's agency, a boiling pulse of it, the anticyclone eye on Jupiter, revolving in my fragile, Bandy chest.

•

I'M AT THE STAIRWELL door with Sperry in my way. He whips his arms around like ropes, absurdly telling me I must "relax, relax." Behind me somewhere, Tahnee or Garcia curses in Italian, meanwhile my shoulder sends Sperry off-balance, and he sits down in a disarray of women's boots and shoes.

Down every other stair to the piazza, no depth perception——bloody streaking across the wide church steps, onto the boulevard, along the Tiber wall. I flee down white stairs built into the wall, down to the river's concrete rim, and crouch, and regain the sleight-of-brain that asks one to believe one's will is free.

Don't walk down there at night, Garcia, maybe Tahnee, said a week ago. Boat ramps, broken glass, cardboard homes. I drip a little parody of blood into the Tiber, musing without wonder at millennia of blood of wars, assassinations, muggings, inquisitions, washed along.

But could it be what happened right after he hit me wasn't hopelessly unglimmerish? Had the structures in the fugue had windows, I might have detected your reflection.

On the holm in the Tiber ahead, there's a hospital, and I hear healthcare's free in Italy. Head down, I walk that way *drip follow drip I follow drops to you to you.* Tomorrow I'll strike my head with a stone? What else might work——electroshock, sleep deprivation?

◇◇◇◇◇◇◇◇◇◇◇◇

I N AN EYEPATCH STUFFED with cotton fluff, I travel south along the Tiber rim. Three indigents cook sausages over a fire of empty fruit crates, and the scent is very fine. I'm sleepy. Four p.m. gold light on shattered glass on the paved riverbank...and Leya, what if you are an adult, one who travels alone, who left home because at last you've lost the glimmer, too? This question hurts, not in my head or chest. I don't know where it hurts...burned Bandy bodies, question-trees deracinated, in my head I'm softly screaming like a song. My mouth is open. I'm sleepy and quiet.

A narrow pyramid marks one edge of the Cemetery of the Foreigners. Celt planned to take me here. Three curious names collected from the stones:

Aeneas MacBean, Esq., Late Banker in Rome.

Otto Henrick Minck.

Edmund Peregrine Townley. *Hello.*

Hello.

I'm Edmund Peregrine, my little sister's in Slovenia.

Aeneas, a virtuous pagan. Otto and his eight revolting sons?

At Keats's arm lies Joseph Severn. At the feet of P. Bysshe Shelley (1792-1822): Gregory Corso (1930-2001) and

William Shelley (1816-1819). *Bury me here.* What year do I die? I've read there is an age past fifty when one's sense of beauty sharpens briefly to a point, beyond which that sense decays.

1930-2001? Another clever joke. Though I have been suspicious for a few years, here in Rome it has become quite clear: despite what calendars and tombstones say, the whole conspiracy glitched at year 2000 like a mound of sand with one too many added grains. The one too many never tumbles off the pinnacle alone, it takes a little hematitic avalanche down with it, the system collapses, stabilizing at the nearest metastable date, 19??, 18???

I become very suddenly frightened (this happens to me recently; it's like a piling up of air, a wing too large to be a bird's buffeting above me; something's swooping at me from behind) and badly want a carbamazepine. I wouldn't do that to you, not when I'm about to find you, and it always passes, and I'm calm, beatific almost, at the grave of Edward Trelawny (1792-1881), who found Bysshe's body.

No name on Keats's stone:

This Grave

contains all that was Mortal

of a

YOUNG ENGLISH POET

Who,

on his Death Bed,

in the Bitterness of his Heart,

at the Malicious Power of his Enemies

Desired

these Words to be engraven on his Tomb Stone

"Here lies One
Whose Name was writ in Water"
Feb 24th 1821

•

"YOU OUGHT NOT PUBLISH so immediately," Bysshe replied, condescension unintentional, and John, inaudibly coughing in the wind (he had, a moment ago, walking under leafless alders, off the path, discovered vaguely in himself a warmth toward this baronet) said, "Why do you suggest that?"

Bysshe had kneeled to inspect a toadstool. "Only to see your powers increase before fools without foresight note them half in bloom. They will make a slavish noise at your expense, if you allow it."

"Isn't that St. George's mushroom?"

"No...no, as they only come with spring and are not quite so slender."

John held his elbows in his palms and watched the older poet's back. "What would you do, then, if you were, impossibly, me?"

"I'd have us both write epics. I would have you as a guest at my estate."

Bysshe laughed, a single note, *but crooked, incompetent booksellers, lawyers, apothecaries*—he was thinking of his enemies. He thought he could convince himself they knew, as if by sorcery, where he was walking, off the path, this minute. Then the fear subsided, and he stood and tapped his boot-tip with his supplejack, a gesture

Ghost at the Loom

unfamiliar to him, puppetlike, *who are you? standing
awkwardly inside me, unborn ghost*—
~~fugitive from jeering masses,~~
~~my Shelley or another passes~~
~~backward through / the sand,~~
~~the Death Bed of another~~
~~Shelley and / another~~
~~epic, but the replicas /~~
~~lack some essential quality,~~
~~so I shall have to / leave this country.~~
"It is good of you to offer that," said John. "What is
the mushroom, then?"

"That kind is called, by plain folk, liberty cap. Did I
tell you my epic will be on the subject of liberty?"

•

A BROWN CAT DRINKS water from a curved leaf by the base
of the stone. I ask it insignificant questions, and it rolls
and winds, a lemniscate about my ankles, scratching its
back on my shoe, the grass, my shoe. I shift my shoe.
I close my eye. A man in brown clothes sits against a
vinewrapped wall. He holds a book and pen and watches
me. He writes. I squat, hand on the grave, my own book
on a cracked flat rock, and cross out and re-record more
faithfully the epitaph. I write some lines of verse and
cross them out, then write some lines and don't:
A blaze beneath a blossom
tree, a wind forks

wind and names—hail
fire, green John—saint me.

Whose nest fits on a grassblade?
But I have to go now.

Writ in blank rest, please—
this house, I—

stedfast as thou
blazing shade—

I wish to not die.

"Hello," I say to the man by the wall.

"Hello," in the tone of an Englishman mocking Americans.

I don't remember what we say at first.

I say, "You came to see Keats's grave?"

"Keats? No, I haven't read a poem since I was nineteen. I guess I read tech magazines primarily, the breakthroughs, like a blind man in your country has been taught to drive. They fixed his eye up with a retinal implant, now he drives with the top down. But it's very good, Keats, isn't it? How about your eye. How're you?" He looks me in my bandaged eye. "You're slightly bleeding."

"I'm okay," I say and give him my hand and tell him my name.

"Johann Bell." His grip encloses mine entirely. He must be six ten. Gray-red thinning hair. He's near my age. "Well, pity he was born too soon."

Ghost at the Loom

"Who, Keats? I don't think that's correct," I say. "He wouldn't have been Keats if he'd been born in 1999 or 1821 or whenever this—"

"Isn't it he'd be something of a Keats the same," says Bell the giant, "different input only, better maybe. And he'd have a shot at real immortality, that is, longevity, like centuries of consciousness."

"What are you," I say, "scientologist?"

"Quite the opposite."

TWENTY-FOUR O'CLOCK, FOUR BLOCKS north of the palazzo, I grip a bottle by the neck, the red wine mostly gone. I can't come find you yet, and so I lurk with a bottle sloshing, waiting for John. I guess you understand, even from your uncorruptible remove, what money is.

My eye stings—it is this rotten cherry stuffed into my skull. At night, there's too much light—it is spilled wine and dye. The Bandy world had clear black weather and the otherzodiac. No balance, bull, no scorpion or twins. Instead, a tower trailing wires, a horse's tooth, a long guitar, a question-hook? My good eye blinks, my mind blinks: *momnos, memnos*.

Wine makes me want. Roman night alleys are runways—cuffs, sleeves, curved cracked terracotta white leather language. Maybe each woman sees me, one-eyed bottle-handed lurker. Each looks once and walks on. Each, I imagine, is gentle to someone.

I slide along a wall into a doorway's indentation. Paro's mercury locket's in my pack. I take it out and spin the cobra, quickening the globules in its head. Swigging, back against the door of some apartment building, feinting as if to press a random buzzer on the panel, studying the hand that does, chain of a necklace wrapped around it.

I've not become someone who knows this city. It remains a barely Roman Rome built of dead English poems and fragments of mirages of home. I mean that all these stones have not become *pietre*; they are *stones*, the saints are made of *stone*. Well-chosen words become a wall of carved and fitted *stones*.

There is here, though, the edge of something, a deeper skein. I can't articulate exactly...hints of you in dusty light on marble, hints of Bandy houses in a sudden broken symmetry in certain architecture, when a series of miniscule not-quite-seizures shiver my head and neck. I'm freaked with unselfconscious hope. Moments come when my dead Western poet's nostalgia (I mean what comes when I am *dead*: when I cathect on artifacts carved and fitted by minds now dead) waxes, as I idle here, receiving whatever blows to the eyes might help me look for you, when I, through that nostalgia, start to see beneath the thinnest veil of Leya hanging over everything that does not make loud noise, certain century-haunted faces in the paintings, faces having nothing to do with you, yet inexpressibly important, starkly, anti-solipsistically important. Sometimes a line in Shelley seems to reprimand me for how much about myself and you I've made my search. Arcades of pillars, obelisks in the piazzas, ridiculing my insistence on their tree-row and electric-tower qualities.

I'm finishing the wine. A bony, prickly, quilly sense
of inarticulateness, a premonition of failure, scribbles in
my head—you seem for a moment not to exist.

I'm waiting here for John, who, never mind his faith
in lack of faith, his disregard for tribalism, so he claims,
will still inquire, "Hath not a Jew dimensions, senses?"
of blond strangers in museums and bars.

J OHN: "THIS LOOKS LIKE a third-rate brothel minus the whores."

"You don't go to whores." I'm packing my backpack in my hotel. We're going to his hotel. "What was in London?"

"Research." He picks up the pillow I've been using and sniffs it. "You really are a pitiable Jesus. I am going to give you some more lucre."

"I accept."

He removes a laptop from his attaché and opens it on the bed. I lie on the bed, my head near his leg. He shifts through world financial markets. I lie at my post, gazing over his leg into tin mines, beverage factories, life insurance, derivatives of wartime infrastructure contracts. Ticker symbols, copper-green arrows, arcs of numbers, commodities, cattle, corn. Tin soldiers kill and replace each other. Behind my eyes, blood beats a bit more heavily, and I feel full of superfluous health.

"I feel okay," I say.

"Guess what I taught them all in London?" with a vigorous working of his lips. "They've got their class system all screwy. It's apocryphal. It should be taste, not capital. The rich need education to have better taste, and the few tasteful people there really are as shabby as you."

"I have two shirts. They're both fancy shirts."

"Oh, I know. You're better than them all, better than I am even."

"Sure."

His wallet is beside him on the bed. It's made of lizardskin.

"But I'm not *tricking* you, tricking you! You really are the most aristocratic twenty-first centurion I know, you have the real nobility, a cultured, civil savage, and a poet, and no wife, really terrible to women, not a sexist, but so childish, so they tell me, childishly difficult. If I could be rich as my da and as noble as you, I'd go to whores. You do know 'Paro' has more dendrites than you've got?"

"I've never met, or even seen, a whore...please don't say Paro's name like that."

"Your girlfriend is from India? Her family must be so thankful a real American took interest in their daughter. I mean, *you* don't subscribe to the stereotypes, but if everyone else does, don't you? Doesn't the negation of the *merde* they think and say exist in you, and so the *ombre de merde* in you takes up really almost as much space as the original?"

"I don't know what that means."

"Like this: I have a French girlfriend, I know this doesn't mean she's sexy, but I like to tell my American friends, 'I have a French girlfriend.' Fine. I have a limey girlfriend, doesn't mean she's posh and proper, doesn't mean she loves and hates and yanks my upright citizen, my unwashed George Washington upupupsetting her uppity empire, but I like to tell my friends extremely nonchalantly, 'My girlfriend's from England.' Now I have a *German* girlfriend, things are getting weird, but people, they are interested. She must be *unheimlich* in the hay—hey, I don't believe in any of this cancerous hysteria, but everybody else does, so how do I feel when I say, 'Yeah, my girlfriend is from Belarus, she's from Iran, I'm doing her a fucking favor.' Rural *India?* Cambodia? She's from some outpost up the Congo? People tell me how 'amazing' that is, that we managed to 'connect' across the world. I'm basically an anthropologist. There's nothing hypocritical about them, anthropologists, they're holy folk."

"I just don't care about these things...she's not from rural India."

"That's what I'm saying. You don't care, but everybody else does, so you play along unwillingly. The negative still takes up space."

Shadows of oars float silently across his screen-lit face, from which they lance across the wall and out the window. Someone, an old man judging by the tone, yells, "*Andiamo*, Mama!" in the alley one story down. John sells some tin. Oar-shadows, lances, the fan on the ceiling. Eli told me once, when he came to give Mama some papers, an ingot of tin makes a sound like a cry if you bend it.

John: "If I'm absurdly wealthy and/or erudite but not domesticated by the morals of one of the conventional classes, what am I? A hyper-pseudo-non-aristocrat, a hyperborean, is what I told them all in England, and it's as true as herrings are communists. I told them, upper classes are disgusting when it comes to mannerisms, patronage, and friendship; lower classes are just plain disgusting, crime is art to them; and there are so many disgusting middle-class conventions, sexual and otherwise, I won't start to enumerate, okay, but what I'm getting at is that the educated, noble savage, reconstructed from the mashed-up twentieth—there is no other twenty-first century noble type!"

I say, "There is no twenty-first century."

Bronze lizardskin, with tiny arrowpointed scales—he puts a card back into the wallet and closes the computer. "No," he says, "the trick is to be wholly unpigeonholeable, savage but not philistine. Like for example, you don't ask if I've been working on my 'book.' That would be philistine. You know with an instinct—you know what I'm doing—like an animal starts running when it smells smoke you know, that I'm the most contemporary kind of artist, in that I produce no art. There's so much surplus grain in wealthy nations—"

"That's what Paro says."

"There's so much surplus milk and meat in wealthy nations it's an obligation of the citizens to transfer portions of their energy to cultural production. Yessiree, it's like a tax. Art classes in the schools, each child and undergrad is making something this week. Drawings of mom. Glazed, wobbly pots. Short stories about when the puppy or Grandpa died."

Ghost at the Loom

"I'm going to Slovenia. I need enough for that."

"I'm also going to Slovenia. I actually was there last week. I had some business, can't tell you. Discreet, you know, negation of the negation."

"You weren't in Slovenia."

Sometimes when a human speaks loudly (or when John, whose calmest voice disquiets, speaks at all), you become, in my image drum, a brittle form, a forked branch inlaid in a half inch of ice, a girlshape on her back on a white quilt lit up by the vertical, icicle bulb through aquarium glass and fishless water in your room...when you didn't get out of bed. A glass of water on the night table. Half a grapefruit balanced on edge on a plastic plate on the table with water and three pills, little green zeroes, to be taken hourly through the evening. Your foot off the edge of the quilt. Your toe, my finger, your toe, finger, toe, interlaced. *I will bring you away to a college with me when I go. Eli said I'm going.*

"Yes but Jesus," Minus says, "do you know angelology?"

"You can't come to Slovenia. I'm meeting Leya there."

"Now *that's* profound. As long as you accept that no one's family or lack thereof's a source of pathos anymore. The Family's ceased to be a source of blood, except in third-world countries, and Japan's not one of those disgusting places, you know, without double-ply soft. In Japan—we're in Japan, okay?—there're twenty-seven words for *sign*. Okay, okay," a gesture, thumb and index, as if zipping shut his mouth, "but let me just say you are obsolete here, see? Your whole pathos is outsourced to Japan, then China, chop-chopped into subcontracts. You've got to go back to America, where folks look at the backs of their heads in the mirror and think, 'This is my face...' What? But look, I like you even more today than yesterday, when I was not around to hear you say things like you're meeting——wait, but what——*what* but? What but. What but," to himself, intrigued by these syllables, "hwut, but. I mean, do you know what I like?"

"You might like these." Chocolates I bought for his arrival——I get off the bed and take them from the dresser's only drawer. "Here."

"I don't eat out of that kind of furniture." He puts them in his pocket. "What have you been doing?"

I don't tell him how I hurt my eye. I tell about Shelley and Celt.

"That's disgusting. What about the last few days?"

"Preparing for Slovenia."

A shadow-interrupted shaft of sun increases through the window on the glossy back of his computer. In that black gloss, my boots in the corner are dimly reflected. I go to put on my boots, but go instead to the computer and pick it up to move it from the sun, and John is looking at his telephone. I hesitate——the plastic's nowhere near to overheating——smelling pomade in John's hair. I put down the computer. I'm a bureaucrat in someone's mildest nightmare, my function to abortively move objects, and my lower back hurts, and the patch is coming unstuck from my eye, about which (I know and can't explain why) John won't ask.

He checks himself at several angles in the smeary mirror. "They eat horse there. I would like a Slovene woman to ridicule me and send me away without satisfaction."

"You can't come with me, though."

"Okay, but to be not serious for a moment, you ought to let me come, because you really are an invalid, I mean you really are defective, and the only reason you're allowed to go around in two shirts, both fancy, is that you interest, not why you think you do, a wee minority with access to depraved amounts of resources. For all this to continue, we are either going to have to figure out how to make profits off of tar sands oil or shale, or else genetically develop fungus or your blue-green algae that shits gasoline, or else the Kalahari, the Sahara, and American Southwest have to be tiled with solar-powered atmospheric carbon capture modules. That's a *shitload*, as the French say, of synth gas. That's Jesus, I don't think you understand, each object we enjoy, each dainty treat's the 3-D surface of a deeper object with a hidden dimension that's the amount of energy it took to get it to us. With a certain type of eyes, you go into the grocery, you see each box of pasta is in fact a little beaker ounce of oil!"

I have been skulking in the northern parts of Rome, where Gigot's people don't go. Yesterday, near the Villa Borghese, the giant from the cemetery walked along the sidewalk toward me, until I saw he was not the same man.

I imagined him stopping a few feet from me. "My judgment," he said with a faintly Scotch accent, "will not bend to your opinion, though I think you might make such a system refutation-tight as far as words go. I knew one like you, who to this city came some months ago, with whom I argued in this sort, and he is now gone mad, but if you'd like to go, we'll visit him, and his wild talk will show how vain you are. He lives in the Julian Alps, in a town called Jamnik."

"But I didn't tell you my system," I said near the Villa Borghese, but no one was in earshot. Then I had to come back here, to my hotel, because Minus would be coming, and I needed sleep; and now Minus has come, and we are going to a restaurant.

There is a lovely woman several tables down, with a face like Alexa Wilding's in Rossetti's paintings. Minus has already seen her. "I hear you've *borrowed* USD from 'Paro.' Whereas anything I give you is a gift. Look, look at me." He's eating bread before his entrée comes. "You have to fill up on this base material, they charge you for it in Europe, idiot. Look at me."

"I am."

"I'm not democratical at all!"

"I know." I'm using Wilding to visually interfere with the sound of some English-speakers behind me, cheerfully arguing about the merits and deficiencies of what must be a video game in which one drops warheads on Russian cities. John hears them, too, but noise to him is nectar.

Ghost at the Loom

"I just finished telling you why *you're* the aristocrat. You think *I'm* a self-respecting idiot?!"

"Be quiet, John." I don't like when he's loud in restaurants or museums.

"I mean, this whole thing makes me want to regurgitelaviv all over you. Democracy? A bunch of children solemnly debating whether to accept nutritional instructions from a doctor or a candy manufacturer. Just tell me where we meet and when."

"Vienna, maybe."

"Good, Vienna, when? And talk to me about this craziness you're into now. I mean, it started in Vienna, everybody misbehaving, everybody crazy knows that, but I have to take you someday into deepest England. That's the last place left where you can waft your Orientalistic djinn bottles and sip on bottled tears to your art's content. I just wish *I* had something to be miserable about. I'll think of something, give me thirty seconds. I know—that I need much more sophisticated acolytes."

I do get tired of John. "I didn't want you to come here."

"No, but you didn't tell me 'Leya' was in Europe."

"I didn't know until a week ago."

Why don't I like it when he's loud in restaurants? Who decides what I like?

"That's lies." His blaxploitation accent. "Lying— lying like the president."

"I don't like when you talk like that."

"Then you're untrustworthy."

I stumbled over Mama once, long past midnight, in the hall. I'd risen to get water. I was maybe fourteen. She was sitting on the floor in blue jeans and no shirt. She'd spilled some water on the wood and drew with a finger in the water...then, years later, I died riding in rain in New Jersey. I thought I saw you, and the wheels shot sideways under me, you standing on the grass between the highways in a long sweater of Mama's at four a.m., and I slid on my back on the grass, a scrap of headlight ripped an L-shape in the back of my leather jacket, and you weren't there, no one was, and I lived and rode on to Manhattan.

I ask Minus, "Where's my motorcycle?"

"Middle of my living room. Three supers carried it...oh, wow. Remind me I said that. Great title. *The Uberintendents*, a play in one act."

"I'm trustworthy," I say. "Sometimes you're part of the problem. I don't like it when you hijack situations."

"Part of the——" He holds his beer up. "Tell me what this is."

"Beer."

"No, what kind of beer this is." He indicates the brand.

"A beer," I say.

"Okay, you pass. I'm proud of you. But this denial, even if it's noble and absurdly healthy, this is not the same thing as immunity. If you weren't just another monoglot American, I mean, if you could understand what all these Europeans here are saying to each other—what, because here, there's architecture? Part of the problem. No, you're wise, I get it. Psychologists are idiot-wrong. Self-helpniks? Wrong. Because certain problems must be denied. Otherwise, cancer. You get cancer of the persona. Cancer, Sir Dagon St. Anthony Tomahawk-nose XVI. Let's have another Nobel Prize for Christian de Duve, discoverer of the lysosome, because I think that's how they're going to cure it, cancer. Whereas I, I don't deny, I don't repress my problems. I'm not a liar and look at me, cancer. I'm part of the problem. My nose has cancer."

You wouldn't even know to say it's beer. I'll be there very soon. What would you say? *Dead bottle.*

•

NAKED, FROM ATOP A pile of stones, Trelawny somersaulted into a deep river pool. Bysshe watched, fully clothed. *In the pressure that hurts one's ears they say, I would I would crystallize in it, some rich jewel. Or a coal full of unexpressed fire—*

Trelawny surfaced. "That I learned from savages! Upon an island nearby Java whilst I served the benevolent crown."

"Horrid crown," said Bysshe.

He traced by sight a line of water running from the hollow of Trelawny's wishbone down into the black hairs, down the hanging arbor vitae, off its tip, into the pebbles, *geometrical, bisectable,* and half behind his open eyes and half on Earth, he saw da Vinci's *Vitruvian Man* superimposed, and he said, "Why can't I swim? It seems so very easy."

"It's because you say you can't," Trelawny said. "Determine it, and so you will. Execute a header off this bank, and when you rise, turn on your back. You will float like a duck, but you must reverse the arc of your spine, for now it's bent the wrong way."

Bysshe spent his mornings reading, standing at a pedestal. His small head rested slightly forward on a delicate stalk of neck, and he had no beard. His frown became a narrow opening, as if to breathe through a reed. Waistcoat and shirt and trousers off, he kicked away his shoes, removed mint-colored socks, and limply dropped into the river.

Facedown, self-consciously Vitruvian at the clear pool's bottom, in black sand and stones, he looked for Mary first, but then not Mary; who was this, another *epic but the replicas are only words, of ink to dust to walls to windows light to lead to gold I will be gone, to grace? To asphodel, for grace is half too strong a word, it glances off the rhyme with glass, off the path, to asphodel to eglantine to infantine, infidel, fontanel, cries, the Magi*—arms grappled along his ribs, legs touched his legs. He was hauled upward, into an Italian wood.

The men lay on their backs, a lace of sun and cedar shadows on their skins, the poet breathing roughly.

"Well," he said, "I always find the bottom of the well. And they say Truth lies there. In another minute, I should have found it, and you would have found an empty cage."

"And what, my savage friend, is Truth?" Trelawny said.

Ghost at the Loom

"The most perfect jest. No one has found it. I was looking for it, such that I might laugh underwater, but I did not."

Trelawny picked up one of Bysshe's socks. "Knaves are the cleverest," pulling on the sock, "they profess to know everything. The fools believe them, and so they govern the world."

"And yet," said Bysshe, "astronomy is working above, geology below. Chemistry is seeking Truth. In another century or two, we shall make a beginning. At present, we are playing blind man's buff."

"And what would Mrs. Shelley have said to me had I carried back your empty shell?"

"You won't tell—not a word!"

"Shelley, I would not." He regarded with pleasant confusion the poet's pained features. "No, you distress yourself so, and when there isn't any need."

"Perhaps," Bysshe said. "It is a great temptation." *I am not safe, what do they call me when I am not present, histrionic, hysterical didact. I can hear you thinking.* "Another minute and I might have been in another planet, if old women's tales are true."

◇◇◇◇◇◇◇◇◇◇◇◇◇

I RIDE A THIN-WHEELED MOTORCYCLE east, along the Venice-to-Trieste cliff highway, overtaking caravans of tankers on the Adriatic.

I called Eli this morning.

"Leya's in Slovenia" was one thing I said.

Worried and I think impressed, he wired money.

I called Mama. "Leya's in Slovenia."

"It isn't strange...to hear that. When I think of her and see her, it's a place with trees and mountains."

"How do you know what Slovenia looks like?"

"I was looking at it in the atlas in your room."

"When?"

"I don't know. Maybe yesterday. I'm glad I'm helping you."

I printed a map of the Julian Alps at a cyber-kiosk, dropped the eyepatch in a trashcan, took a tram into the Jewish Quarter, took out of my sock two violet €500 notes from John, and bought a very old French motorcycle.

Out on the Via Salaria, there was a motion in me disconnected from that of the motorcycle. All my ignorance, my flawed beliefs, were moving, growing darker, sharper, faster—crosswinds and the sun, a flaming brain, a compass rose—and faster. All the famous dead were falling from the balconies and clouds, red shatterscatters on the Roman road.

My jacket flaps, the noise of a flag. Insects die against my chest and face. A tunnel leads onto a wooded ridge. Accelerating over stripes of sun. Trieste flickers far below, crescent-shaped along its harbor's edge.

I cross the border, still accelerating, sun stripes blurring into one another: finally truly on my way to you, I am as if detached from my body in motion, projected out into a fragment of a self-mythology, a folktale with a half-life so short the folktale can't be studied, all one knows is that it was about the boy who rode too fast toward what he thought was open country, hit the wall of Paradise, and fragmented into a thousand undelivered letters.

In Kropa, I eat ostrich steak, black bread, and calamari. Humans are polite to me and do not seem to be revolted by Americans.

Conversing with a man who parks his motorcycle next to mine—"And what do people say about Milosevic's trial?" I ask boorishly, or some journalist asks with my voice.

"It was not our war. That is, I hope, clear to anyone. The southern states are full of the insane."

"You've no opinion on it, then?"

"No, no. What brings you into Radovljica?"

"Looking for my sister."

"Yes? Sadly, I must meet my wife at a garden shop, but good afternoon."

I tap the metal helmet in his motorcycle's basket. "I don't have a helmet."

"No, I see."

"What do you say about Napoleon?"

"Please, I don't like to be rude, but I must meet my wife. She's preparing a party." He laughs without amusement. "Not a large one."

A crooked trace up into alpine quietness, slow work on a light bike. Mist drifts down the peaks, across the road. No signs, no towns, rock and dark trees, a hawk or buzzard hovering against a huge cloud.

I throttle past the sign for Jamnik, around a curve, out of the trees, and am arrested, braking, staring out across a valley of square miles, and places like this proved God to Aquinas, but I feel—not a proof, of course, or angel of anything—maybe you can be...something out past these words.

A chine juts from the mountainside into the valley. At the chine's end is a small stone church. *You don't like churches? Leya, I don't know.* The art in Rome was nearly glorious enough to block the enervation pouring off the crowds.

First house alone on the road before town all summer. Structures in the trees ahead. I've gone too far, nearly into the town itself.

Ghost at the Loom

I ride back and find a gravel drive, invisible the way I came, that drops off the road through a gap in the guardrail, down into a sprawling, weedy courtyard. Amateurish, sentimental works of sculpture, crumbling steppingstones, a rusted spade, and in the courtyard's depth, a house. Weather streaks the windows, which emit no light. One statue is a soldier studying the southern sky. He clutches his fist against a chest wound, rifle in his other hand. Around his neck, a wildflower garland hangs—between his boots, an egg-sized stone, speckled with unweathered gold and emerald paints. So you are truly here. Such heavy strangeness. Fives and sevens, these cycles of wildflowering beats on my dark image drum.

I lean the bike against the soldier's leg and go into the shadow of the entryway. A water-damaged note from Paro pushpinned to the door! I curse inexpertly and take a pen out of my backpack and deface the note, but, doing so, see in an upper corner, in what must be your adult handwriting: *at the church*, written over Paro's writing. I am looking at this for a long time. It's my handwriting, but shakier.

A delicate nausea comes and goes. I've asked to be confused, but beautifully, and what is this? I'd say impossible, this note, you here with Paro's help, except, if Mama's house is a house you can exit, isn't everything permitted?

No. If I don't eat the carbamazepine, then other people must not meddle. Even Mama couldn't tell me where you are. You wrote to *me*. I feel as if a promontory has shot out beneath me—someone with my mind is slipping toward the end of it—shot out so far I could almost believe you if you told me Minus, too, is involved.

Five and seven-petaled flowers scatter in a mental wind before a diving, incoherent image hits my drum, too hard—I can't think about Minus or Paro—nebulosities of stone and snow and brutal crowds, college students drinking-running-yelling in New England streets, French soldiers retreating from Moscow, but none of these, nothing so easily sayable. *Scythians, Hittites*, Aryans migrating out of the Caucasus, *what are they riding?* Something like boat-shaped horses on rolling land. From inside the drum, looking out through stretched skin into the circular view of the valley, I intuit your shape throwing rocks at the horsewater tub, which, when hit, rings like a distant cellular phone.

Does it ever seem, inside a moment that, by definition, doesn't last, that you alone last, everyone/everything else is a discontinuity? I'm about to see you, see you, physically? Broken frames around pieces of thin time, scratches, pentimenti. *At the church*—but Leya, do you even know what churches, mosques, and temples are? I don't mean *I* alone last. *You*, I said.

A dry mud path, no wider than a wheelbarrow, no footprints, down to the end of the chine. Nine stone crosses in the churchyard, three by three. The steeple is a triple cross. I enter the grid of graves, look off into the

Ghost at the Loom

valley—too much to intake at once, farmsteads, scattered
pine hills, rainclouds ten miles out—and slowly spin to
blur the details. Feeling old and young, I spin a little
faster. Clockwise, slowing, stopped, hand on a stone
cross to steady myself. The clockwork Earth whipstalls
in space and chatters broadcast static starward, military
codes, trance-dance-club anthems, radio evangelists...

I know, but not to think about the noise is difficult
when I am always in it. Interrupt it, Leya, interrupt—
remember you you remember Bandy voices?

Emberember...

Spin the opposite direction if you're dizzy, Eli took me
once without you to a park and said spin spin and
that I could correct my balance in my fluid inner ear.
Counterclockwise, trying for a long time not to think
about the commonworld or anything a part of it.

I thought, at first, it was a stand of weeds: a wild-gone
garden, purple chard and short corn, on the slope
beyond the church. How difficult is it to truly look at
you, a highly conscious being? Shadowy, a thin young
woman crouching in a patch of chard. Are you a little
girl? If I stare at your glancing profile too long, will you
turn and look at me directly and obliterate me somehow?

You eat peas off a bush, splitting pods with your
thumbnails. I'm close enough now to smell the plant's
sugar, the clear green blood of the pods. One by one,
you pinch peas out and eat. The two-inch wingspan
of your moving lips. I crouch beside you, sideways

watching you watching me sideways in the quiet other than your munching sounds and the rhythms of crickets. I have loved to watch you eat. You do it with the unselfconsciousness and business of an insect.

"May I have?"

You put one in my mouth.

"Another."

I chew two peas, and you put the last one in your mouth and turn your fingers down and splay them to drop the pod.

"I watched you, Rider'spinning."

"Yeah?"

"You're very good at Rider'spinning."

"How long have you been out here?"

"This morning."

The valley behind you, now in horizontal light, is easily transfigured by my image drum (which more so lately overlays the commonworld, but this is no more than a glimmer of a glimmer, glass panes in nine or ten isolate farmhouses catching the low sun, relaying the signal, closing the circuit, the signal I send to the sun by staring into its corona, the blinding core safely blocked by your head) into a painting of the topmost layer of the underworld.

"Why aren't you home?"

"Mama turns the lights off in the house."

"You're in the Alps. It's so bizarre."

"I like peas, do you like peas?"

"I do. What are you doing out here? Are you with anyone?"

Ghost at the Loom

"Rider'shh, don't ask me every question. I like when you're quiet." You stand, the sun that was behind your head now reddening behind your hips. "Pick. You can see the church or treehouse, which one first?"

"Treehouse."

So I follow you down to a precarious pair of birches at the chine's end, up a ladder of broken branches and old wire, a nervous climb to a nestlike platform between the two trunks, poorly built of wire, planks, and branches.

"What is this?" I brace my weight against the trees and not the planks. "I'm skeptical of this. What was this, built by children?"

"Falconers. They had binoculars."

"Who told you falconers? Is Paro here?"

"Hm?"

"Was Paro here or did she send that note for you to give to me?"

"I told *you* to."

"I don't remember if I've even told her you exist."

"I want a falcon."

"We don't have those. Falcons are for rich people in England," I say. "There are crows...crows in California. I assume you have a house key to that house?"

"You have."

"No, Leya."

"In your backpack."

"I don't have it in my backpack."

"Rider'stop, I put it in."

"Just now?"

"I said don't ask me every question or it hurts my head under the skin. You tell, you tell me things, pea. I haven't seen you for a little while."

Past your grown-up child's face, the trunks' diagonals divide the valley into asymmetric sectors. Now you look at me and look away and look again, and I look away, and what can I tell you? I can tell you stories in this letter—it is not too late for that—but not out loud, not when you look at me from such remoteness: you decrease me to a point of missing self, a zero-dimension. We're anesthetized inheritors of some disaster. We don't know what it was; we weren't born; we can't talk about it; it would be dishonest to, to borrow sorrow from the families whose survival has resulted in our lives. I make up stories still, but all my stories now are self-attacking, half-ashamed:

A sister and her brother once lived at the bottom of a hill, but then a fire damaged or destroyed all papers from which any record of them could be drawn with certainty. Flaked-away sections and dark carbon ripples effaced all but the passages that easily could be about a thousand other families. Just when they thought they were about to find a passage back to when they ran away from Mama in a window in a white dress watching them run up the hill, a passage they'd been looking for for years, there was a hole in the manuscript wide enough to drop my pen through.

Ghost at the Loom

"I'm the one," I say, "who taught you different birds, remember, finches, falcons. They were in a brown book in the box made of wood in my room. Leya, am I talking to you properly? I don't know how to talk to you as an adult."

"Finches? Rider'good, and if you turned into a little pea because it didn't have a mouth, you can't say anything...you can't? Then I will tell you things."

I am afloat in alpine blue, utterly confused at last, and there is beauty in it, even if no glimmer. You are here. We're in Slovenia. It might as well be Venezuela, anywhere we don't know anything about. The commonworld roars in and out. The way you talk...it hurts my head. *I'm sorry if it hurts, I had to see you.*

"Tell me then," I say.

"I am, but don't forget sometimes I'm not clear right now...because this isn't such a clear day."

"Okay. Tell me."

"Want a pillow?"

"Thanks," I say, "but I don't think there are any up here."

This is the story you tell me in a tree in the Julian Alps:

"Falconers went here to build a house. You were there. You didn't know who could take care of you. There was a little egg peahead who came and sang me then, and then when you opened your eyes, a van with lights on top was leaving with them in it. Sometimes I see a man lying under, between the wheels. He calls me on the phone. Don't worry, he's not you. I heard Mama say, 'Leave Rider'stay.' Were you outside the fence? 'Take three of these. Drink all your water. Go find Rider'stay. You are a story I tell my son to make him stop growing.' We're not people, well, I said it's not so clear today, I'm not, but sometimes I talk to your friends like you say what happened. Then the man under the horse, he was your friend. He left a message. Rider'good, do you miss Eyeball?" and you laugh, a stratospheric, thin, apologetic sound. "I'm really not so clear today."

I don't know what to say. The wind lulls. Among many still leaves, one flutters. "Look." I point. "Why that leaf only? Chaos theory. That's—"

"Woodworms."

"What?"

"Writing worms." You're pointing at the tree's vermiculated bark.

I say, "I guess that's right. Do you read books?"

"I told you."

"And you talk to Paro?"

"Sometimes I talk to your friends."

At the "t" in "talk," the tip of your tongue appears, rough dark red, raggedly healed where you've bitten it off since I saw you last.

I say, "I saw your tongue."

"They told me if you cut a starfish leg, another whole fish grows."

"Who told you that? Must have been me, years ago. It has the same genes. It's a clone."

Ghost at the Loom

Then, for many minutes, nothing can be said. It's as if you're not here, or I am not. The wind leaves and arrives and seeds little chaoses, random numbers in the leaves...

"Rider'secret."

"What."

"We have to see the other thing. Goodbye this little house." You kiss an inch of wormpath on a trunk.

"Okay. We'll go look at that church, and then you let me take you somewhere else? Not back to Mama right away, don't worry."

"You're a *bad* wood worm, you have to think of women more. You have to copy me." You feint as if to kiss the bark.

I swiftly kiss the bark. "I think about women all the time. I think about you a lot. Are you a woman? You're twitchy. Are you cold?"

You shake your head. The leaves behind you shake as well. The commonwind arrives and leaves. The otherwind almost arrives but flees.

"So Paro cares about me? So much she's discovered you?"

"No, Rider'she doesn't know, as long as you don't ask me every question...no more hurting me."

"I'm not." Something is lightly crushing me, I can't decide from what direction. "Please, I wasn't trying to, are you okay?" It's like a wheel, a millstone, and the product of the mill is this disquietude, this dust in me.

"One question a city from now on, Rider'asker, one, or else a bad thing has to happen."

"Per city? Where are we going?"

Planks are missing from the back wall of a stall in the church's doorless stable. We duck into a room, a sacristy I think, strewn with old bicycle parts. An open wooden door in one stone wall leads out into the narthex.

"If you want, stay here. I'm going up to play." You walk, on your toes, in the aisle, in the sun-and-moon dusk light down through some stained-glass windows. A scarecrow Christ haunts the common landing of two winglike staircases, one of which you take, touching his leg as you pass.

Above the stairs, pipes dominate the great back wall, not Roman gold, but dusty iron-colored pipes. The whole of this church is unswept and shabby, not ruined, but not often used. The pews smell faintly of wharfwood, boatwood. You're at the top stair, stepping onto the landing. I stand in the aisle, and you sit (inside a parapet of small pipes) at the keys, and I can't see you now but I can see the shadow of your arm extend and then the shadow's fingers poised to touch a key.

This organ does not work or is not on. The keys click in the quiet. I can hear notes, if you like. Uncommonworldly notes ricochet off my image drum: finches, piccolos, foghorns. You begin to sing—too softly to be understood—then stop, then start and build and narrow to a vocal point. The point floats up and down...out through the holes in the warp of the commonworld, out past the riptide, signals, clocks.

"*Anan ananai.*" Bass chords on the organ, two, five, seven notes, falling back to the two sustained, overlayed by the seven again in the range of your alto voice, so the words come out from a five-seven-nine-woven chrysalis, post-Bandy language I don't understand. "*Ankarigarawnkanka...*" catching and uncatching in the hollows of the apse and nave.

I drop into a pew.

"*Oroi oroi karawnka...*"

Christ of unknown dark material. It does not seem alive or dead or Christian. Nothing here obeys, or balks at, any commonworld religion, nothing like in Roman chapels. It's as if we are not in a church, as if this building's been desacralized without heresy, heresy having no existence outside the context of whatever religion it offends——my hands becoming

feminine, discarding euros,
flutes of wine, and clothbound
books into an ocean, drumming
the back of a boatwood pew.
Wing-shaped
visible echoes
spinning from rims
of the wine-colored shadows
of nine stone crosses. A shiplike shape, a crow-
black juggernaut jack-
knifed up off the swelling
soundwaves, piloted into
a zodiac of windows

in the soundwall slamming
in my chest, each twelve-
     tone window
stained, staining in turn
each unison pitch and accord
you stretch my inner clock with, circular,
ovoid, now linear, so
that the distance,
    window
to window, rest
to rest, totaled, is
black time too slow
for sound to be not seen,
my senses vinelike,
 intertwining on the windows.

Your shadow convulses, its arms flying up to the sides of its head, hands batting at space, as if trying to cover its ears. It falls behind the parapet of pipes. I scramble from my pew, bolt, trip, smash my knee on a stair and, through the pain, break out/in/through a texture like the surface of my drum, but thinner, slicker, *knee-deep in an ocean, black sand, there are stars between my long black toes.*

It's night when you wake. I carried you out of the church, up the path, to this blank-walled, alpine house (unlived-in, plain, so unstrange-thus-utterly-strange) and laid you on the doorstep to look for the key you must have slipped with a pickpocket's quickness into my backpack. Indeed,

Ghost at the Loom

it was there, in the bottom, nestled with that note from John and the carbamazepine, and so I carried you inside and laid you on this unmade bed and, for an hour, considered pushing a carbamazepine into your throat with my finger, but then was ashamed and put the bottle back into the bottom of the pack, and now you're smiling at me with your eyes closed, seemingly unhurt.

"I don't know how to talk to you. How do you want me to?"

"You had your question here already. We don't have to talk so much." You're talking, but you won't open your eyes. "I could be clear tomorrow."

"Good."

"If you can let me back to sleep."

I T TAKES DAYS TO sell the bike in Ljubljana, and I've written nothing. Days of our reunion, which should have been so important, are a pair of empty pages facing one another?

Now the bike is sold, we're in a cheap hotel, I'm writing to you, using the room's windowledge as a desk, and I say, "Where should we go? Did you fly with a one-way ticket? Leya."

"Rider'what."

"Don't ask you questions?"

I have found you, but there is a blankness here, a sense of anti-climax? I'm ashamed, if so. It has to be some incapacity in me. Something is fastened, or keeps catching. Something keeps declaring you a decoy. Or you're here, it's you, except I haven't found you yet. The glimmer still feels faraway, and you are close enough to touch and faraway. My hand has gained a twitch. My eye is healing well. You are, I suppose, this young woman with waist-length hair and a falcon nose, and I am your brother escort. Take you from city to city? An iris-ringed tunnel reopens between us somewhere?

"Rider'spain, I don't know."

"Do you want to go to Spain?"

"I'm hungry."

"Where there? Barcelona?"

It's as if I miss a word or sentence here and there of what you say. Is this a hopeful sign? Is your attention also cut through by brief passages of blankness? Blanks between pages *stanzas, metrical brickwork, rooms without windows* of focused attention. For me, there is a near-oppressive quality of workmanship—*of rhyme*—between the blanks. For you, the negative, the complement, must be the case.

"Pamplona," you answer, "and that was your question."

"That wasn't my question. It doesn't count unless I know it does. It has to be a solid question, not just a little logistical question like—why Spain?"

"You don't know. I don't know what I say. You make me talk. I don't like to. You like it but I don't you like it."

"Does it hurt to talk?"

"That's okay...I'm happy here with you."

"You're *happy*? Leya."

"Mm."

This means, I think, you are. "Nn" would mean you aren't.

I say, "That's not my question, and neither is this." I'm helplessly bullying, trying to cheat, but you nod— you're happy here with me. "Pamplona? This isn't my question, either. Pamplona?"

You've found an inch of white thread dangling from a button on my shirtsleeve on the bed, my folded shirt, the one I don't have on. You're picking at it—this is meaningful, but really not: "Oh, Rider'cities don't mean something else. They're just the words you like. They're just my paints."

In Rome, in moments of naiveté, my task was to return you to Mama, or, I thought, return to you, or protect you from Europe, myself from America—none of these is it. Will I begin to know with you with me, with extended exposure, something to do with certain lines from Shelley I've been falling through, like *what thoughts had sway o'er Cythna's lonely slumber / that night, I know not; but my own did seem / as if they might ten thousand years outnumber / of waking life, the visions of a dream / which hid in one dim gulf the troubled stream / of mind*—that any return to the glimmer is one tangled tenfold compared to returning to you in space, in "southern Europe"?

"What do you mean paints?" I say.

"I play piano cities...that was it."

"Was what?"

"Your Ljubljana question."

On the first of three trains to Spain, you say, "On time, Paro said," as if you know her and communicate with her somehow, but when were you out of my sight? It arrives, the winglike buffeting behind me, then it's gone. I think it comes when I get too close to becoming unconfused. My mouth is open. I am not yelling and holding my head like a little boy. I have to take care of you.

Ghost at the Loom

"She's in Europe, too," I say, "makes sense. That doesn't mean we need to go to Spain, though. We don't need my friends. I can play this drum at a station for some euros."

In Trieste, I play the small flat drum I bought in Rome for an hour and am ignored. Too many longhaired Americans drum for free in Europe at stations in summer.

I call Mama. "I have Leya."

"Sometimes people don't know what to do. Are you in a train station?"

"Yes."

"She shouldn't be there. Bring her home."

"I will."

"I'm making jewelry today. I'm making earrings." Then, with her mouth away from the phone: "Leya, have you seen my tiny hammer?"

"Leya's not with you," I say with self-surprising force.

"You have her, though. I guess you'll have to fly tomorrow."

"I don't like that, Mama. Don't pretend you're talking to her."

"A few days, maybe...you do have money?"

"No. Do you? Do you know how to wire me money?"

"Probably you need to help me, Rider." She's audibly rummaging—what is she knocking together, stones? "You need to come home."

"I can't yet."

"Well, you have to. You have to bring Leya home."
She's becoming upset. Her voice thinning indicates
this.

"Mama, I can't yet. I need some money."

"I can mail it to you. Where are you?"

"You don't have money."

"If you bring Leya home I do. Some people don't
know what to do."

"Okay." I have to semi-lie to Mama, see: "But I don't
really have her yet. I'm close. I'll tell you when I do."

It takes me another ten minutes of twisting and
circling to get off the phone. You're beside me, watching
an outgoing train, a sleek one, recently built. It looks
like ingots on a conveyor belt.

"Don't cry," I say.

"I'm not."

"I thought you were."

"But Rider'look, I don't have any tears."

A woman walks between us, rudely, swiftly, close
enough for me to smell her perfume, a white, urban
scent, no botanical referent.

I step through this chemical ice to you. "If I ask the
right questions, what happens?"

"Is that your this city question?"

"Yes."

"Your sad will go away," you say, and eye contact
becomes unbearable.

Like Pascal's Wager. Am I to believe you? Certainly
it will not happen if I don't.

Ghost at the Loom

"What do you mean?" I say. "I mean, do you know what that would mean?"

"Knows, knows."

Stomach-deep, subsonic rhythm (from a train, a heart, my image drum, from you, impossible to say which) in the wake of you promising *knows, knows* has run me through with need to be not here, not public, forked me into two one-legged runners parting at a forked street, but a windy heat, a rush of childish self-protection, forces them backward, together. What's happened here? I feel *followed*, like a child feels in a night street running home with nothing following him.

"We have to go to Spain," I say. "I can't get money here."

I'm an adult, on a railway platform at noon, and you're following me toward the timetable display.

"Why not?"

"Just believe me. You don't need to think about money."

Through a city I don't see the name of, you glimmer (not roughly, not a seizure), triggered by sunlight strafing, strobing between buildings. The train slows, speeds, and you come back, not talking, but alert, in the seat across from me, solving the little riddle of living in the middle of eternity untroubled by the rhythm of the ties, which is, for me, a measuring of time, foreshortening to a false depth my sense of age, of having traveled, but I think to you an instant is no more a point of departure than an unasked question:

I said last night in Ljubljana, "What time is it?"
I said it again.

"I thought you hadn't asked," you said.

Little riddle in the middle of one so large it threatens
to beat me senseless, beating and swooping behind my
head, but subtly, barely noticeable now. Little soluble
riddle enmeshed in one so large as to be almost nothing.

The second train stops in a region of fields. Italians
behind us say there's a cow on the tracks. What are you
writing on the bottom of your teacup with a pointed
sugar-breaking spoon? Shadows of Morse clouds crossing
the fields.

Why not believe me if I say I wake from a doze, you're
asleep, and when I open this to write to you, the facing
page left blank isn't blank anymore:

Dear Friend,

**I send you this, but without my name. I wrote it
with the idea of destroying it, but now I find it is
too long. Two of the characters you will recognize,
and a third is also in some degree a painting from
nature, but, with respect to time and placelessness,
approaching an ideal. You will find the whole
visitation, I think, in some degree consistent with
your own ideas of the manner in which poetry
ought to be written. I have employed a style of
language to express a station of the mind which**

Ghost at the Loom

education and a certain apocalypse of sentiment have placed above the use of vulgar idioms. I use the word "vulgar" in its most extensive sense. The vulgarity of rank and fashion is as gross in its way as that of poverty, and its cant terms equally expressive of base conceptions, and, therefore, equally unfit for any future. Not that the familiar style is to be admitted in the treatment of a subject wholly ideal, or in that part of any subject which relates to common life, where the passion, exceeding a certain limit, touches the boundaries of that which is ideal. Strong passion expresses itself in metaphor, borrowed from objects alike remote or near, and casts over all the shadow of its own self-bloodied sword. But what am I about? If my grandmother burns churches, was it I who taught her?

I do not particularly wish this to be known as mine; at least, at all events, I would not put my name to it. I leave you to judge whether it is best to throw it into the fire. So much for self——self, that barb of grass that sticks to one.

——your friend

The third train crosses the Pyrenees. Umber raw rock, hewn in bites from the planet. I read aloud lines from the books Celt loaned me, stolen half-mistakenly:

"...nor are the strong and the severe to keep the empire of the world. Thus Cythna taught, even in the visions of her eloquent sleep, unconscious of the power through which she wrought the woof of such intelligible thought..."

You tap the page. This means, I think, you don't dislike it.

"Bysshe's his name," I say. "He had little sisters."

I called Eli today from a mountain station. "If you talk to her, tell my mother we're okay."

"*You* are," he said, "your mother is another situation."

I said not to worry about you. I think he had hung up.

I read you Byron in the foothills at night.

"Don't out loud."

"Why not?"

"Don't, Reader'rider."

So we read together, silently, a few more cantos.

"I don't like him."

"I do."

"He's too hiding. You like him, you have to. I don't have to, too." You push my foot off the bunk with your foot, then smile to reassure me. "*You* are little bluebottle eggshell head and didn't you know I'm clear right now, because it is a clean train and a blue day, and I'm happy but I just don't want you to speckle my brain with that book about I don't know."

I try Keats on you in the morning: "...locks to shake and ooze with sweat, his eyes to fever out, his voice to cease.

Ghost at the Loom

He stood, and heard not Thea's sobbing deep; a little time, and then again he snatch'd utterance thus.——'But cannot I create?'"

"Yes."

"What?"

"John."

"Keats? Do you know my friend John?"

"I saw her on the train."

"Saw who? Is Paro on this train?"

"Rider'stop." You uncurtain the window. We're leaving a hamlet station. Two olive trees grow from some broken asphalt: gnarls, silver, spasmodic leaves, thousands, eyes, hands, nerves. *Dear friend, please try to keep your mind out of the world, it has enough in it already.*

"John, my friend John is in Europe, too. Does Paro know that?"

"Shh...we're not in a city."

"Do you know my friends? I know, don't ask you questions, one per city, but sometimes we can't play games if it's important."

"Sometimes?"

"Sometimes what?"

"We can't play games?" The simple way you say this, like a disappointed three-year-old, sends the acid from my stomach to my chest.

"My friends," I say in a tone of apology. "Paro is about to be a lawyer, if you know what that is. John plays games with banks. One of them will give us money, then we'll go without them somewhere."

"Why will they give us that?"

"That's a good question. I don't really know why they do."

Maybe out of perversity.

At Pamplona-Iruñea station, I shake you by the arms to wake you, take the blanket off you, and find myself faintly disturbed to see (a hint of betrayal, *of whom by whom?* absurd, but difficult to shake out of my head) the complete poems of Shelley pressed between your thighs. I shake my head, as if there still is water in my ear, though it is language, now I know, not water.

Naturally, we're met by Paro and her friend Sravanthi on the windy platform.

Paro: "I am shocked. We came down to the station only on a whim. I really am amazed. How do I know if you check your email? Most women never would tolerate you."

Sravanthi: "Like me, I wouldn't."

Paro: "You look different, more brutal. No, I like."

"It's my eye. It won't scar."

"Good, that would be awful." A red festival flower behind her ear.

I say, "Do you want to know what happened?"

"When we are alone."

They wear white blouses and new red suede pants flared over new white boots. I'm so confused now the confusion's spilling over into something else, a clarity, a resolution not to trouble anymore with commonworldly

Ghost at the Loom

hows and whys. I found you, that's enough for me. For me they have a red bandana. It is the ninth of July, the festival of San Fermin.

◇◇◇◇◇◇◇◇◇◇◇◇◇

PALMS ON MY CHEST, Paro pushes herself to arm's length, her hair a tunnel suspended between our faces. When have I spoken of you to her? Once, twice, something mumbled like, "I have a sister," so why should I speak of you now?

She isn't asking. This is generous of her. Or sick and tricky. Either way, it doesn't matter. We have to remember, I'm no longer curious how this has happened. As far as I care to know, you are, to Paro, just "his sister, just met at the station," not of interest, a silent young woman, a harmless, docile psychotic, a minor burden.

"What do you mean," I ask Paro, "when you say see the summit? That's not something you would say."

"Not as a metaphor, crazy, we want to read about the G8 summit on the Internet. This hotel's Internet is unsetupable. The *room* is good."

"You like the room."

"Without getting up, can you lift up this thing, turn it over, can you—" I obey. It says, on the reverse surface of the little table, HECHO EN DINAMARCA. "—thanks," she says. "I thought so. The table and chairs look good, but nothing works in this hotel. We might go back to Genoa in two weeks, to see if protestors upset the summit."

"Vienna, you mean. It's already over."

"The G8 is in Genoa," she says. "You do not follow politics."

She is above me, half wet from a shower, hair in a byzantine rhythm of overlapped loops. This woman born in India who's memorized the U.S. Constitution, who knows which belt and jacket go with which boots to which restaurant—some humanist could write a wise, important book, a whole life, beauty, education, and decay, with Paro as protagonist—she's wasted on us, though, and you can't care, but I do taste a note of guilt.

I say, "Sravanthi's seen to your various needs?"

"We have been here just twelve hours since Ibiza. There is nothing more——" She pulls the hair below my navel. "I have no way to express it, but Ibiza hurts my heart. We did not want to leave it. We cried on the flight...where is your necklace?"

"Right here in my backpack."

"Your chest looks odd without it. Put it back on when we finish."

Very glossy, Paro's lips, no different than my memory of them. Her eyes, though *punched in the head punched in the Pleiades*, the blank black in her eyes is unfamiliar. Truly a reptile's eyes behind tank glass. She's tricked me—someone has. My mood toward her swings with her hair as she sways to the music erupting from the street two stories down: a note of guilt, of intimacy, human womanhood, a source of peace? It swings into a blank black wall. I disappear.

I'm back. Framed by the glass of the balcony doors: red pyrotechnics in dark purple air. I slept through the day. The other bed is empty, sheets disturbed.

I ask too softly to receive an answer, "Where is Leya?"

Paro slithers to the bedside and spits my chromosomes into a Spanish soda can. "You do not take care of yourself," she says.

She flares her lips. She's looking in the mirror across the room. Her face gains angles. She, without reflecting deeply, understands she must confirm what she appears to be to others, not to me exactly, but abstracted tens of thousands, sharpen and anneal the outward parts of her into a shatterproof image: Mach-speed, millennial cosmopolite with rhomboid ruby earrings. In one motion, she arranges, executes, and reloads a rendezvous with that self. She is radioactive, reclining now, semi-pornographic, laid out lavishly across the path of decay of the Western idea of the nude. She will look at the mirror again, immediately after I succeed at what she's waiting for.

I say, "You could wire some."

Bronner laughs, a loud, high-quality noise, from which I duck away. I can still hear him well, holding Paro's phone a foot from my head. He talks, but a blank has arrived, and when it leaves, my attention has shifted from ear to nose. A nose is a finer sensor than an ear or eye. Telephone plastic and hotel laundry and my unclean shirt. Do I smell strongly to you? Different, I imagine, from when we were children. Can you detect if I've been in a room?

Ghost at the Loom

Bronner: "Why? So you can spend it on champagne?"

"Yes."

"What do you do again?"

"I don't. I mean, I can't be hired, socially. I can't look people in the eye when they're lying...they don't know they're lying. I don't like to expl——"

"How's Mae Band?"

"Exceptional."

Sravanthi, possibly, is eavesdropping. Her head is very still, ear aimed at me. I step into the bathroom.

Bronner: "Big blond head——head of hers?"

"My mother's hair has not turned gray, if that's what you're asking."

"So I have to show you around Paris?"

"You've been to Paris?"

"Sure," he says, "I buy in Paris."

"Nn, you've never been to Paris."

"Sure."

We talk for a while about Mama, nothing I'd put in a letter to you.

"You plan to call me once a year?"

"Yes, sir," I say.

"And what?"

I didn't know you were in here. Sorry to walk in on you, but you're not upset——you're at the sink, regarding yourself in the mirror.

"Why?" I say to Bronner. "Well, why not? It's just paper with white people's heads on it."

"Not if I wire it."

You turn on both taps and smile at me, and the ache to protect you is so strong I hear nothing Bronner says for minute or more.

"—my ankle," he's saying. "Surgery's not cheap."

Inadequately sheltered from the shoving mob, you rock, heel to toe, inside the circle of my arm. Paro must have given you these red and white festival clothes.

"Soon," I point, "bulls will run in there, and sometimes someone dies."

"They die?" You indicate a pack of men pouring red wine on each other's white, Greek-lettered jackets. In the lee of the logbuilt barricade, two men choke and slap each other in the dust.

"Sure," I say. I'm being shoved around inside our generation. Everyone I do not know is here. Impossibly, you're also here, and in my image drum, a thin white tree with magma-colored roses grows out of a broken monitor amid a wall of active screens—world news: the running of the bulls—and I can feel the brittle lightness of your body knocked and knocked against me.

"Why are you holding your stomach?" I yell into the escalating noise. "You have a stomachache?"

"I have a little baby egg!"

I don't have time to think about what this might mean, because a man is trying cheerfully to walk through us. Sravanthi pushes past us, too, and, standing on my foot, climbs up onto an unattended vendor's cart. Because she is subordinate to Paro in some vague,

Ghost at the Loom

primatological hierarchy, and because this both disgusts me and disrupts me with reluctant lust, I, as she climbs (maybe to feel what it might be to be one of many young male persons here) give her red suede ass a slap, which yields a yelp.

Paro puts her bottle down carefully on the cart and slaps my shoulder. "What was that?"

"I don't really know. I was trying something."

"I said," she yells inside the mob noise, "what was that!"

"I'm about to drink this wine!"

She puts her mouth to my ear. "Did you do that because of what I said that time at the party!"

I lurch away. "What party!"

"Why are you being not a gentleman!" She slaps me again, softly. "What are you thinking!"

"I think no one will die, but there'll be injuries!"

Her mouth is on my ear, "What are you thinking about me right now!"

"What time is it?" My mouth on hers. "People are slapping people."

"What were you thinking about me?"

"Not you, Leya!"

"What!"

I feel an unfamiliar, admonishing perspective in me, asking whether I assume these young people whooping, pushing, singing anthems are, in fact, anti-sublime. I find I have no ready opinion. Maybe they experience intensities of anti-critical compassion, brotherhood, neo-hunter-gatherer love, sweat and meaningful violence. I am curious. You, of course, are not. Could it hurt you that I wondered for a moment here if I, on the rim of the commonworld, might cede my mental heart to it or you if either would take more than half?

I'm eleven feet tall astride the barricade. You, below, behind me and the barricade, untie and tie my shoes. Paro and Sravanthi stand with half-bent, ready knees inside the bull run, in amid the drunks and braves.

Two bulls already ran. The second tossed a man against the barricade, ten yards from us. Revelers dragged him under the logs. Medics dragged him into a truck.

A rumble from inside the city, expletives in many languages. We are a bottle's throw from the cervix of the stadium, in which bulls die. Flight instinct, contagious, transmitted by sight—not sight of bulls, but of running people, precedes the rapidly oncoming rumble, pulsing runners to the edges of the run. Some scramble up the logs.

A third bull runs. A man falls and is trampled by his friends. I'm ready to drop and catch you, but your grip is easy on my ankles. Paro slithers, shrieking with glee, between two barricade logs and stands and puts her hands over your hands on my feet. I scan the chaos for Sravanthi—there she is, a rather lovely, menacing, visceral woman running, whooping with the many men, the bull behind them, toward the gates.

Ghost at the Loom

On the stadium's exterior, a graffito: TOURIST YOU ARE NOT IN SPAIN LONG LIVE BASQUE COUNTRY. This barricade is real to you, I don't know why. Mere meters from these animals, fiercer than horses, you don't have the tightening in your face.

"I'm ready with my question for Pamplona," I say, dragging everyone's luggage along a cobbled road. Paro and Sravanthi have gone to find us food.

"Little speckled head," you sadly say, "you had your one already."

"I did not. What was it?"

"Why are you holding your stomach."

"That wasn't my question. Leya, play fairly. You said if I ask the right questions, you were clear then when you said that!" I'm not yelling. I don't mean to raise my voice.

But now you seem sadder and enter a silence you'd have me understand is helplessness not stubbornness.

We wash our hands, feet, and shirts in the Arga. I watch you, moving away, near Sravanthi, a hundred yards upriver, *an adult*. I don't need to follow you? But the city is packed to overcapacity. Paro was able to get only last night at a hotel, from which we stole towels and blankets, and we'll sleep tonight in the park with hundreds of drunk human beings. I tried to tell you, you'll sleep between me and a tree or wall, you'll be safe, and you told me to "shh." You wanted to wade upriver. Your toes were hot, you said.

Smaller than my hands, I don't mind Paro's feet. They stand beside my head on a flat river stone, toes in my hair, and a human part of me threatens to surface and drug me with notions of passion, obligation, put me to sleep with my cheek on the hairless, dancerly bridge of bones and feminine muscle and skin, and maybe I could say love to her, painlessly, an anesthesia even, but the skeptical director, that perspective in my head with no face and a head like a zero, lurking, tells me: *Amsterdam 16:05 tomorrow tell her not to come half-love, you husk-love, mask-love and how many nights in her bed in New York.* I don't know. I don't have proper memory.

"Stop, please." She reclines beside me, pulling my shoulders, my face to her neck.

It's a problem of authenticity. So many stimuli have to align to make me believe in Paro or myself. You alone are real to me.

"If I say stop, you should." Paro scratches the crown of my head. "You stop." *I'm sorry.*

Sometimes the authentic thing/place/state seems near—it's as if I gain speed, like I'm riding the breaking crest, my senses curved together in time like a wave always breaking toward shore, but the shore retreats at the speed of the wave: if I'm reading or writing a line with a wave of its own, its multiple senses suspended, salt-crystallized, or if I'm naked with Paro or fighting, dancing, riding, drumming, jabbering with John, I gain speed; but these are not it, not it.

On Horse Hill, the glimmer captured time and dammed it to a trickle.

Ghost at the Loom

Paro's saying things like "Rider, can you stop?" and "Thanks for coming here" and "I appreciate you. Ask me something? Ask me for something."

I am compelled to ignore her, as if by your instructions. Armadas of bottles and cans. Circles follow skimming insects. My hands and the ends of my hair and her hands in the river. You walking upriver.

O N A NIGHT TRAIN, in rural Allier, through fields of
dark grain, Paro atop me—rail percussion beating
out a rhythmic backbone to the nearly silent song from
your bunk below, a new song, half in English, half
ananai—Sravanthi asleep in the top bunk across the
compartment.

To sleep and travel at once is theft. Theft from
time. Promethean fire. A spark of that in me, an
early memory:

Eli had borrowed someone's RV. On a highway,
with you in the forward bunk compartment at night,
under quilts, I unpretended that I touched your
head to check your dream, a private, non-repeating
world, good. I don't remember, maybe the Bandies
were eating. They liked little seeing-eye berries and
windybird drumstick bones that had sweet yellow
marrow.

I spied through an oblong window on the
taillights and headlights. You, asleep, I, half-asleep,
alive before we'd heard of death, were stealing miles
for which the understood price is hours, waking up at
the effortless destination, somewhere with redwoods,

California. This specific spark from commonworld and commontime is stolen, taken with us elsewhere.

To rest and study and travel at once. Paro's tactful, slight motion and silence, her legs atop my legs, her back to my chest, my flaccid cock between her buttocks. Turning pages with my free hand, I follow the recipe—

> *Wit may flash from fluent lips, and mirth*
> > *distract the breast,*
> *Through midnight hours that yield no more*
> > *their former hope of rest,*
> *'Tis but as ivy-leaves around the ruin'd*
> > *turret wreathe,*
> *All green and wildly fresh without, but worn*
> > *and gray beneath.*

—flicking her clitoris to Byron's demi-demon rhythm, striking the flint, and the feeling from childhood is back, satisfaction, theft, effortless efficiency, albeit deviated out of grace: to read and stop her lust at the same time, to the same time.

◇◇◇◇◇◇◇◇◇◇◇◇◇

ANTI-MNEMONIC WHITENESS THE COLOR of quiet noise. This first day in Amsterdam seems to have fallen into a blank. I know we checked into a hotel and slept. It was light outside.

◇◇◇◇◇◇◇◇◇◇◇◇◇◇

I SEE YOU, BETWEEN MY fingers, naked, arms around your knees, head jerked to one side, steam and water blasting from the showerhead, with vomit on the surface of the bath.

"What should I do?" Sravanthi's screaming in my ear.

A key sound, turning in a lock—*did you hear that?*

Hear who?—you turn your head with queer fluidity, cheek to knee, and whisper.

Paro: "Rider!"

I am staring at a wall.

Sravanthi's at the tubside on her knees. "Who cares if she's naked, help me get her out!"

"What did she say?" I say.

"She's having a seizure!"

Paro slaps my shoulder. "What is 911 in Holland?"

"No," I say, "just help me make her clean."

"What is wrong with you!"

"Nn—clean. Help me clean."

We hold you up under the spray, and your head swings around on an as-if-boneless neck, and when your face swings near my face, you are looking at me with incongruous clarity, with spray ricocheting off your back and shoulders into my eyes; and then, with the vomit washed off, we carry you out to a bed.

Sravanthi: "What has her doctor said?"

Paro: "She should see a doctor. Does your mother know that? Rider, look at me—your mother knows that Leya needs a doctor?"

"No, she's been to plenty. This is it. It's not a problem."

"Then why do you scream *fuck, fuck*? Rider! You scared us so badly."

I didn't scream. "I didn't scream." *I sudden't dream.*

Sravanthi sits down on the other bed. "You understand she is an epileptic, also possibly autistic." She takes a metal brush out of her bag and tends her hair. "There could be also dormant MPD."

"Doctors said it's neurological, years ago." I remove my wet shirt. "If they found out more than that, I'm sure my mother isn't telling anyone."

"Asperger's syndrome possibly," Sravanthi says. "She should be medicated for the epilepsy."

"Leya wouldn't like that."

"You are an idiot," Paro suggests.

"That's also John's opinion," I attempt to say. My voice seems to come from my stomach or lower. My mouth is closed.

"What if she swallows her tongue? She could die."

"She never does," I mutely say.

Sravanthi: "Does she vomit always? She could choke on it."

Ghost at the Loom

"She's only started that in Europe." This concerns me, but I do not want to talk to them about it.

Woken by the sound of water, I get up, having dreamed you had a seizure in the shower. You're asleep in the other bed. It's early night, and now the door is buzzing. Paro comes in with two just-purchased mp3 players and a brown paper bag full of pastries and starts berating and quizzing me.

Sravanthi's laughter from the bathroom wakes you. Paro's yelling at me now. What I say next in a quarrel of two idiots I won't remind you. Soon they leave to purchase marijuana and go dancing, leaving Sravanthi's brush on the opposite bed.

I offer to remove Sravanthi's hairs.

You look into the paper bag. "I don't want to brush."

"It's getting tangled, though. You want to read."

"It clears me."

"These?" I point into my backpack at the Byron, Keats, and Shelley books.

"I don't need to right now. It makes me better... when I talk. Did you notice that?"

"You told me you don't like to talk."

"Rider'clears me."

But I don't know how to talk to you.

•

EXITING THE PATH, INTO a copse of conifers and thornbushes, Bysshe and a male companion stepped onto the hunting grounds of a six-year-old gypsy, whom Bysshe stopped to study with obscure longing, as he might a bird or doe, and yet not with a naturalist's separateness, for as he studied he, he felt, became more bird than man. She was slight, with tangled points and shards of black, extensive hair, and her head twitched to one side *tic of malnutrition, tic douloureux if one of these French doctors should examine her were she my child, indeed she would be fed milk and oats and given education—bare-legged, squatting, in a gathered smock with wool patches. She had partly filled a sack with snails.*

She was so murkily collected by the little spiral worlds, she did not see the men until they'd watched her for a half minute.

"But I am struck," said Bysshe hushedly, "by her intelligence. I mean to say, such as is latent in her countenance."

The man behind him nodded neutrally.

"And in how humble a vessel," said Bysshe, "and what an unworthy occupation for a person who once knew perfectly the whole circle of the sciences, who has forgotten them all, it is true, but who could certainly recollect them, although most probably she will never do so. She will never recall a single principle."

Human beings, he supposed—not in this order, a conflux of images—make candles from tallow, slaughter cows, forge hammers, stitch jackets from leather, build houses in bad weather, crack bones for soup, and, from such industry, surplus enough obtains that each night he may

Ghost at the Loom

spartanly dine, then lucubrate to exhaustion. He intends to walk this way again in the morning alone. *Alone?* A strange, non-identical twinning occurs when the wind blows from just the right point of the windrose. A girl's hair tangles. A bit of rhetoric becomes inextricable from another. One's mood attracts one's less contented self's mood.

She hunted snails still, retreating as she did, and a riverflat stone slapped the moss. A stone clacked a branch overhead and fell to one side of the men, who looked onto the low, coal-mined hill above the copse, from which a boy threw four more missiles, doppelgängers of the snails as soon as they came to rest, not so much aimed to strike as to make it known she was not unwatched by kin.

•

"Are you awake?"

"Some birds outside made dog-bark sounds."

"I need to ask you something. Did a man named John talk to you?"

"That's your Amsterdam question?"

"Okay, though really that's not fair. I guess I need to know."

"He's sleeping. He's not here."

"You do know John, then? Did I tell you about him?"

"I don't know. Everyone's sleeping. Isn't it night? I'm not clear right now. It's not a right question."

"I think he's in England. He came to see me just before I found you. Did you talk to him somehow on someone's phone?"

"*You* did."

"What?"

"You promised to stop asking."

"So you're saying yes, you did."

"I don't know if I didn't. I don't know their names. You're hurting it."

I didn't mean to hurt it. "Hurting what?" I say.

I'm still here. Red clocklight three a.m.

"*Analoo kerawnkeroi, oroi oroi alee.*"

Face to face, on our sides, eyes open. What is this language, Pelasgian, Scythian?

"I wish," I whisper, "your songs were longer."

I've been thinking for a few minutes about noise, not the vulgar, ubiquitous noise that attacks us—something softer. What if laws against whimsical notions coming true weren't so draconian: then we could be, instead of animals with lungs, teeth, and sore feet from walking in cities, merely a signal, a subtle noise; having no more to say, we could leave like circles of radio static, return to the a.m. white sky full of bodilessness...thinking how can I keep you away from this letter ending, from the phrase at which I somehow stop, and the remainder of the page seethes with unwritten noise...how to revert to the default signal...the highway light threads, white and red, in California, flowing opposite each other.

"That's my one-line song," you say, "my one song."

"You can make another."

"There's another, I forget."

Ghost at the Loom

When you sing at night, a dried-rose brown obscurity unfolds and folds behind my eyes. I'm in a sad, small, merciful place. I could say I'm a fraction of a narrow persona, a secondary character in a tale no longer told to children. No one knows why he goes or comes. Sometimes he asks you to sing. He alone asks you that; he is at peace in a way few would want to be. This mood, under the whirling oars of a ceiling fan somewhere in Europe.

"Can't remember things," you say. "I'm always tired."

"I worry there is something with your health."

"I have a baby." You cup your hand against my ear. "Inside, Rider'listen."

Nothing, maybe someone crying nearly soundlessly (it's just the open window and a North Sea wind, an adult crying, not a baby). On your face, a foot from mine, the expression is utterly inward, as alien-blank as the face of a seashell, like faces I imagine on the girls who breathed the vapors drifting from clefts in the rocks at Delphi.

I get up to close two books flapping on the table by the window, and I close the window, too. I am marooned between two sleeps. Each is an open, windy sea. It's as if you're still singing somewhere. I return to the bed in which Paro sleeps. They must have come in without waking me. I'm awake, but somehow not becoming older, marooned on an hour abstracted from time, an isthmus of amber between *oroi* and *oroi*.

I'M AT THE WINDOW. No one else is up. It's nine a.m. and tranquil, nothing like the amber last night, though. This is tranquility as if behind a cracking dam, which, in my image drum, is mounted with a tower (similar in line and materials to the residential tower across from our hotel) with a weathervane slowly rotating atop it, an iron raptor with an iron book in its beak. My inward eye moves down the tower to a crude oil-colored inlet. Too late for the raptor and book to be consequential symbols. They are mental detritus. What can I build from detritus? Now the dam and tower are in pieces. Someone's kicking scribbles, swastikas, and pentagrams across a puddled warehouse floor.

It's noon, and Sravanthi returns to this laserlit sushi bar and places on the table a transparent box. The box contains a type of fungus called philosopher's stones, clumped like amphibian eggs.

Paro opens the box. "Did you pay with your card?"

An earthy stench spoils my mouthful of eel.

"I know," says Sravanthi, "isn't that crazy? The man at the shop said these are thought to be the most potent, even more than Mexican or Thai varieties." Sravanthi thinks this is funny: "And he had a forked beard like a—who had forked beards?"

"*Ex-ci-ting*," Paro sings. "Where do they say is the best place to do them?"

Chemically, they're no worse for you than a heavy night of gin. It's Paro's appetite that troubles me. Talismans must not be gulped. We have to get away from Paro soon.

But maybe a drug, like a punch in the eye?

I say, "How much MDMA did you eat in Ibiza?"

Paro: "Do not say Ibiza, please. It hurts my heart."

"Your brain. How much?"

Sravanthi: "Absolutely not your business."

Paro: "I did take more than we planned. The sea is *perfect* there."

Sravanthi: "You were fine."

"Don't speak," I softly say.

Sravanthi: "Ha! *Don't* speak. Your ego is disgusting to me. Do you know it makes us ill?"

A waiter fills my glass. We wait for him to leave.

I say, "Aren't you a doctor? Weren't you in school for that?"

Sravanthi makes an insect-shooing gesture at me as she says to Paro, "I think we should eat them inside the Van Gogh museum."

Paro: "Rider?"

Sravanthi: "He's busy, he has plans to sulk in the hotel. Besides, he doesn't like hard drugs or being a tourist. He doesn't like Van Gogh or tulips or hash."

"These aren't hard drugs," I say, ignoring her insinuation that to stay at the hotel with you means sulking.

You'll watch bulls goring people in Spain but won't walk around Amsterdam. Something frightens you here? Sravanthi: "No?"

I say, "No, I would eat them."

"Eat them with us," Paro offers.

As soon as Bronner wires us money we'll escape. Yet you seem not to mind these fashionable witches who have kidnapped us. Nor do you mind graffiti on seventeenth-century buildings. What troubles you other than my questions and your clarity of mind? You pass through new old Europe with such impassivity, it's as if you've lived here for years.

"I think," I say, "Ibiza hurt your brain." I am alert to, but without control to stop, these shamefully passive attempts to rekindle the quarrel that will justify escape. I lack the direct methods men like Minus boast.

Paro says, "That is ridiculous," and Sravanthi, under the table, kicks my foot.

I am unsteady, not quite violent. I say, "Don't do that again."

"Then don't be pushy. You are not entitled——"

"Shh, enough," I tell Sravanthi. I tell Paro, "Let your brain recover. I'm about to tell you something honest, that your eyes are more reptilian, less potent-looking than they were before I left."

"Can you believe?" Sravanthi says. "Rider is giving you brain advice."

Ghost at the Loom

Orange flowers float in Paro's tea. She primly removes one from her mouth and lays it on a napkin. "It is almost nice, that he is concerned."

I do care for her—if there were clones of her, hundreds, all slated to die tomorrow, and to save one clone I could hammer a nail through one of my hands or feet, I'd save four. That's right, I care four times as much as the average man possibly can for his one uncloned wife. *The logic's sound, of course, except you fail to take into account Muslims, Mormons, Germans had they won, the ancient Hebrews, also half the businessmen in Moscow and Hong Kong—thus spake John.*

"Look at him, though," Sravanthi says, pointing with her little finger. "Now his hair is dangly, so much better-looking than it was." She reaches as if to caress my hair. I jerk away. So here at least are two clones. They have a joke about their little fingers. They are doing it right now. I keep forgetting what a pointed little finger signifies to them.

"I may never get to dance like that again. I will be old and busy soon," Paro lays her chopsticks down with practiced melodrama, "and it hurts to think about that beach. We woke up still dancing."

"Your pupils are too big," I say.

Sravanthi: "Oh, you stop. It certainly is not the best thing, but a few doses won't do permanent damage."

Paro: "Do you want to ruin my last wildness? Do you even know how old I am?"

"I can't stand listening to us," I say.

I'm sorry, Leya, should I tear these pages out?

Sravanthi: "These are necessary talks."

"They're not if they recur eternally. Then they're a form of...death-in-life."

"Well," Paro says, "but is this not the first time we have ever talked about this?" Like a better-than-average actress asked by the director to appear disgusted, she pushes the box of fungus at Sravanthi. "Vana, if I leave now, will you pay?" To me she says, "I will not do drugs with someone who is not entirely on my side, and can I make you leave and let me enjoy myself with Vana? No, but if you are a gentleman you might volunteer...so?"

Precise—these lengths of snapper flesh, arranged on a black, square dish—eight-petaled star. I am still hungry, my intestines in good health. For about ten seconds, nobody speaks, then Paro stands, sneers at me, and leaves the bar.

I spill the excellent sashimi from her dish onto mine. "Van Gogh museum?"

I shouldn't leave you in the hotel room. You shouldn't be with Paro, should you? But I can't resist attempting this. In Rome, a fist transported me, however briefly. So a box of psychotropic stones...

Sravanthi: "If you don't think that's too sacrilegious."

"Sacrilegious? To eat a few stones without Paro? No, see, at the summit in Vienna, at the Congress, you were there, when divine right was revoked, it was unanimous, but it was quiet, right? The diplomats were all deaf-mutes. You know what I mean? Wait, you're a doctor?"

Ghost at the Loom

"Hm? Not quite, not yet." Sravanthi laughs. "Do I know what you *mean*? Not at all, who does? You're notorious for nonsense. I just meant, might it not be disrespectful to view paintings not as they were painted?"

Oxygen! is the missing ingredient from Amsterdam's wind— this consideration causes me to stop on the sidewalk.

"Hey," I say to no one.

Quick arrhythmic gulps—it's just that I, entranced by scenes (the businesspeople dodging slender trams, these tall, round-headed Netherlanders striding like negligent shepherds through foreign flocks of the stoned, the semi-homeless, postcolonial workers, whores), neglected to take air.

Breathing with conscious measurement, I pull Vana's hand. "Sravienna," I say. "Viana, which way is the——"

"You be quiet." There's a rainbow pamphlet in her other hand. She pulls me—we are running. School is out. Children run, too, perpendicular to our trajectory, across a little bridge. Strange succulents fork from between bricks of the canal. I slow to learn more of their image, but Vana pulls me—over bridges, through a square, onto a thoroughfare.

I pull her back—a taxi misses her—my boot-heels slipping from the curb. She flutters, skirt and jacket, in the road. There'll be no accidents on this foray. All patterns must complete themselves. I feel this in my spleen and gall bladder and pancreas.

A bolt of laughter ruptures from my mouth. I hear my noise and am surprised by its satiric mordancy. It seems to say: I am a devil, elegant with ram's horns, polished cane, and tailored suit; I spit vermilion tulips when I ridicule the world.

She's whirling in on me. She slaps me on the hip, emitting wave after wave of thermal energy, daring me to *hey! you're in the video with* "Jesus! Watchout!" smash the idols, break her from the coven. *She will give you one minus one wishes so choose wistfully.* Totemic, anti-Teutonic tulips, *spit spit*, landing planted, stem-down in her pamphlet, in the sidewalk cracks, o my elegant, sudden spawn, drinking from the gutters.

"Didn't Paro say we could," I say, "last year at that party, if..."

"Unbelievable. You really are. Well, if you like, if there's an opportunity. You have?"

I shrug.

She says, "I have an old one in my purse."

Did you, sir, throw something at me? A soft, fly-sized missile strikes my cheek. I can't tell what, among the specks and slithering spots around my feet, it was.

Blue-nailed fingers dance about my face. "Our tram, our tram is here!" She taps my forehead with her lunacy-colored claws.

What cyborg engineer? A metal millipede, excreting/eating humans.

"Urgh." I hold my stomach. "Zoroasteroid." My eyeballs lick the trotting away of her legs, which taste

Ghost at the Loom

like...information. "Makes sense, information in the place of oxygen, wind on her skin. Telephone numbers are part of the wind," I explain.

Pedestrians dodge the millipede. We're in it. Cars accelerate toward us, daring head-ons, escaping sideways. "Who designed the civil engineering in this maze?"

"See," she mumbles, "Van Gogh's trees."

"Of course!" I say. "Like in a footnote, in an index. Trees designed it." Swung against her by a turn, "I agree! It's just it's hard to speak, because it rhymes—I don't mean sonic rhyme exactly, more that everything's in something's image men straw men dum dum dumb drummer boys, it's like a synesthetic thetic total rhyme, like God, I'm having trouble, hold on." We collapse into the seats behind the driver.

Nose to the window, Vana says, "I think I changed my mind."

"Change how?" I blither. "How how hee. Maybe you didn't like museums before. Your hair rings rhyme with airwaves, sub-sub-bendling, recombinantium peroxide, black rings blond if bells can't see if I eat stones now I can speak the way I think plus or minus one?"

"Be quiet," Vana says. "I'm driving."

"What?!" I mean to say but somewhat yell. "*Who* talks about God? I don't talk about that. I'm a grown-up. What?" No one answers, so I say, "*God?* Well, this is two-thirds, this is, technically—I feel it now. Oh, *thirds*, I'm glad you said that, thirds."

The millipede accelerates—we curve, we jerk through points of harsh mutation, zones of sky becoming zones of stone or trees.

"Fuck *me*," someone hisses.

"Oh, I love it," Vana says, "such a calm society. It's normal to hallucinate inside museums."

"I don't know about 'normal,' maybe tolerated, maybe barely tolerated, but the purpose of a government—I can't—how do we dewy dewy know the Dutch, like most Americans I know, *want* madpeople in the streets, parks, gentlemad—" I gasp for oxygen.

"American dissenters do not vote. Perhaps," she says, "the Dutch dissenters write on ballots not just walls. Is this place a plutocracy?"

"Just walls...*so* glad you said that. That's not how you talk when Paro's here."

"I already *have* an MD."

"Oh. That's unfortunate."

"Unfortunate," she roughly breathes, embracing me against the braking of the tram. "I wonder, can you even bribe policemen in the Netherlands?"

We walk the Museumplein. Casual scholars sprawl with books in swarming green *what is*—

"This," I burp. "I feel such...rhymings, rhymies."

Vana points into the sky. "We both do. Do you want to rest here on the grass and know for certain what these clouds are doing?"

Do not stop from place to place. "No? I'm telling you the true, the—"

Ghost at the Loom

"What do I have to do to get arrested in this country!" someone yells.

We step into a line. An undulation starts in the skin of a young man's face and ends in the woman's next to him. Fineness of gauge: individual strand of an old man's hair. I stand behind him, inching forward, mesmerized by the gray art of his shiny *protein, touch it.* Vana's fingers in the belt loops of my jeans. Follow the ancient hominid, his warped and warted neck.

I throb and fixate, shooting syllables at words at walls *a bread a cod, red ribbonacci, kun run koo me dive wait thirteen. Apropoprophets?* Keep in line! The line is integral to our success, because *A is not A, that's logic. Mole is not wart, that's cancer, spake spake Sonnenreich spake*—

"Kookooo," I say over my shoulder to warn Vana of the blue glass gates impending and our graybeard guide escaping via speaking to a woman through a hole in the gates of HELLO, WELCOME TO—

Vana thrusts a fist of euros underneath my arm.

"You are a baby elephant," I realize.

"Me?"

"Yes. Don't let go." I guide the fist of money through the hole and wait.

An azure woman stands behind the glass gesticulating, speaking English, but I can't make out the words. She must be passed.

Vana gasps: "Can't think of anything I'd rather have than baby elephants. You thought of baby elephants. They leaped into your heads?"

"Double vision," I say. *Must pass in, mammalian cortex, go go go!*

The woman speaks again. I'm still unable to decode. I look away and hope she'll stop. Seconds, maybe minutes, bump impatiently against my back. She slides a spread of bills to me, two tickets, too. I take it all, turning, homing on the beacon of the old man's skull. He's yards away, inside the building now.

The ligaments between the bones of what happens, the bones washed offshore past long glass piers, impulses of a loose awareness, not mine, whispering *caveat, caveat, viatic plutotechnocrat, excuse me sir, you can't do that.*

A city of domed buildings heaped to appear as skulls, with streets and terraced gardens, navigated by a man, a tourist in an untucked byssus shirt, outraged *that obelisk is naked, give it something to cover herself, for it is my daughter, my ruined o*

Thickening, curved, chartreuse nerves, affected by a question: rights of man? Jacob's ladder lightning.

Books on a Liberty-statue's stone shield, broken off with her hand attached. Books on utopias spun on the shield, singed by flame beards. Until an atlas opens, and she pisses into it.

Chives growing forked from a cup of soil.

She sits and makes thread. She touches the wheel. It rolls into the street.

Black eyeholes twisting. *I was quilted on the universe's false-anthropomorphic face.* Euclidian planes, pre-

Ghost at the Loom

Columbian worlds, wooden tables supporting empirical arguments.

A half-empty carafe. The surface of a glass of artemisia was rippling, registering footsteps leaving. Café tables in a slanted street. The other chair is empty.

She runs with a cablegram held to her head, protecting her hair from rain.

"You mean absinthe?" Vana says in the voice of a small girl.

"That's what they're drinking in this painting. Want to go?"

"Where?"

"Someplace safer," I say.

Humans stalk on slanted, stilted legs behind us. I am watching them. They study me. Each face knows me.

"Go?" she innocently asks, except her lips, a purple bow, forked arrow tongue, are silently explaining *everything*: idiots, geniuses, cowboys, Indians, Jews, Palestinians, bombs the size of elephants, and finally that, at any given instant, two-thirds of the world's chairs are empty, one-third of the world's women are lonely. "Are we coming down?"

"No," I say. "It comes in waves. This one is so clear, though. You have to help me, though, remember what I was about to...Paro wasn't helping me."

"A sign said this place is an archive."

"What?"

"*Archief. In het Nederlands.* The sign said that."

A Rider steps out of my back. I can't see him, but feel the subtraction acutely. He's going to live here forever, an archive life, without my excesses of pride and alienation, a life of mature study. He'll set up his desk between two paintings, occasionally greet museum-goers, never need food. A simple desk under a window in which each day rises a spheroid heart, an unbright star distended with futurity, posthumous; a heart engorged with data, not with blood.

"Oh, go. As in *go*? I think," she gulps—she fills her lungs, "we can. I think I found it already."

"Found what?"

"Upstairs." She leads me through galleries, up and down stairs, more down than up—

"We've been apart in here?"

"I know," she says. "I found you."

—to a blank place ending in an archway blocked by brass poles and a burgundy plush cord.

"Who's in there?"

"Nothing," she says. "No one looks."

"But they have cameras."

"I did it. No one saw me, I just did it."

"You can bribe the police." I step over the cord.

A corridor leads to a paintingless room in which the following ideas have been collecting for no one can say how long like hair in a drain: having eaten a spider, the sick eagle—it is Death—stares at the sky, from which it determines that A is not May, June is not noon; one-third of eternity, though, is three-thirds of eternity. Vana's bare legs and the hexagons warped on the window distort my binocular vision until it becomes monocular and thrusts out into water-textured fields, into the trams, the deadly

Ghost at the Loom

elevators, drug-entangled syndicates of other unknown minds. It plants a rigid flagpole in the field of my other-warped self-recognition, demanding unification of the world's warring nations, meanwhile populations blossom on the tree of constant *e*, two-thirds of history's Don Juans are deceased, and Vana's skirt is lifting in a branching wind that sounds like my voice coming out of my ear. Blind people drive convertibles in America.

No kissing, you two. Are we moths with stems or flying orchids? *Write down what you're thinking, I may need these ideas later.* Minus is the god of half the numbers in infinity. Square-root one of his acolytes: imaginary I remain. Tangled ankles in these jeans I've worn for weeks, I'm thrusting my insectitude into the loveliest human I have ever touched. I have stones in my belly and a black-winged lack of control, my clever-seeming false Cartesian soul abandoned in a café in Arlés to watch my body through a window doing what it diligently does.

Riggid ragged rawntawn, softer, *riggid ragged* echoes in my stones. Earholes cut into the words, *my god I think in words? What does that mean what does it halve to mean? Inside the belly, these are wings, you see them clearly on the sonogram here, here, and here, you can't go home point one* four one in circles, words in circles, towers built of words and numbers, masts, rigging, elevators into space.

A thread of something called Objective Beauty can be traced to π. I'm thrusting at a vulcan sphere that Vana shelters *mayday!* in her body like a child *fire in the pollen! Pull out! System error! Go!*

Inhuman heat increases with the friction, then, remotely: *i.*

The next intricate iota of my life is blown away in Amsterdam's green wind. I'll never find it. I won't try. It will not lead to you.

At the crest of the next wave of clarity, my questions are:

By what means did we exit the museum? Can one bribe the Netherlandish police? What square full of lampposts to lean on is this, and why so few people in it? When did the sun go down? Where's Vana? What is my next-city question for you?

Watch me pull the handle on a moving door with a long window full of red and white diodes, *HEY. HEY are you the*——?

Sentences in Dutch, firing at me from an open taxi. I fall into it and spew information at a man composed of tiles. His throat expands and bursts but certainly does not. Shrieks of laughter slope along my anvil skull, rebounding into plastic hexagons along the dash and elongated rubber bubbles on the door.

I spew *rag rig erminder kooo*, but inward, down to Sonnenrig and Sonnenrag, who fight over these scraps and bones, and further inward, all the way to zooming zigzag streets outside the taxi, to the light-ray grids and fractal genealogies of butterflies that are the skin of all visible, physical things——so much in a clump of fungal

Ghost at the Loom

stones and no glimmer?—this skin across which I waltz without moving: nobody knows I'm dancing.

I attempt to glimmer. Time curls, curls and curls, approaching the immobile center. *But I don't bemember*, howling from the cabman, *who are you the messenger*—"What? No, Beethovenstraat. The room's not in my name. I left her at the restaurant. Sashimi, yes. Sonnenreich. It's Jewish-German."

He expands. "Are you a Jew!"

I belch with great force.

"Shake my hand," he says. "I'm from Den Haag!"

A queer pain in my heels. I say, "He died in an elevator. I have to call him. Take me to the phone." I shake the hand in front of me.

I'm on a cell phone, Vana's, up the street from our hotel. Her phone was in my pocket. You and Paro haven't called it.

"Eli," Eli says in San Francisco.

I say carefully, "Hello. This is your son."

"That's correct."

"I am in Amsterdam."

I'm about to say more but, standing in lamplight, I'm looking at what? A piece of public art? Some civil engineer has planted a torso-high pole in the pavement, the top of which sprouts out at compass points into four horizontal poles, each capped with a polished steel sphere. In the north-pointing sphere, my curvewarped face, for less than a second, is also John's, with unbrotherly eyes, bluer than Danish streams. There are abstract, Opheliac gown-shapes of green going round in the irises' counterclockwise currents.

"That's good," Eli says. "It's a well-made town. You know, my dad, he would have thought—"

"I know."

"You know? Are you saying you've heard it before? I was talking about my—"

"Don't worry. I just told the man in the cab."

"The cab? You talk to taxi drivers? You know what you need? A part-time job in construction or something. It'd help with your writing. You need to listen to the speech rhythms of laborers."

"The *what?*"

"At least in Amsterdam the hospitals aren't cartels. They have good hospitals, the Dutch, if he had made it to one—"

"Italy, too, hospitals. Your father died here in an elevator," I say carefully.

"Since when do you interrupt me in the middle of a sentence?"

"Don't yell. I can hear you extremely."

"Am I yelling? Am I?"

"Coming down off potent mushrooms."

Several silent seconds.

"Purchased legally to boot!" Faraway from his previous tone, eager now, vicarious, measured, playful more than heckling, most of all letting me know he is not "square," indeed, he once "was there," fornicating in

Ghost at the Loom

daylight in protest atop a color-shifting U.S. flag outside the Pentagon, or so, at least, it should have been.

"Yes, and I wonder, might I speak with my father?"

"We're talking, we're talking. Hello, my lost son."

I mumble something friendly-sounding.

"So you're all drugged up in Amsterdam."

"Scattered, clarifying rapidly. I'm calling with a proposition, an idea."

"I know the feeling."

"What are you doing?"

"I just finished lunch," he says. "What's your idea?"

"Buy us tickets from Vienna to San Francisco? Leaving in fifteen days."

Because, Leya, I've kept Mama panicking long enough. If no glimmer in fifteen days, I'm taking you home. If glimmer, we'll stay where we are till we starve, or I'll drum in the street or tend bar, or money and humans will cease to control us: we'll eat mental fruit and drink Bandywine and sleep in the beds of our dilated pupils.

"Fifteen?" Eli says.

"I'll contribute five hundred."

"That's alright. I'll pay."

"And will you also tell my mother?"

"I don't talk to her, you know that, but I'll email her. I'll tell you though, last time we talked, she did seem worse. She's a real problem for you. She continues to be, and I can't get too involved, but don't think about that right now. I accept your proposal."

"It's a good proposal."

"I'll handle the airfare."

A Rider from earlier exits my head, is already far down the street, without much of a mind, though it knows no return into me is possible. It is a sloughed-off snakeskin self, who, because it has sucked so much prismatic venom out of me, is disgusted, has abandoned me in Amsterdam, and the sloughing has left me raw with a prickly, meager euphoria.

"Yes," I say, "but did you know these stones affect me extremely. For example, I can't recall parts of what I did today. Numerologies, false math must come from you, not that you're not excellent at math, because I rarely talk to you but can tell you, probably, something for example—for example, I've been reading, finding clues for example, in poems in the riddle, the big one, like: Would you have deep grief like you did for your father when he died here in the elevator in a hotel if she died? Here comes another what."

"Another what?"

"You see," I say.

"If who died?"

"What I was about to say, can you think of another—of any potential I don't know, potential *universe* in which one plus one could be three?"

"Uh hm. Well, that would be a problem of semantics. Not a truly mathematical problem. Listen for a second—we can set the ticket up by email, but you'll call me when you're in Vienna? So I know you're getting on the plane?"

"Yes, but do you want to talk a little more?"

Ghost at the Loom

"I do, but I already didn't take another call, and they're calling again."

Vana's in a towel next to Paro on a bed, and they don't acknowledge my entrance. Vampire mannequins, nodding their heads to trance music videos on a British channel. Such strong, sudden, puerile hate for them, but it passes because you are here, in an armchair, reading Celt's copy of Hogg's biography of Shelley, your feet in my backpack I left on the ottoman.

I sit on the arm of the chair, accept the semi-offered book, and softly read aloud to you: "Bysshe, leaning forward, listened with profound attention. 'I have heard this argument before,' he said; and by-and-bye, turning to me, he said again, 'I have heard this argument before.'"

You put your hand atop the page to block the words. "Rider'comeback, did you go somewhere?"

"I walked around. I ate some philosopher's stones, little mushrooms."

"Not *somewhere?*"

What are you saying? Have I been in error assuming you'd rather I not even hint at what's missing? I'll answer, but can't if I'm looking at you; that's too much. "I get closer to *somewhere* in the book you're holding than by eating philosopher's stones. That's the name of the kind we ate. It was fine. A distraction."

"From what?"

"Leya, never mind."

"I would like to taste a philosopher's stone," you say, enunciating oddly.

"I don't think it'd be wise to multiply what's in those stones by what's already in your head."

"Then not, Rider'knows. I don't care about those philosophers, but I would like to see some piano *before* we leave Europe."

"Who said we're leaving?"

"Before we leave."

In fifteen days, is that enough? Hints arrive, but never *it*—suggestions of Bandy limbs in shadows under trees, suggestions of where to go next in the sound of my shoes, hints in poems in the books we carry, slip-away pieces, but what are these pieces of? Not glimmer exactly, but something akin, something vanishing, old on Earth, immense but so delicate, something the twentieth century nearly destroyed, but a thread survives.

A thread threatens no one? It can't be the reason one utterly alters one's life? Once, it wasn't so light and thin. Didn't Shelley let it crush him? Byron felt it there, the complex ghost between the paper and the words, behind his head (he turned, but never with sufficient speed), and then he lacked the grace to not deny it. How can something so immense be so easily torn by snickering. Then somehow it was 1999, the snickering had reached a level of uniform deafening storm.

"We're going to Vienna. They have music."

"But I think...it's sad to be known about like this." You pet the book.

Ghost at the Loom

"Yes."

"Like in this story," petting the book like a pet, "I'm sorry my story in the falcon house was so...in pieces. I like this one better. Today, I feel better."

Amsterdam station. You're still in these red and white festival clothes. You must have changed six times since Spain, but I can't recall you in anything else.

"I told you," I tell Paro, "John's in Europe. I told him I'd meet him."

She loses the last of the calm we've been holding unstably between us and calls me a bastard and other names, and her words fly at me through a drift of smoke from Vana's joint. "And I do things for you you do not even know and——" and she goes on.

You don't appear disturbed. You are probably deaf to sexual quarrel.

"You're contradicting yourself," I say helplessly-shamefully-tritely.

Our train announces third-to-final call, I blank my face at Paro, to whom you've turned your willowy back, and she says something loud, then something quiet. You lean on my arm, mouth open in a tiny o, and Paro laughs unhappily. Vana waves, almost conspiratorially, but no, there's too much disconnection in the gesture and her face: if there's any conspiracy here, it is not one of persons against other persons.

I lift you aboard. We sleep through Germany. Just after dawn, you have a small vomiting seizure, but no one sees you.

THE LAST OF BRONNER'S wire is spent. We go to Brüll's Op. 24.

"John's coming. He takes care of us," I say, "don't worry."

You don't like applause. It's true, there's something false about it, when it comes right after beauty.

"I could live here, with pianos and some books for you," you say. "I want to go three times to symphonies as long as we lived here."

"Three times a month? Don't answer. That isn't my question."

"I think you could find a little cottage house."

Is this the solution, drum on the streets of Vienna, find a room for rent, and live with you until we go carefully mad?

"It'll flood by the weekend," warns an Irish backpacker at our hostel. "There's already a crisis on in Prague."

Here is your rice and lemon soda. I'll drink water from the bathroom, which tastes like it's one percent blood. Stay here in the room if you no longer care for Vienna and/or rain. I'll continue to go out for foods you like and gifts (here is a tiny pewter horse I found for very little money), but you must answer some of my questions more deeply. I know I've been foolish in choosing my questions. No more commonworld questions. John won't arrive for at least a day, a day we must not waste. We're together without Mama watching us. She was too often in the window.

"Oh," you say. "I'm going to put this here?" The horse on my pillow.

I'm wandering in this hospitalesque hostel room, from the all-white bed to the window and back to the bed. My question is: "What was the zodiac there?" The signs in the sky above Horse Hill, like the ones in the sky above Earth, but bluer, dense blue stars. "I only remember a tower," I say, "and a dog and a horse-tooth."

"I don't know."

Are you lying to me? Are you able to do that?

"Rider'no, what zodiac."

"In you, me," I say. "You know where I mean."

"What is it?"

"Twelve pictures made of lines from star to star, not the stars above Earth, above *there*," I say.

You remove from the back of the chair by the bed the fake snakeskin belt I bought in Rome.

"My belt," I say.

You stretch it, hold it up. "But speckled...pictures?"

"Pictures, stars." I'm looking at you, but it's like you aren't here. What do I mean? I don't know. I'm confused. I return to the window, one-inch open. Rain xylophonically plays on a hollow ledge a few inches below, and some faraway streetlight or lit window sets a yellow square into the band of black that is the open inch. There's no taste in my mouth, and I'm thankful we don't have a light on, because if we're going to talk about this, better my senses are reduced to—it's hard to say what...it's as if, for a moment, my whole grown man's body is one raw, ripped-open ear. A boy could fall out of that huge ear in the dark.

You hang the belt back on the chair. "Did you think I'm a woman?"

"Just now?"

"At the tree in Jamnik, you said, are you?"

"Never mind," back onto the coward's path, back away from the starry edge, the end of a small world. "Zodiacs are never mind," I say. "They don't mean anything—you don't have to tell me anything." I return and sit on the edge of the bed, *I'm asking you.*

"I know, I don't feel clear right now."

"You don't have to do anything." *I'm asking you.*

"Horse-tooth, good dog, bad dog, tower."

"Guitar?"

"Guitar, curve tree, cinderblock, spy bird, window, straight tree, long."

"That's eleven," I say.

"Long was two."

"What's long?"

"You, threads, you said them...star to star."

I've strained you. Your voice doesn't sound right. You tap on the back of my head, I think to have me look at you and not the window crack. You say, "Are you a woman?"

I shake my head no.

"If I'm a woman, you are, Rider'never mind."

I tilt and shake my head: the yellow square warps, becomes an abstract nostril, and an infantile taste-memory of citrus soap plays briefly in my throat.

A night or two later. "We're moving into John's room at a bigger hotel."

"Rider'why?"

"That one won't flood," I say. I feel a bit dizzy.

"What are you Rider'looking at? My hair?"

There is, to force it into English, a center of mental gravity in the room, a fragile place between visual thought and the impulse before a sought word resurfaces, a rendezvous arrived at by crossing out what I might say before the Roman letters clarify across the surface of my image drum, where wordlike shapes are swept and scattered by you, by the image of a woman's head turning, her *hair full of English*...

All this triggered by the way you watch me, head on your shoulder, birdlike. "It's tangled," you say, "don't be sad. If you tilt your head for a long time, everything opens."

"Opens."

"Yes," you say.

I tilt my head. This reminds me, I no longer feel like there's water in my ear. "We're going to leave Vienna soon," I say. "We're leaving Europe."

"You already said that."

"No. I didn't."

"You're going with John to see music without me tonight."

"Did I tell you that?"

"Nn."

"I can't have you around John too much. He's not good for you."

"But sometimes—oh," you sound surprised, "but now it's *very* clear. What should we talk about? What do we like, you Rider'like to read the most, you like it more than talking. Let's talk talk about what I've been reading. Look, look, look, I finished your book about Percy'bysshe but why so little he should have written more about when he was little, and you put the pages backward. Who taught you to read, little fingerprint?"

I tilt my head the other way, and wordlike shapes regather just beneath the surface and approach *ragrag idraggedrawn*, but fail to arrive, to *mean*. "I didn't write that book," I say.

Intensely, yes, I want to talk about what you've been reading, and I am about to try, except a minute snap-thrum like a guitarstring breaking far away makes me turn from the window and say, "What did you say?"

"I said, I have to cut these," it appears you've stolen Paro's eyebrow scissors, "ragged ends. I feel so clear right now," and are about to trim the longest feathers of your

hair, your hair in my head now filling with words fully
formed:
> each hair
> a list
> of lists,
> of dark salt
> lattices,
> columns of
> stock prices,
> hairs in a
> loom, a piano,
> a flowchart
> of delicate
> misinformation
> on falconry,
> dead English
> poetry, mental
> pathology, the
> coming flood—

◇◇◇◇◇◇◇◇◇◇◇◇◇

BYSSHE GRIPPED THE MAST, Byron the helm. Long strands of rain pointillized the deck and water. On the shore, at Diodati, Mary wrote in black ink with a jackdaw quill, hearing thunder as the wheels of vast, grotesque machines.

They would capsize, Bysshe surmised, regarding his companion through the spray: *afraid to die, and I am not?*

Byron: "No more to be done!"

Bysshe: "I do not swim!"

"I swim for two!"

"I've no intention of being saved! The rocks are too distant, and you will have enough to do to save yourself!"

"I swim for two!"

"I beseech you not to trouble!"

Byron slid along the deck to Bysshe and wrapped his legs around the mast, removed his coat, and said, "There's naught to do but sit and wish like sweet birds for a better sky."

Bysshe, who would drown——not now in Lake Geneva, six years later, in a storm at sea——removed his coat.

•

ONLY I, A VERY small English boy, and his older brother are in the men's room. They piss to either side of me. The older brother reads aloud a sign in German, French, and English: "'*Bitte nur während der Pausen zu spülen. Ess-vee-pee ne tirer pas la chasse d'eau pendant la seance.* Please do not flush during the performance.' I'm going to wait outside, okay?"

The small boy doesn't want his brother to leave him in here with the man in tall, scuffed boots, but his brother does leave, so the boy chants a courage-mantra while hurriedly finishing, "Do not flush! Do not flush! Do not flush!" and then flees without washing his hands.

I exit the men's room and tell John what's happened.

"Now that's very humorous," he says in a head-patting tone that means: *I'm proud of you, I didn't know you could be lighthearted.* "Everything is relevant."

"I don't think that," I say.

"No, we all know what you think, and yet this is all very twenty-first century, what you're doing here, flushing my virtual money down Europe of all toilets, as opposed to proper melting-pot America, the way you dress, the way you can't please women. What's the problem here? The problem is there are too many data points, potential counterfeit equations. Eurail unlimited-pass-holder divided by Wandering Jew equals—"

"That's your language. I don't think like that."

He's fussing with his belt buckle, which has Chinese characters on it. "Because you don't think as well as you could if you tried, and I know how you 'feel,' but I just can't digest your lactic mysticism."

"Leya used my belt, to show me something, the other night."

"That's enough about that. I mean, read your Shelley, that's fine, but keep in mind material systems, like for example goldfish ponds and multinational corporations, aren't characterized by what you 'feel,' but *quite frankly*, as the French say," switching to a mock French accent, "by transferences of energy resulting in intersubjectively observable organizations and disorganizations of state." He flicks something off my collar. "The way you were talking about imagination at dinner, sometimes don't you sound a bit like old New Age?"

"The opposite."

"Oh, no? I'll trust you, then. You just had an emotional foible, you know, a moment during which you needed me to be understanding, and I was sarcastic and a bad friend. My instinct is to blame. You know my background—I mean, by the time I was eight, the neighborhood childlife had formed into a shadowy, wayward band. My dog, a poodle, was slain by a bee from a bee farm truck that crashed into an early version of the minivan. We cooked and ate the dog. The fire, I recollect, was fueled by date palm leaves. This was Miami Beach in the early eighties. In that stifling political environment, you, a humanist and pioneer of liberal thought, can imagine, this kind of lost tribe underworld was all we had."

Ghost at the Loom

He picks up a schedule of musical events written in German, turning pages too quickly to read them.

"I'm not a nobleman like you. I don't have secrets. I'm not a priest of Denial, so people like me," he lists people in New York who like him, "—more than they like you. 'Paro,' too, but, right, that's over, but what I do is I sacrifice myself to make you noble. No one can be anything by themselves, I mean, without a conscious observer, me. Also there's the social responsibility angle, and I'm not talking pinkos. I'm saying what if there's an isolated tribe or orbital habitat somewhere and nobody's allowed to have a proper name. Around me, you're just 'Friend.' In this tribe, when you're talking to me, you're 'Friend.' If to one of these Lamarckian recessive-Nazi ushers, you're just 'Patron of the Arts.' They say, '*Bitte*, Patron, proceed into the chamber,' for some chamber music, classical gas. Dear Friend, no one has a fixed label. You can only think about yourself relative to whom's at hand. Nobody's hoarding beads or spears or anything. This is a possible utopia, you should be into this."

"Did you just say 'dear friend'?"

"In the tribe. Your name's Friend in the tribe. I'm being hypothetical. Although you *are* my friend."

"I'm not for your utopia."

"Neither am I. We aren't into democracies," he says to some passing, septuagenarian Austrians. "We aren't into democracies," he says again, and they smile warmly.

"And," I say, "I'm sure there's been a tribe like that already."

"That's *my* problem. You just keep fondling the curve. I'll cover the outliers. I'm a noise cowboy."

"The endless noise," I say.

"You want to hoard beads? Hoard beads. Just don't go anywhere without me anymore, even if you know who tells you to. You know, because I talk to your father— Jesus, *my* father talks to your father."

"Nothing shocks anyone anymore except unapologetic, outspoken elitism," Minus declares in our hotel room.

"When do you want to eat?"

"I don't know." He removes a hand-sized computer from his pants. "Eggs, I want ham and cheese. I'd like some oysters a third-world pearl diver got the bends for. Chicken, leg meat, I want French bread, Comté cheese or old Manchego. Ach, shut up. You know I don't know why I go around with you. You think you're quiet, but bedlam leaks out of you. I can't even hear the little quails indigenous to my brain. A shovel's getting them. The tiny, chirpy ones. Each time a quail gets brained, another one *just* like it hops out of a rabbithole. I swear, it's not even political, it's not why-how I want to help people. I'm just the babysitter. Okay, I want pork. Paté?"

"I want to read for an hour." I go into my backpack for the Shelley.

"But idiots, people who move their mouths while reading, are always saying, 'Nothing shocks anyone anymore.' You tell a plebe, a yeoman, *or* a duchess you're a genius, they are *shocked*. It's the crime, the crime.

Except if they know you're not. Then it's 'funny,' and everyone crawls back to vaginal points of origin to watch the telly, little holy Joes. I love the plebes and yeomen, I love the duchesses. It's dukes who need a whiff of nitrous Zyklon."

"I don't think you are a genius."

"No? I have a perfect memory," he warns.

I go onto the balcony. Out on the glacis, the backs of Ringstrasse buildings, in various stages of construction, radiate a spontaneous atheism, which swiftly decays, back to the potentials of the cortex, to the limbo radioactive metaphors decay to.

"Hiding from John out here?" I say.

"Rider'finder."

"Not clear right now?" These aren't Delphic questions. You know they aren't.

"Don't know when I am clear?"

"I don't know. I guess I know when you are...if I think about it."

"Knows, knows."

"I test well, Dagon! I test well," John screams from the room.

You ask permission, "Mm?" holding a €1 coin out over four stories of air to the street.

"What country was it minted in?"

"Spain."

"Okay," I say.

You drop the coin. The gesture seems devoid of symbolism, though we do need money to continue this.

"John," I call into the room, "may we have some more money?"

He comes out and snatches the book from my hand. "Sorry to *obturb* you, but I'm not a genius? You were saying? What, but if I tell you a secret, it still is one. If you tell someone else, it still is. At what point does a secret cease to be? The motion of exposure of a secret's similar to motion in slap-happy Zeno's paradox. Nonsecrecy is more than the sum of exposures. It's all just an ostrakon chipped from the pot. I mean, I test well. If I get too drunk, I vomit. Don't you see? My normal speech is better than your poetry," he grimaces, "but I need your good company, so you can't 'read for an hour' right now."

Shelley's book is slightly open, hanging at John's hip in his hand, in a general stillness with local trembling of the pages. On a still day, dry gold grass in California, you can see it moving if you study it. It registers wind your skin can't feel.

"I have a *real* problem," he continues, "more than you or anyone with problems. Let's say someone made a documentary of my life—or what, you don't want in to the Society of John? Great women belong to it. Martyrs have had sex changes to enter it, why not? It's always down one leg or the other. I just don't have a circumstance, you think you do, you're lying, and it's genuinely beautiful. I do admire it without sarcasm. I'm vulnerable." He swats my shoulder with the book. "Enough. You moccasin-head. Mass, lightspeed, energy.

Literacy, pluralism, pleurisy. You've got the worst of us, you do, the Jews, the worst half is in you."

"I just don't feel superior to people."

"That's the *top* half, your top half, you know, if you're not—wait, what? You what? You don't—but's that's fantastic! Jesus, I guess you won't shock and offend anyone, then. Your egos are safe with Sonnenreich!" he bellows out into Vienna.

•

"YES, BUT I AM formed, if for anything not in common with the herd of mankind, to apprehend minute and remote distinctions of feeling, whether relative to external nature or the living beings which surround us, and to communicate the conceptions which result from considering either the moral or the material universe as a whole. Of course," said Bysshe to the doppelgänger in the unlit mirror, "I believe these faculties, which perhaps comprehend all that is sublime in man, to exist very imperfectly in my own mind."

The doppelgänger's voice was feminine and sympathetic, as of some loved voice heard long ago: "You're safe as long as you stop asking questions. If you don't, she'll have to stay here in a square white room, like the room in this mirror, but the negative image. Someone dropped her on the left rear quadrant of her skull, as you see here indicated by this darker area of bone, when she was a baby. We, for one, will testify it wasn't you."

•

IT'S GOING TO RAIN again. You shouldn't be out on the balcony jacketless.

"For example," John continues (he's been talking, talking mercilessly since he came outside), "this little stick you've been carrying around."

He tries to take it. I won't let him. He already has our Shelley book.

"Let me supply you with a parable," he says, "important for your future pseudo-sanity you understand this. Once there was a man who went out on a hiking trail, a wide trail, right on the border of winter and spring in New York, upstate, and the trail was still mostly covered by rethawed, refrozen, melty, icy snow, and this man plucked a twigless stick, a shooter like this one you've been making Austrians nervous with, from the side of the trail. Now not too many people came along this trail, but if he waited, maybe four per hour came, and so this sneaky citizen inserted the stick into the snow, thick end down, arranging it to look very much like an anomalous but natural sapling in the middle of the trail, yards away from any other, and of course there was a Jesus phalanx of such saplings off to either side off-trail. So Sneaky hides out in the Jesus, off behind a spruce, meanwhile a few lonely hikers go by, and the first one to pull up the anomaly, whether due to dendrological good sense or a vague hostility to individualism, Sneaky jumps out from behind the spruce and shoots him eight times in the head and torso. There you have it, as the plebes and yeomen say. It's not just a parable, either. It's awful, the killed guy had a family, on the news. I mean, his whole family had careers as news show hosts. Maybe his son was a weatherman, but that counts."

In the Stock-im-Eisen-Platz, I say, "Why aren't you ribald, John?"

"I'm having a very bad mood."

"Why are you sad?"

"I'm not *sad*, you symptom, I'm having a mood, I said."

We've walked today beneath all kinds of gargoyle cryptozoa: gorgons etched with disk-shaped leaves, small titans, inconsolable angels, feathered apes. Bituminous sludge, running swiftly in well-designed gutters, does not leak into the street or splash on the sidewalks.

There's a Turkish cannonball embedded in the Stephansdom. On the west side of the street, a "birth house" (if I'm translating correctly, where a woman may give birth without being forced to disclose her name) is inconspicuous between a stable and an Internet café. The children are, I guess, put into foundling homes and given food and education. This government has done much for the rights of the illegitimate.

I say to John Minus, "You're having a very bad mood."

Stone posts with iron hats protect the sides of famous buildings from potential traffic accidents. Rectangles, thousands—plazas, cut stones, windows—are starting to box in, to trespass on, my mental images: a block ago, I saw you waiting in my head in the hotel window and your hands were rectangles.

Don't leave the hotel. John and I will be back soon.

I say, "Do you want to look inside that flower shop?"

He nods. I'm glad he does. I will bring you a flower.

Sometimes I provide the medicine for John. I make it out of what's available. For example, he is just a little boy, and when he's sad, I tell him stories. This flower is a Jew's white hat. The woman under it is worrying, *Who will intercede for me in the next world?* I think it is her father's hat. John agrees, it is a hat-like flower.

"But," he says, "you can't really think except in German," eyebrows dipping toward his nosebridge, like they do when he's lying. "In English, basically it's a disaster."

This one has a blue-pink nexus and antennoid stamens. On the stamen tips, the frontiers, are the nectar-merchants' settlements. I try to tell Minus about the war and final dissolution of the charter of the merchant league because of lobbyists and class struggle in the blue-pink capital. Without the charter, trade continues semi-anarchistically.

He translates the names of flowers into English.

"My father has hepatitis," he says.

"I know. He's had it for years."

"You're looking at a narcissus," he says.

I'll pick it for you, when no one is looking. "Thank you for translating," I say.

Ghost at the Loom

He picks a hair off my pale leather coat. "This used to be my coat, you know, but this is your hair."

"Yes," I say, "that is one of the hairs from my haircut. I got a haircut this morning."

"My hairs are blond. They don't show up on that coat."

"That's true."

"You're looking at looking-at-yourself itself," he says. "Okay, what I just said is all you get for an hour, just meet me back at the hotel for dinner. I'll feel better then. I have to do something without you, okay?"

He thinks he provides the medicine. I don't think he goes to whores. Maybe Paro followed us to Vienna. She said she was going to Copenhagen.

"Paro's in Copenhagen," I say.

"*Probably* we're all in Copenhagen. Meet me back—I can't be around anyone right now, goodbye. I can't be around you."

One of the Vienna mornings: "Please don't leave this area," I say to you, "I'm going for a walk."

Along a row of lindens, saying nothing to myself at first, with Schumann's Op. 44 on John's headphones, then murmuring *patterns of forms of patterns of forms* until the three words are one sound, the sound of seeing sonic branches, these scherzo pianowire telephone wires pole to pole in the heart-shaped leaves, heart-brain full of patterns of symmetries forming and breaking, arborizing to a double fugue, brown hearts on the path chewed by worms, remainders, bits of violinstring—what if nothing troubled me? I'm a corporate diplomat, an American pirate in Austria who, if not at his office, walks in the park and stops at a fountain and reclines there on a stone bench, pulsing with incurious existence, and his sister (she's "in town for the weekend") waits for him on another bench, reading some book about poets from England.

Different morning in Vienna, same park. I'm having a fixation, looking at the black heraldic bird on a smashed alebottle cap on a path between trees—far less than a glimmer, not even a "vision," but Shelley, I think, would have called it a vision. It beats on my image drum: wingbeating dactyls slap-skip off the tabula rasa, five, seven, repeating and threshing the lip-red air above a girl with my face on the back of her head like a carnival mask. I can't decipher what I'm saying on the back of her head. She isn't listening. How can she? A beak as long as her body has caught her by the neck and pins her chest against a chest too broad and darkly luminous to be a human's. A heart seven times her heart's size beats the beat of hers into antediluvian submission.

The pressure increases, her chest against a lamellar surface of hammered folds, as of Japanese swords welded edge to edge—the dam/drum bursts, spurting earthy water. Muscles in her calves and groin go slack. The mask falls off the back of her head at my feet on the path, and I nudge the half-buried cap with my shoe, exposing the other black wing of the bird that ceases to be visionary with great speed and no sense of loss, but a sense of division by large numbers, maybe similar to how a Christian sees herself becoming not herself but part of God? And yet the God I am becoming is a mindlessness. I feel the lack of Mind around me, permeating everything. It's *beautiful*—my jaw is twitching.

You've skinned your elbow running after a cat in an empty sidestreet off the Stadtpark. Points of blood get on my hand. They make red lace on my brown hand.

"Why are you holding your stomach?"

"You don't have anymore."

"This isn't a question question, it's just a question."

"Oh no!" you whisper. "It's the answer question, if only you didn't not have anymore."

"Your stomach's the answer question?"

"Oh, no."

"But this isn't Vienna," I half-lie, half-play, to see what you'll say.

You look worried. "What city is this?"

"Copenhagen."

You look at me carefully and say, "I didn't want to hurt it."

"You weren't going to hurt it. Cats get scared for basic biological reasons."

"No. I can be pregnant, if I fell on purpose."

"Pregnant? I don't know. I guess you can be pregnant."

"I have a baby."

"Yes, okay. I have one, too." I cup my hand and put it to your ear.

"Not that kind of baby." You push my hand, gently, with something akin to, but not quite, regret. "That was your Copenhagen answer."

But, it suddenly takes great will not to yell, *we're in Vienna, we were playing!* I'm suffering something akin to, but not quite, panic.

I don't know what to say to you. I don't know what you mean. If there's a door to you with a book-shaped lock, you see I try, but lack the mind to write a key with teeth that fit between the words in a lock-shaped book.

You're in the hotel room, asleep. I'm in a Thai café with John, who's preaching, yelling at me: "What you're saying is embarrassing! If only you had read your grade-school neurobio, you'd already know there are these wrinkly little nodes that govern our perceptions of infinites, eternities, that class of thoughts, and epilepsy, certain cases, causes every neuron in a node or larger area to fire at once, and even if you think in German, in the motor cortex this means seizures. This means Jesus— in a node that's dedicated to attempts to think about the infinite, a total firing causes cracked-up lookingglass hallucinations, often with religious themes, depending on the personality inside the brain affected."

"I know," I say, "about this total firing. One will happen soon. I feel it on the way. That's why I brought it up. I don't take blockers anymore."

Ghost at the Loom

"Sure you don't. Let's have one, then, a big one, tell me right before it starts, I'll put my pinky finger down your throat, and you can *accidentally* bite it off, and then we'll all drink blood and toast Enola Gay, and as for telepathy, Dagon, a society of skeptics, SFBPC, you ever heard of that, in San Francisco—hey, that's where your da resides, coincidence?—this whole society has offered millions cash to anyone who reproduces telepathic anything but in a seriously controlled environment."

He feeds me peanut beef on a fork. I chew with zeal. I am a zealot. I don't believe in telepathy.

"Even with your kind of mind," he's saying, "zero evidence for paranormal—I mean, I have memories from when I was a kid that, seen from an adult perspective, can't have possibly occurred. Take this one for example, just like lots of people have, a sort of game, I'm showing all my wrinkly little parts to someone's daughter who's in school with me. I think her parents just had moved from India. This little girl, I mean, we're eight or something, and we're friends because we're both the only non-white people in the school. Her hand is on my naked, tiny ass. Now this just doesn't happen in America."

"You're white," I say.

"I'm white?"

"Okay," I say and chew and smile at John with beef in my teeth, but in my image drum, an eight-year-old me (it could be you, too dark to see) is locked in a windowless room, yelling over and over something like *I am real, I am real!*

I'm in a nightclub off the Ringstrasse. Long glass surfaces, a hooded DJ, four/four rhythms. I tap tabla talas on our table. John, who has been preaching celibacy to a young blond Salzburgian woman, returns to perform his arrow-shooting dance, alone, orbiting our table, prideful in his neat self-mockery, *for none shall mock what I mock with superior authority,* sloshing a glass of vodka and juice on his new black English suit, *if I do anything that can be understood as vulnerable, it's actually ordnance, see, the present and the future are about preventative war and preventative medicine.*

He gyrates in the golden strobes and seems aflame, a monk protesting lack of something certain to protest. *Dear John,* I'm pointing at my chest and then the door, *you see I'm getting up to go, the music is too loud to tell you.*

I walk faster when the wing begins to beat behind me. I forgot I don't have money for a taxi. John has the umbrella. Twenty blocks from you, I detect the first pull of a riptide in my right brain: my left hand twitches, seeming not a part of me. They start like this for you as well?

You must be sleeping. Beating, beating, feet in my chest and my heart on the wet cement and the wing beating time and building, threatening to phase-shift into final form: a storm of dismembered falcons and angels and crows. I'm scared, and yet eager to go——

Ghost at the Loom

carried off to the scene that is always here behind what's here, but that I'm so infrequently allowed—now, as landlocked Vienna floods, off like an ejaculation in the space behind my eyes o god in an alien city at midnight, each pool with a halfmoon, each street object charged with numinous ipseity. Who *are* you?

Obsolete god made of blowing pages, cities written quickly, you who turn away. Whose eyes are yours, the drops of glass light making little cataclysms on the pavement. I run on the Ringstrasse in sideways rain. Rain and my vertical voice erect a cross of sound. I'm running on one leg away to either side of me, a body utterly unstable, yet it does not seem to be destroyed. *Who are you, blowing away?*

•

THEN BYSSHE HAD A bad dream, an anachronistic tear in the weave: that his heart has been taken from Mary's belongings by whomever stole Einstein's brain and took it to Kansas, and his heart is taken to Vienna and placed in a stone box trimmed with feathers from Levantine birds. G8 summit participants carry the box into the Augustinerkirche. In other boxes, his intestines, spleen, and lungs are to be buried in the crypt under the Stefansdom. His scooped-out body lies, in jeans and an open, high-collared Italian shirt, in a coffin covered with narcissi. The Viennese come quietly in.

Someone has painted an unsarcastic exclamation point on the cannonball embedded in the wall.

The father superior says to the coffin: *Who art thou? Who wants to be admitted here?*

The high chamberlain says in Bysshe's voice: *I am His Majesty.*

Father: *I know him not.*

Chamberlain: *I am the Emperor Franz-Bandy, Apostolic King of Rome, Prince of Spain and California, Grand Duke of Amsterdam, Duke of Horses.*

Father: *I know him not.*

Bysshe: *I am William Shelley, Edward Williams, Edward John Trelawny, Edmund Peregrine, John William Polidori, John Keats, John—*

I know him not.

The chamberlain kneels and says in as gentle a tone as he can reproduce from memories of you talking to me in my sleep: *I had rather not have my hopes and illusions mocked by sad realities.*

Father: *Then thou mayst enter.*

◇◇◇◇◇◇◇◇◇◇◇◇◇◇

WHY AM I BRINGING you home? I don't want to go home. Mama's pulling me somehow. Head on my arm, Leya, sleep—and yet, this worries me. How many hours per day can someone sleep? Thirteen, fourteen.

Despite fickle flashes of "vision," despite that, by human standards, we're closer now than we've been in two decades, I am not *with you.* I'm in a plane. Coming down over San Francisco, an alternate history pulls taut in me, then fires its images: imagine you had gone to school, learned to speak American vernacular, got a job at an ice cream shop, a boy date-raped you; imagine you fell further from the glimmer than I have or could, and now I've brought you home, not from Vienna but from some crash landing somewhere with your latest vulgar man; you have cartoonish tattoos on your stomach, legs, and back; you sleep against me in your headphones with death metal leaking out of them; your illness has become the dullest tragedy.

◇◇◇◇◇◇◇◇◇◇◇◇◇

BUT IF THAT WERE the case, would this letter differ at all? I am your brother. I would invent Europe to defend your honor.

◇◇◇◇◇◇◇◇◇◇◇◇◇

My dear friend,

I indulge despair. Why do I do so? I will not philosophize. It is, perhaps, a poor way of administering comfort to myself to say I ought not be in need of it. I fear this most recent despair springs from you, from your constant nearness, as if behind a paper wall. It is a passion, a passion, too, which is least of all reducible to reason. But it is a passion, it is independent of volition; it is the necessary effect of a cause, which must, I feel, continue to operate.

What shall I tell you, which can make you happier, which can alleviate your sickness and your dire belatedness. Shall I tell you the truth? Oh, you are too well aware of the crossed out lines in that. Perhaps, if I had known this in my youth, you would be different, forward into something else, I cannot say. It was the opposite for me, a dire earliness, an odor like the tuberose, that overcame and sickened me with sweetness.

Shall I say the time may come when happiness shall pour down like balm, like mercury, upon a night of wretchedness? Why shouldn't I, or you, be false? You seem to me, if anything, a prophet who may only tell the past, and that in error. You are welcome to it, given the general principle that the insults in your world powerfully overbalance its pleasures. They will tell you to cease to think, to cease to feel; you ask me to be different than I was in life; and I fear I must obey before we can talk of hope.

I have read your letter attentively, almost as if it were written to me. I find there can be bigots in imagination as well as in the lack. I, perhaps, may be classed with the former. Distraction and denial are among the highest moral virtues, the foundations, indeed, upon which many others must rest. It seems a bigot such as I must then believe that he who has neglected to cultivate fully these virtues, who still requires from the creatures near him sums of money, food, caresses and the rest, never will return to her, whomever she may be, though she is only separated from you by another paper wall behind the one that barely keeps you separate from me.

My charity is this advice. Take any system of religion, lop off all disgusting excrescences, tithes, superstitious adjuncts, retain virtuous precepts, qualify selfish dogmas (allowing as much irrationality as amiability can swallow, combined with a bit of self-conceitedness); do all this, and I will say, yours is an errant system which can do no harm, and, indeed, is highly requisite for anyone for whom it is too late.

Finally, what is a ghost? Not a soul still on Earth when a body is dust, for this is superstition without a doubt. A ghost is but a stranded coil of information in an era hostile to it. I find such a conception has, at least, the virtue of distraction.

I, therefore, request that you continue as you have behind this poor screen, this tapestry of faint glyphs read backward, as, it seems, you truly do not know the deformity of wretched errors you of necessity overlook. You do not know you often are as vulgar eyes behold you, for you believe you are outside responsibility to the enslaved. I cannot judge a system by the flowers scattered here and there (your blues and pinks, your crowns or skullcaps liberated from the heads of wanderers who lean too far backward, observing the sky), but you omit the mention of the weeds, which grow so high that few botanists can see the flowers.

You shall hear from me again soon. I will send some verses.

I heard from J. yesterday. He said little more than: I'll be by with claret and a cake.

My dear friend, your affectionate
P. Bysshe Shelley.

MAMA DOESN'T ANSWER AT the front door, so we walk across dead sea fig to the yard's fence.

"Mama's car is here, not Mama."

"No, I think she is," I say.

Sea fig is chthonic, needs no watering. I lift you and our bags over the fence, return to the driveway, run, and hurdle the fence. Thick weed, in rows in the yard, looks plotted almost. Opaque curtains hang in every window. There are roomlike areas of tree-shadow and house-shadow and direct and ambient light in the yard, this half acre of land that is the house outside the house, and the shadow rooms wax and wane and become each other. You didn't say to take you home or not to.

We're at the back door. You squat in the fork-tipped weeds to take a key out from under the purple-and-black-painted cinderblock. "She changes locks," you say, "she knows how to." You stand and fumble the key. "Are you, Rider'cold? Come see, feel my belly, is it cold here, whisperbaby?"

"I don't know what you want me—"

"Shh."

I take my hands out of your hands and pick up the key, which scrapes twice as it turns, and I prop the door ajar with my boots I remove. Tree-filtered light and air enter with me, and you wait in the doorway, looking out, while I heap our bags against the antechamber table's legs.

"Because," you say, "sometimes the babywhispers sneak, and I can hear them sneaking."

"Leya."

What are you looking at? Something in the yard or on the hill.

"Leya."

"One or two?"

I say, "I know I promised no more questions, but you need to tell me what you mean."

"Rider'never mind. It doesn't matter now. A bad thing has to happen."

Are you saying something is my fault, too many questions, that I lied we were in Copenhagen?

I say, "Did a man do something to you?"

"Shh...not me, who I'm sometimes, it did it to her... 's all it is, I'd like to leave." You partly step into the house and pet my shoulder, pointing at my backpack with your toe. "She isn't home. She took too many photographs," enunciating *photographs* in that new, discomforting way, the way you now speak once or twice a day for a sentence or two, as if a breath, a small cold curl of wind, has blown aside the curtain in your voice. Then the curtain swings back: "I'll go with you to New York maybe, don't you want, I want to read more of the books in your backpack before I—"

"Answer, are you pregnant in your body?"

This is when you lift your shirt, your stomach flat, translucent tan, one dark visible vein. I stare at that vein. I'm full of will, but will without an aim. Unless it's will to block inadmissible subthoughts about what you're telling me. You've backed away, into the yard. I'm following you. I lost the glimmer, but it never was an innocence exactly.

Something tunnels in the weeds. They slant and flow around a hidden plow.

"What's that? That's Eyeball under there," I say.

"Her nose, look, there's cloudy eye and all white eye. Look, each nostril."

We crouch in the needlegrass. You lift Eyeball's paw and put it in my hand. I like to dig my fingers in the dry gaps between Eyeball's toepads. You push at her facial folds, exposing glaucous eyes, empty even of the look of animal intelligence. They do contain a warped, silver image of me behind you, both of us macrocephalic, as in the back of a polished spoon, your figure less defined, inside the borders of mine, like a double exposure. This is nothing, though: the commonworld is full of little locked-up gates to smaller worlds.

"Bring Eyeball in," I say. "She wants a piece of meat, I think."

The inner antechamber door is also locked and with a different key. This room, built by the man who lived with Mama many years ago, was once part of the yard. The window between this room and the next was

Mama's watching window. Pulling off the screen, I boost you through, then Eyeball, feebly kicking.

Mama's bedroom. All of her lamps are still here on their many surfaces. Furniture covered in papier-mâché. Snips of dusty fabric swept into a corner. The quilt on the bed depicts a seraphesque form in profile, fernlike wings—a newer quilt, not here when I lived here. There's an odor of tangy wax.

"She doesn't sleep here anymore," you say, but not, I know, to say again that Mama isn't home, which we know isn't true.

Clay pots in a curved line on the hall floor contain unlit citronella candles. Past the quilted sisters on the hall's walls—these are Mama's daughters, too, black queens like queens on cards, but cards the size of you—into the kitchen. Music's playing in the fire-and-piano room. Mama must have put a stereo in there.

The kitchen countertop is cluttered with jam jars, pepper jars, glasses, champagne flutes, and inside each, a moth or butterfly. Many are umber moths. One is a monarch, one colored like a snow leopard, another burgundy. She's not so different from other people's mothers, carefully arranging rooms and objects so her children, coming home, adult now, feel familiar. And/or the jars and candles have been, or are set up to be, photographed. Maybe John goes home to salad, challah, brisket in the oven, thanks his mother, and she tells him she was cooking anyway.

A purposefully loud noise through the floortiles says she's in the cellar. It's a hollow concrete cube, perhaps an old WWII shelter, which you've never entered and will not, and, as a child, I, too, would not: too little air, the walls were bare, and it was where the man who lived with Mama stored his extra tools.

I pull the pantry doors and stand before a library of new and ancient cans and jars and pastas and a square of light open in the floor, through which I climb, and Mama, on her knees before three trunks of old supplies, says, "Help me with these lights? Tell Leya play me something...keep the pantry open."

You, your head obscure in the square of dark at the laddershaft's mouth, chirp, cricketlike, quiet, cricket in a sealed jar.

"Why are you down here, Mama?" I say. "Are you feeling—you know?"

"I'm fixing my darkroom. Go tell Leya go and play for me."

"Can't," says your voice above my head between the crickets, "can't," and my mouth twitches, as if I'm pretending to ventriloquize you.

"Yes she can," says Mama. "Tell her turn the music off and play for me. Just put the CD on the stack of books, she can't find cases anyway."

"Answer how you feel," I say. "Why is the yard so weedy?"

"I don't weed it. Hand me those." A box of dark red bulbs.

Ghost at the Loom

"Why are the sea figs dead?"

"That was Leya."

"Leya killed the sea figs?"

"That was Leya," she says, "going into the piano room."

"Mama."

"Do you know what…do you know how much I want to take your picture?"

"Not right now."

"Don't worry, just to document your face." She plugs the track of red bulbs in. "It may be good. I think it will be a very good portrait," pulling little twists out of the power cord. "Could you turn off the white."

I turn the white light off. "But I don't want my picture taken down here. Tomorrow maybe, maybe in the yard, with Eyeball."

"That dog's blind."

"She won't be bothered by the flash," I say.

It is a black-red corner of the cube (the inside of a sharp point, pointing north into the roots of Horse Hill) I am looking into when she takes my hand and lays it on her arm and tells me, "Rider. This is here."

"Okay," but I retrieve and pocket my hand, because if I touch Mama too long my image drum becomes a room, no doors or windows, and something is wrong in there—I can't get in or out.

"I don't think," she says, "that you were doing well, with certain people."

"If you're talking about John, I disagree. Supposedly, he keeps me balanced."

"I don't think so. I guess you're most balanced here. I'm talking about Leya."

"Leya."

"Leya wasn't doing well out there," she says.

It's been so long since I've seen Mama: lines have surfaced in her face—like hints of city maps—although she never leaves this town and often not the house for weeks.

"You went around alone," I say, "at Leya's age. You traveled."

"Not Leya, she was sick. You should have brought her home immediately. Did you even one time take her temperature in Europe?"

"Leya's home," I tell her in the tone that says I am the clearer-minded one. "She isn't sick. You never talk to doctors."

"No?"

"No, don't be Mama in the way I don't like or I won't stay home."

"What is this, what you're saying?"

"That we shouldn't talk about that—basically, I did what you wanted. I'm home."

"But I don't know what to say to you if you already know everything."

"Just stop before we get into an old loop. Tell me something else."

She says, "I didn't travel very much. San Miguel de Allende. I had a job painting."

"Painting what?"

"Just thousands. Thousands of stones for a pond, for the bottom of a man's pond at his house in Mexico."

Now a silence, one I can't enjoy, is here, a silence full of lost words coming back, the prow-like front edges of words, too soon. Let me have a seizure, just a little one, a little quilt of wordless paper pulled over my face. Blank. I don't like it down here. I'm looking at my hands. They're old, not a boy's. I'm talking to Mama in a calm voice: "What about when you were Leya's age?"

"I don't know. I went to Montana. I told you already, but you were a baby."

"Tell me now again, if you want." I know she won't, but, bizarrely, she does.

It's a folktale she tells me, short and torn. Rifts in the paper wall. I can't see how to fit the tale into this letter without leaving in the noise leaking in from the rifts. From down here in the darkroom, I can't quite hear what you're playing, but you on piano is leaking in, too. Mama never talks about before your birth, or if she does, I don't have proper memory. Her 1970 Montana is a wall of fraying word-threads, word/picture dualities, and pictures opening and closing into words across my image drum; they make a snarled palimpsest, a threading-over the dualities already there, from books, from this letter, from wrecked lines of unwritten lyrics adrift in my head, from Europe, from long before that.

•

MAE CALLED TO THE boys on the road shoulder. Feathery towers of rain on the hills. Blackfeet call this place the Backbone of the World. *I am invisible out here,* a memory of her brother on the telephone said, weeks ago. Another voice was also there, behind his voice, staticky, as if the lines had crossed *as horses crossed the trail above the mine / a windowbroken wheelwindbroken ship / sailorless it slept on the abyss / without a surge. The tides / were in their grave. The moon / their mistress had expir'd,* a female voice, but with a knot of masculinity, as if hers had conceived a son that then was reabsorbed. Two boys, one with a deer rifle, one with a small guitar, climbed into the truckbed.

Leaning out the window, Mae said, "Which of you knows Matthew Band? He's my brother."

"Take us up to Browning?" said the boy with a guitar.

"Help me find my brother and I'll take you both to Mexico."

Her radio was on. The stations faded in and out and through each other. *Bone touch bone in leviathan's tail / guitarwood ship without a sail / as far from the sea / as possible I walked in touch wood to paper to blank / some books with me.*

"What's he doing up here?" said the boy with a rifle.

Mae: "Where's Touch Wood Hills? He said he's at a house with men with names he didn't say. They're making acid."

Rifle: "You sound like the Bureau."

Guitar: "Those hills are in Canada anyway, a long way away. If you can take us up to Browning, there's the Bureau man up there."

Ghost at the Loom

"Not that Touch Wood. I looked for it in the atlas. This is just a couple little hills called that, my brother said you call it, near here, not in the atlas."

Guitar sat on the tailgate. His fists on his knees were like little bald heads. His sleeves hung from his wrists like hoods. These boys lived in the commonworld. They did not go to school. Last night, they slept out on a blue tarp in the sea of dust behind Guitar's father's trailer, dust atop recordless rock, a land in which no Babylon awaits excavation. *Touch these darker areas of bone / there's a man on the phone / at the door / with a book-shaped lock / no compass or clock / you have to think of women more.*

"I play, too," said Mae. "I have a guitar."

Rifle laughed when she said "guitar," disliking liking how the whiteness in her put some gold and green in places where the girl he sometimes said he'd marry had black and black, and that girl had no truck and no guitar. "White Rabbit's why you came up here? Is that the truth?"

Oh, you are too well aware of the crossed out lines in that.

When a man behind a roadblock of chainsawed trees aimed a pistol at Rifle, Guitar greeted the man in New Blackfoot, and Rifle put his rifle-bore against his own head, laughing.

The man behind the roadblock spoke to them in Old Blackfoot. *What did he say?*

"What does he say?" said Mae.

"Go down to Browning," said Guitar, "good idea."

"Ask him about my brother, Matthew Band."

Guitar called in New Blackfoot, "We came to find her brother who's the one who cooks it," and in English, "White Rabbit?"

It was Matthew coming down the hill, between the stumps and trees, over the roadblock, landing near the truck's nose, but when he leaned into her window *broken wheels under the van / upon whose brow Famine had / written Fiend*, Mae saw them, the bad crystals in his pupils, with his irises eclipsed to narrow loops of yellow. Matthew faced the sun. In one pupil, Mae observed her face pulled oblong and the sun behind her as an ovoid flame, dimmer red than real. *A hammer with a solar mass / a waterwheel pick up pick / up help us strung ship / smashed St. Elmo's compass.*

Rifle tapped the truckbed with his barrel quietly over and over, and maybe Mae said something like, "Get in or...get your things, we have to go to Mexico. They're getting all the Indians. You have to come with either me, the Army, or the Navy." *They came at a woman-shaped hour / when the long glass piers / were priested by soldiers / with guns in the mouths of their halfbloodredflowers.*

"The Navy, I guess, if I had to pick one," Matthew said, "*ómahk-ahkiohsátsis.*"

"What is that, Matoo?"

"How to say ship, I think."

Ghost at the Loom

"Come with me, then."

"No one's going to find me out here. See? Not even you. I'm out here," Mama's brother said and slapped the roof of the truck as if to say it should've been a horse and now it had to go and he, too, had to go, go hide from armies and navies and sisters, and he backed away and sank away into Touch Wood Hills.

◇◇◇◇◇◇◇◇◇◇◇◇◇

MAMA STACKS RAGS.
"There are mangoes," she says.
"Fine."
"Come here."
I do.
"Play with my hair?"
I shake my head no and climb the ladder to the kitchen. I can see you through the archway. You have put on one of Mama's knee-length sweaters. I go in to you in the piano room and build a fire in the fireplace: paper, one big log, and bits of oak and dogwood from the yard. Mama keeps wood here in a crate, some dogwood sticks, but not the right length.

"Rider'quiet..." barely pressing minor chords, four-fingered. Folding your hands across the middle octave, firelight crescents on your cheekbones, when your foot comes off the pedal, you say, "But you can't do something and you know..." a soft harmonic follows the release, "you can't for me, except just take me when you go."
"Go where?"
"Back to Europe? Cities don't scare me."
"Neither did bulls."
"Rider'quiet, take me when you."

"How do you know I'm going?"

"Are you going?" Same chord again and again, and then a higher minor chord, the top notes dragging tattered, rusty extensions. I'd call a piano tuner for you, but would Mama let one into this house? "I have a friend," I say. "You know John. I can't do a lot without his help. It's up to him, but I don't think to Europe, not again this year."

I stand behind you, not touching your fingers, but feeling these phantom extensions of their movements in my own, I'm *guarding you. I am your older brother. I am right behind your head.* But there are times, especially when you're asking me for something, times I fear I'll never find you if you physically are near, and this becomes our metronome—blood, quartz, sap in twigs popping, cricket legs, crow-flaps, shoe-slaps of scared humans running from strong ones, the thought that something could happen, that you could be dead—this inaudible sound, which has been hidden under words and chords, is tapping the back of my head.

I am touching the fringe of your hair, not like it was in Vienna, not *your hair full of English* right now. Straight, black, languageless.

"My friend. John," I repeat, and you, reminded or restarted, play.

"Like in your book," you say between the chords. "You like to say his name. I heard you talking to him yesterday on the phone."

"You read my little clothbound book?"

"No. I read your published book," enunciating *published*, "that you sent to Mama, and you dedicated one small poem to John."

"Don't look in my cloth book."

"I didn't look."

"Are you going to sing?"

You start a melody on black notes only. "But you can't do anything, you egg. Sometimes I am alone too much in here."

"In the house?"

"Here." You tap the air beside your head. "Rider'home."

◇◇◇◇◇◇◇◇◇◇◇◇◇

*H*OME: WORD LIKE A round deep drum struck once. I go with a stick, without you, onto Horse Hill. Forms that once were purely *home*, gold needlegrass and trails with hoofprints and no footprints, have become entangled, at the border of mind and sight, with the swarming echo-shadow-grass of Amsterdam and cobbled Roman alleys.

Granted somehow suddenly intense will, I dismiss these echoes, but what's left? The trails appear suspended in an ether that mocks any suggestion of their leading to or from another place. The border of grass and sky overpowers material objects below and above it: day moon, clawfoot horsewater tub, concrete culvert, flying dark bird—immaterials. If a few lichened rocks seem to float in this ether of gold, they are here not to signify hardness or oldness—just blindspots, just gestural shapes overpowered by wheatlike grasses. Hill terrain: but there has been an opulent, mysterious flattening of space.

I planned to hike to the electric tower to see if it's true a child could have climbed it, but now the symmetry—the dishonest construction—of that act has turned me around.

I'm in the house, reading in bed, writing notes. I'm in the yard. It is time to sleep. A faceless, dullard self beside me asks, what *is* time to sleep, what is *time* according to sleep. *Nothing,* says the Minus in my brain, *sleep can't accord, it's not a creature with a brain.* I even have a pregnancy test I bought at a drugstore in America yesterday. As if I could give it to you and await a report. I should stop reading and sleep—rereading what I wrote to you tonight.

◇◇◇◇◇◇◇◇◇◇◇◇◇

Rider,

My new book is out. 190 pages. *Bad Poems* is the title.

Why I wrote: you surprise me because in New York you were such a peaceful guy but [Celt] emailed me this morning saying you're a girlfriend thief, a book thief, and a brawler. That's hilarious. I shouldn't laugh. Please disregard me generally. Until I hear both sides I'm not judgmental and yes impressed with the fuck-up as a whole.

Write back,
Will

I PULL UP MY shirt and look at my stomach. An oddly high moan exits me. I push my shirt down, sit on my childhood bed, and crack my fingerjoints and toejoints, then go to the kitchen and drink soymilk from a bottle. Underfoot, the darkroom clanking sounds of Mama remind me of something...too far back, a metallic zero in the back of my head. I put back the bottle, snap shut my mouth, drop to my chest, and hang my head down the laddershaft into the darkroom.

"I'm here." She sits cross-legged in a ring of pots and plastic tubs.

"I'm ten," I say.

"You're ten, little egg?"

"Nn."

"Did someone scare you, little egg?" She shakes a canister with both hands. Forearms, wrists, and hands—these thin, spearlike extensions from her sleeves.

"No one is dead," I say.

Mama in a violet bathrobe, black in this light—hair wet, braided. "Isn't that funny, Rider?"

When Mama says "isn't that funny" there's never any humor in her voice, have you noticed this?

"But I'm glad you aren't getting married," she says, "not to anyone. I need a little help with money."

"You need money? I can get some."

"I know, soon, but not from Paro."

"No, from John. Did Leya talk to you?"

"Will you make a little cup of tea? The slippery elm, it's in a tin behind the rice. Tell Leya play for us."

I hang my face against a ladder rung. We have been in this house of stasis for at least a week, not often talking like this. Mostly I am at my books, Mama her photography, and you, I don't know, sometimes the piano. Other times you must be in your room with the door closed. Photos, clipped to taut strings wall to wall

Ghost at the Loom

down here, show things that can be still found in the house, unmoved: moth jars, me, a little girl's shirt, a stick as a bookmark jutting from Shelley's biography a few weeks prior to his death.

"It's in the round tin," Mama says.

"I'm leaving soon."

"That's not the best." She pours developer into a tub. "It's best to have you home. You finding Leya was the right way, don't you think, for you to have a reason to come home."

I stand up to avoid the stink. I still hear Mama speaking but I can't hear what. I fill the waterpot.

"Play for us," I say toward the fire-and-piano room.

The water boils. I'm rifling through boxes, most with no more than a teabag or two. The cupboard contains no cups. An act of mildest rebellion: I take a teacup from the counter. There's a crack in it, a stimulating, winding crack, like a coast in a map; here's the seaport of Blank on the Gulf of China, and here, further on, is the inlet of Leyamakemamastop.

"Mama," I yell at the pantry, "I'm throwing away a brown moth! You have lots!"

"Yes you may!"

I wash the insect from the cup. I pour the tea and climb one-handed down into the cube. You'll never use this ladder, but, if you did, I think you'd feel it, too, an urge to hold one's breath before continuing down. Harriet Westbrook, 1816, first wife of Shelley, drowned herself in the Serpentine. She left me this note: *I could never be anything but a source of vexation...too wretched to exert myself, lowered in the opinion of everyone, why should I drag on a miserable existence?*

"Mama, take it."

"Too hot, she can have it later." Mama sets the teacup on the concrete floor.

I don't have any money, but I'd like to give her something. What do I have that a woman might like? I can't stay here, Leya, not in this house much longer; it fills me with abstract pain, abstract colorless colorfields. Exit. Now. *Take me.* I will. The grasses on Horse Hill are blowing, not quite beckoning: they are the mane of a great mindless head in the sundown. I'm down here, remembering suddenly (why?) schedules of trains we took, the emptying of Pamplona, red tassels and flowers, a shop in Manhattan where I bought my wine for a year, John telling jokes about money. I take off the mercury cobra Paro gave me and double-loop it around Mama's wrist. Something in/behind me, utterly without an image, huge, is hammering a small thing that is also imageless.

"Oh...thank you, Rider."

"Sorry."

"That's pretty," she says.

"Will you wear it? You can sell it."

"Where's your unsafe motorcycle?"

"New York. No. I don't know. Maybe somewhere in the middle of the country. John's supposed to have shipped it here."

Ghost at the Loom

"You won't need this?" She pendulates the cobra near my face. "I guess you live here now."

"Of course I don't."

"You have to help me, anyway, with Leya. New York doesn't help."

She's never met John, but his name is a trigger: have you noticed she begins to speak more slowly, even more carefully? It is as if she thinks John whispers lies or undermining truths about her in my head when she's not there—I am the aged, ill, half-conscious monarch, she and he the rival plot-decocting courtiers.

"You don't have anywhere to live," she says.

"How do you know?"

"Because you have to help with Leya. I've been asking you for years. You're not supposed to not be here."

In pure red light, a sharpening of shadows in her face: she looks more European, Austrian almost, a face from nightclubs in Vienna.

"Everybody's mother asks him to come home and then not leave," I say. Is this true? I imagine not. "If I went to New York, I'd stay with John."

"John? No—are you a little shoe? Are you my little boot?" she coos. "John, no. You've shipped your unsafe motorcycle here."

"I know. You think you don't like John. That's fine, because I have a place a few hours north of here. I'm taking Leya with me."

"No...that wouldn't work."

The lit part of the porous wall behind her is divided by her slightly swaying head into two cloudy oblong fields of colorless nowhere: flayed-open lungs, they seem to breathe, though the light is steady. Mama's talking. I'm not listening. I'm breathing with the lungs. My attention returns to Mama's mouth.

"—she can't," she says, "it's funny, but she can't."

"She'll email you," I say. "She does know how."

"She doesn't use computers."

"Leya emailed me. That's how I found her."

"No, my daughter doesn't use computers."

"Yes she does. With me she does."

You can't fight Mama. Don't fight Mama. The wing beats constantly behind me in this house, but barely, and it never builds; it's just a thinnest difference of wind, a thinnest scent of carrion.

"Well," Mama says, as if with deep consideration, "each person's different with each person. People have their versions of each other...what place do you have that's north of here?"

"I spoke to Bronner yesterday. He said it's fine, he's never there."

"Who said?"

I say, "Am I a little shoe? Is this the game? You can't pretend you don't know Bronner."

"Well, I don't know anyone these days." She purrs, she coos, "How old are you? Are you ten? Are you only ten?" *Don't fight. Do what she likes.*

Okay. The first roll is developed. Eight-by-eights clipped to strings and laid out on the upside-down boxes

Ghost at the Loom

around her. She's about to develop the second and third, as soon as I climb up and close her in. These insects in their cups and jars, they're neither sinister exactly nor innocuously entomological. What *are* they, then? They thwart allegorical interpretation. More and more things do. *Counterfeit equations*, John says such things are. Moth cup-or-minus butterfly equals jar?

◇◇◇◇◇◇◇◇◇◇◇◇◇

B UT THE NEXT DAY, the equation is over.
"Where's Leya?"

"In her room."

"The door is locked," I say.

"She likes to lock it. Maybe she's outside."

Mama's cleaning and putting away the jars and cups.
The burned-down candles, in the hall since we came
home, have been picked up and put into a bag with all
the insects and the kitchen and bathroom trash. The
bag leans on the yard door's sliding glass, through which
I stare. Up Crow and the other trees tranquilly weave
in the wind, and the plotted weeds weave and unweave,
and the absence of you is another inseparable thread.

"We need to take your car to get my motorcycle. It
arrived this morning at the shipping place."

"You can't," says Mama.

"Oh? Why not?"

"It's funny. Leya took my keys."

"I have your keys," I say. "I took them from the nail
this morning."

"Well, if you do go out, will you pick up a cotton
plant?"

"What, where?"

"Make sure it's not too young. It has to have good roots."

"You can't just buy a cotton plant." *I can't stay here.*

Key in your backpack?

There isn't a key. Your room locks from inside.

Why wait here for days for your door to open? It won't, and I know this is not by your choice. I'll wait nearby until I have a plan. Leya, imagine a man in the dark, who wonders if he's somehow staring at the sun without knowing it, a kind of understated paranoia in which the voice of self-governance, the one that tells him to look away, stays active, even if he's gone into a room without windows. Or imagine a last crescent of sun no brighter than a darkroom bulb; imagine a man compelled to watch it set. Without the white pain of a daylight sun, that voice is the only motivator: it says, but without words, *the retinae are being damaged.* Eerie, to suspect you're being damaged without pain. Imagine that voice won't go down with the sun.

I can't live with Mama. I can't live in this house in which I ceased to glimmer, and I can't break down your door with my shoulder or words.

DIRT ROAD FOR MILES, with hints of hidden hempfields on the wind. It's dusk. His house is long and low, bought years ago. I've never been here. Gray wood, two doors, a deck, a small white truck. To the west of the house, a pond. He's in the left door with a fatter gut, a narrower face.

I dismount, and we hug, and Bronner stands back and taps my chest. "You lift weights?"

"Sometimes."

"Lift weights. You should run long runs." He points west at some shallon-covered hills.

"I don't run," I say. "I don't like to."

"That's not true if you learn to like to."

Redwood table with a laptop on it, mismatched chairs, the stretched skin of an animal on one wall decorated with not Karuk patterns, maybe Modoc. Two halls lead away from this main room. There's a rack on a wall with two shotguns and a cartridge crossbow. A heap of catalogs and other trash in a corner.

"I'm just here to let you in. I'm on the rez in fall and winter. You know that?"

"You told me on the phone."

"That's a long drive."

"Thanks," I say.

He taps me on the head, above the temple.

"What?"

He taps again.

"Okay," I say.

"Okay."

One window, large, the wingspan of an albatross, I'd like to say it *faces south*, toward you. It faces west. It faces south. It frames a landscape splashed together out of semi-accidental inkblots; there's a psychiatric quality, as of an order imposed from outside the landscape (that is, from in here, inside the house, or else here's where my cracked logic breaks) by a doctor of landscapes, me, myself imposing on the landscape in my head in the— *Rider'stop*—in the window.

"Don't use the guns."

I say, "I don't know how."

"So don't."

"Okay."

Now Bronner's asking questions about Mama. My answers aren't answers. I can't write to you what's being said.

One week apart from you:

Have I made a mistake? I should've stayed until your bedroom opened? I subsist on canned corn, butter, garlic, and defrosted Bronner-shot venison. The door to Bronner's bedroom—I don't open that. I sleep here in the main room on a mattress. I walk in the hills. Dead brown California autumn land, *home, home.* My drums in New York—has Paro thrown away my drums? My new dogwood sword, from Mama's yard, hangs at my side. I walk from oak to oak and draw my sword and tap the earth. I tap a large, tripe-colored mushroom. My epic will be on the subject of impossibility.

I call Mama again. "Let me talk to Leya."

"Leya's in her room."

The squarish pond beside Bronner's house is the size of your room. In the crux of a dead live oak, at the water's edge, I sit and write to you: of finding you in Jamnik, climbing the trees at the edge of the chine, your grown-up child's face and the valley behind it, and what can I tell you here in a tree? Anything to stop this letter from ending. If my image drum were square, I'd see a black queen on a card, the outline of your profile in the stagnant water, and you'd look at me from such remoteness, through the zero of the royal pupil, from a point of missing self, and say: *a bad thing has to happen.*

Two weeks:

"May I talk to Leya now?"

"She's in the yard."

"Not in her room?"

"When are you coming home?"

I hang up and chew on some defrosted bread and make tea and return to my reading, and soon the sun's gone. It's three a.m. I need sleep less and less. I'm listening to a voicemail from Minus that says, among other things:

Ghost at the Loom

"I've spoken to your doctor in Vienna. He was looking through his positronic metaphoroscope into your head before you're even born! Before hard science of the brain. He calls the feeling you're describing 'oceanic.'"

I am not concerned with Freud, though oceans have been in my thoughts. I have been studying rhythms in the books we were given in Rome. I tap the table, having left in some hotel the drum I bought in Italy. I lose books, clothing, friends, drums, money—but I find things, too. I've copied out and linked some passages in Shelley that appear to be parts of a cryptogram:

> An orphan with my parent lived, whose eyes were lodestars of blank blank, which drew me home when I might wander forth; nor did I prize aught human thing. What wert thou then? A child most infantine, yet wandering far beyond that innocent age in all but its sweet looks and mien blank: even then, methought, with the world's tyrant rage, a patient warfare thy young heart did wage.
>
> As mine own shadow was this child to me, a second self, far dearer and more fair; who asked me without speaking to forget all paths which money and despair of human things had made unwalkable. And warm and light I felt her clasping hand when twined in mine: she followed where I went, through lone paths of our immortal land. And there lay Visions swift and sweet and quaint, each in its thin sheath like a chrysalis, some eager to burst forth, some weak and faint with the soft burthen of intensest bliss.

> She fled to me, and wildly clasped my feet when
> human steps were heard; I moved nor spoke, nor
> changed my hue, nor raised my looks to meet the gaze
> of Strangers.

Now more than a month:

Panic, calm, calm calm panic, calm. An eight-footed rhythm. Why can't I ride home! Am I waiting for you to give birth? For whatever you're calling a baby to happen? Or waiting for Mama to let you out. I've stopped calling and asking for you, and the limbo that gnawed me toothlessly in Rome is in this house, or soon will be. I hear it mumbling in the fog. Great slugs of fog, blown from the coast, are here for hours most days. Bronner told me today on the phone that Root's pregnant. It somehow makes sense. But you don't know Root. You were in your room when I knew her.

I've several times mounted my motorcycle, ready to ride to Mama's and break you out. *But you can't fight Mama. Don't hurt Mama.* Mama with her noose of thinnest psychic thread around my head. Then I'm quarantined here? Then I must be ill, and yet, I feel it in my limbs and the back of my neck: I am surging with health, strong heart, strong liver, kidneys, nerves. There are owls and other night-murmurers here. And mine own shadow, too. A parliament of owls lives on the roof, or possibly nocturnal squirrels.

Something runs on the roof—in my image drum, Shelley runs out of the room, having imagined a woman with eyes for aureoles, and he shrieks

Ghost at the Loom

once in the hall, and I have jumped up from the table. As I run into the hall, toward the bathroom, my mouth encounters something mouthlike in the dark, but with vertical lips, and a current, an amperage, snaps through my teeth into a floating image of my brain, wherein you play piano silently; and in your head a brain beats like a fist against the side of the piano in my brain; and in your brain, in your sensorium, one node's a thousand times more active than the rest.

Dear Jesus Dagon Isolato,

Moral illiterate, what are you doing?

What are you doing? What are you doing? I'm your only friend (except for "Willy," barely, who smells like saliva on a bitten fingernail and whose new book is bad and who's the type who sees a speck of fuzz on the inner rim and, without making a mess, treats his beam of piss like it's a solid rod and taps the fuzz into the water, real self-satisfaction). Why don't you just pick up when I call? The guys I call in Riyadh do. Get it? What we have to GET is out of here, because, y2'know, this country's falling down, a building at a time. We haven't been to Fiji, Vanuatu. How about we satisfy me for a change? We're going to do the puddlejump, and I'm deciding everything. I'm crying while I'm typing this, you sick nonpickupper. Jesus, I'm sicker than

tricky dick of these Dark Age religions. There has
been a terrorist attack here in NY you know. You
don't know.

Dixi,
J.

A SCAB ON THE back of my head won't heal. I can't stop
checking it. Sometimes I scratch it off to make it heal
faster. I do this when the scab has proven faulty, having
taken too long to fall off, too long to assure me it is,
in fact, a scab, a functioning part of the system, not
something foreign, feeding—like yesterday, a tick on my
ankle, I found it preparing to bite, and so I placed it
at the base of my computer screen and watched it walk
below the digits of the clock displayed in the lower right
corner. They walk to a definite rhythm: tick rhythm, tick-
walking eight-stick-legged rhythm. Pull off a leg? Sevens-
rhythm. I create, attune to, and decipher rhythms. Still
no glimmer, but my hands commune across the flatness
of the table and my books and papers. Something's
building, curling, iterating. Do you have a Rider'raby in
you, too? Awake at early hours, copying patterns, tapping
patterns, tapping passages, meticulously linking:

> We prolonged calm talk beneath the absent moon—
> when suddenly was blended with our repose a winged
> sense of fear; and from the mine behind I seemed to
> hear sounds gathering upwards! Accents incomplete,

Ghost at the Loom

and stifled shrieks, and now, more near and near, a tumult and a rush of thronging feet the mine's blank depths beneath the earth did beat.

The scene was changed, and away through the air and over the sea we sped, and Cythna in my sheltering bosom lay, and the winds bore me——through the darkness spread around. The gaping earth then vomited legions of foul and ghastly shapes, such shapes as haunt wet clefts,——and lumps neither alive nor dead, dog-headed, bosom-eyed and bird-footed.

My study ramifies, economizes, ramifies. This process is not neat, not without scraps: *Revolt of Islam*, anaesthetized, cut, killed, dissected, spliced with itself, with other epics, then reanimated (not to cast me into Laon and you Cythna, but I need not tell you that; you know the riddle doesn't have that kind of answer), notes in margins, little folded notes in pockets, and my backbone is electric:

Unawake I rose, and all the cottage crowded found with whooping, pushing, singing men, whose red, inflaméd swords were bare. And ere with rapid lips and gathered brow I could demand the cause——a feeble shriek, it was a feeble shriek, faint, far, and low——arrested me, my mien grew blank and bleak, and grasping a small knife, I went to seek that voice among the crowd——'twas Cythna's cry!

'Farewell! Farewell!' she said, as I drew nigh, 'At first my peace was marred by this strange stir, now I am blank as truth——its chosen minister.'

I drew my knife, and with one impulse, suddenly all unaware three of the Strangers slew. What followed then, I know not——for a stroke on my raised arm and naked head came down, filling my eyes with blood.

There is, of course, much more. I only copy out the least convincing of it here, because my hand is tired and has been so for weeks. John says he's coming. John is worried. Should I stop him? Is it working, Leya, isolation? Maybe today I am closer to you, to it, than yesterday.

Approximately forty-seven days alone:

There's been, in objects, wrongness. How else can I say it, though the objects look and feel no different than they should. This box of Root's old costume jewelry is wrong. I find "bad" fruit in a wooden bowl, entirely fresh. I bought it myself in the nearest town. The steel knob of the towel-hanging bar in Bronner's bathroom is laced with intangible wrongness. Sitting, one sees oneself dwarfed, reflected in the knob. This causes a mental effect like remembering, except without a memory. To fill that gulf, I imagine a man in a fine black suit, who carries a walking stick, the steel knob at the end of which has been abducted from the vicinity of a toilet. He intends to bludgeon me with my sitting self.

Also, the wing. The wing beats behind me more often, but subtly, not like in Vienna.

Then sometimes there's the feeling that if I were to begin to rip the walls, I mean the pages of this letter, in the rifts between the lines, arrases of threadlike script

Ghost at the Loom

would hang undamaged, woven right to left and left to
right like English written over Hebrew or the opposite,
and then a layer under that (with a wrongness that is not
exactly mockery, not quite intentional enough for that),
half-weaving-half-unweaving top to bottom, like Chinese.

> The peace of madness fled. O if I were as in my
> boyhood and could be the comrade of thy wanderings.
> A ship was lying on the sunless main. Its sails were
> blank in the breathless noon. Its destination lay
> beyond——that sight again waked, with its presence,
> in my tranced brain the stings of a known sorrow,
> keen and cold: I knew that ship bore Cythna o'er the
> plain of waters. I watched until the shades of evening
> wrapped Earth like an exhalation——then the bark
> moved, for that calm was by the sunset snapped. It
> moved a speck upon the Ocean dark, through the
> gray, void abysm, down, down, where the air is no
> prism, and the moon and stars are not.

John's here. I don't know anymore how many days I've
been without you. I have made John promise not to touch
Bronner's crossbow or guns. On the deck, I show John the
trapdoor underneath the three loose boards. I've found
the key to Bronner's "government collapse shelter," which
contains many boxes of cans of garbanzos, condensed milk,
propane, antibiotics, three rifles, and the subterranean
mouth of a well. Bronner's shelter, Mama's darkroom.
Everyone who cares for me is ready for a bomb. Antibiotics,
Bronner claims, will be worth more than gold.

I tell this to John.

"Not true," says John, "bad investment. Big collapse, not coming, not what's on the agenda. The markets are pleased with the myth of collapse. Still, I'm going down to catalogue. Don't shut the lid, I'm serious. What, do you think it'd be funny?"

"I don't think that kind of thing is funny."

"Better not, I swear. You do, I'll defecate all over everything down there."

I like to daydream that by climbing into Bronner's shelter, I can come up out of Mama's darkroom, find you in the fire-and-piano room with all the curtains drawn and Mama sleeping, and carry you back down the ladder and come up here on the deck. But you're scared of the darkroom. It never would work.

John comes up and hands me a hammer and nails.

"What for?"

"For fun," he says. "I'm going to do some work, you know *work*, in the house."

I'm listless as an old dog on the deck. Damp redwood wind cools my shirtless back. I try to drive a nail through a knot in a redwood plank, and the sound of gnarl being bitten goes well with the beat in the back of my head.

On the deck stairs, there are boards loose to no purpose. Also, the railing wobbles. Sure, I'll repair these stairs for Bronner. This should occupy a few days. *Rider what are you waiting for?* I don't know...a bomb or a baby. I'm dull, a dullard, slow, except on drums and motorcycles. Still, if someone must repair the stairs, it must be me, as John is physically and morally incapable of carpentry.

John likes to make up parables. Here's my attempt:

Imagine an irrational Awareness, something densely interlaced in more than three dimensions, a network, a dream, a language maybe (the language you sing in), something ill-defined, with irrational energies, irrational laws, structures that at lower levels look like chaos, but it all develops upward, and the whole is orderly. Imagine this Awareness then encounters Fact, another intellect incarnate, except this one's entirely composed of empirical elements. A battle of wits ensues between Fact and Awareness. Can Fact be undermined at all by language and imagination? I don't mean can Awareness merely trick itself into ignoring Fact. Can Fact be stronger than, yet somehow impotent against, a sub-enigma, hidden, small (but vast), but there?

John wakes up from his nap and comes out, and I tell my parable and ask him, and he says no, "...and your whole family needs a better education."

I go in where John can't hear and call Mama, whose father in Ohio, whom she speaks to once a year, is dying.

"Is he? Sorry, Mama."

"Sometimes people need to help each other," Mama says. "I don't need to talk about that anymore. I hear her in the mornings when she's sick."

"Will you let me talk to her?"

"It's every morning. What's her temperature, I wonder."

"She's just pregnant in her head."

"Rider."

"I just can't right now. Put Leya on."

"I wasn't asking you for help...if I, if someone has a son, at your age, women, women with their sons at your age don't have anything, but this is my relationship with you. I'm not like this with other people. I go to the store and bank. I talk to people. This is my relationship with you and Leya so you both are safe. Where are you now?"

"Can man be free if woman be a slave?" I murmur to the phone.

Tiny yellow flowers in the grass this morning turned out, as I knelt, to be the jawbone and teeth of a rodent, the petals and teeth of a detail supplied to distract me from you, and it worked for a half second.

"You know where I am," I say. "Put Leya on. I could be at your house before dark if you'll put Leya on."

"Your dog is dying, too."

"I know."

"I'm going to have to poison her. She's suffering."

"Put Leya on."

What does she think—I'll kidnap you? I will, but how? I've written you dozens of emails. Why don't you use Mama's computer?

John doesn't help. I'm in a hole, a little limbo valley, with redwoods and oaks on the wall of hills around me, and quiet crows and falcons that fly sideways when I turn—too slowly—so I never see them hovering behind my head. If hills crumple north along the inner

Ghost at the Loom

coast of California, north from Horse Hill, these must be the hills beyond the hills beyond, the Tug Foot Hills, the Touch Wood Walls, the Drum Rim Wings. I need new sight, a plan.

I call Bronner. He's been smoking, or maybe he has a cough and a fever. His breath is full of snags and stops. *He should be quarantined, not I and John.* Some awkward pleasantries...I'm listening to his breath..."Still there?"

"You talk," he says.

"When are you coming to your house?"

"I might come soon. What do you think?"

"I thought you maybe had some medicine that I could try."

"Some what?"

A fly skims my face. A fly's flightpath is redirected by my stationary head.

I say, "I won't be indirect."

Minus watches through the screen door, writing on a little square of paper.

Bronner: "Indirect? What kind of talk is that? What are you talking about, 'medicine'?"

"So I could just hallucinate a little...you still there?"

"You want Navajo medicine? Why call me? Navajo as you are."

"I am?"

"I'm as Navajo as you are, why call me?"

I stare at Minus. He steps out of view.

"Root's with you?"

Bronner: "Sure, she just moved in with me again."

"I could come up and see you both."

"I'm in a fight with Root."

I'm thinking what to say.

"You bring your mother to the house," he mutters, "Saturday, and I'll come down."

We both want off the phone.

"Maybe get a new phone," he says. "Bad connection."

"Sure," I say.

"Hey maybe some of what you sound like some old white lady calling 'medicine' could do your mother good. She needs to see me anyway. I haven't talked to her in seven years. I'll come down Saturday."

"I don't think she would."

"No?"

"I don't think," I say.

"Okay," he says. "Don't think I'm disappointed."

"No, I don't."

"I'll talk to Root. She has some friends."

The phone sits closed on a stack of books. I stand with my hands behind my back, my back to the screen door, which opens, and now John's behind me.

"Self-medication again? Don't you know," John says, "hallucinogens are for those who lack imagination?"

"Who're you quoting?"

"Everybody," pulling at the hammer in my hand. "I, in fact, know better what to do for you than you do."

"You don't have to do it with us."

John pulls the hammer from my hand and puts it on the table and then puts his fingers in his ears and

Ghost at the Loom

makes a serious-eyed, tongue-out face at me, which, in
my image drum, becomes an oblong mask with eyelike
orbicles and hands or horns or jutting ears at three, six,
and nine o'clock; and the hands tick, and I tap my shoe
to this waltz.

◇◇◇◇◇◇◇◇◇◇◇◇◇

*A*RHYTHM CAN RADICALLY CHANGE *via minimal changes to beats and their placement, so can a well-placed enjambment topple kings*—I stare at this epitaph I've written into my letter to you. I try to collate days, sitting in the blue shade of the old growth, tapping a sparse rhythm out on the sides of my head, sacrificing my head to my hands in the needles and cones, my gestures becoming less irreal to me, more supple than spindly, less puppetlike? John (my nurse, my keeper?) allows me privacy, and the glimmer perhaps is some small unnamed unit of measurement closer, still... the restlessness without a spatial destination. Still the destination's you. Small cones on the forest floor. Any network of points can be seen as a constellation, a map, a mission: go this way and cease to be human. Smoke or breath drifting up from the sacrifice in the morning, in a light wind.

Bronner arrives with dinner from a restaurant. John shakes his hand with Jewish, jittery enthusiasm, grasping for, in Bronner's grip, some dubious alliance of the likewise holocausted. Bronner talks about Mama. We eat. I avoid every question, while John, fascinated, abets and encourages Bronner, and what they say about Mama I couldn't report to you.

This pain continues until a noise of wheels on gravel stops it. Bronner has me by the forearm. He is strong. "Root's here," he's saying.

An adult, a woman, enters: unbuttoned jean jacket, roundly pregnant, rich healthy skin, thin arms and face. Good pregnant health all places but her eyes, which are reptilian as Paro's post-Ibiza. Unless it's me, unless I don't know how to look at women's eyes. She puts down a carrier crate and opens it, and two cats exit the crate.

"Introduce yourself to Rider and his friend," says Bronner.

"Don't tell me what to do. I know Rider," she says. "Whose rental car's outside?"

"John's," says John. "I'm John."

She shakes his hand, not mine, and goes into a hallway, saying she'll be right back. Her birth name is Rose or some flower. What is this, this yearning to follow her out of the room? Bizarrely, I consider for an instant (frantic, an emotion full of hooded lights and garbled handwriting) whether I'm the father of her baby.

I am calm. I say, "Should I go help her?"

"Help with what? She's fine." Bronner's looking at me again like he did at the door, like he's judging my soundness, my strength. "She's going back to junior college in the fall."

Then everyone runs out of talk. Poor John, at last without a quip. So much loud (but also so much quiet) power has been given to, and taken by, the disempowered in this country. Here it must be power of a quiet kind that's silenced John.

I try to still the muscles of my face, this face that is too frequently disloyal to me, not in the sense of revealing my feelings, rather by suggesting what I do not feel, what other people's faces ask to see.

"Come over here." With helpless yet profoundly nonchalant excitement, Bronner leads us to the wall-mounted rack and shows us his weapons and details their drawbacks and blessings, these weapons I have lived beneath for weeks without touching. This takes many minutes. The guns he puts back on the rack. The crossbow he leaves on the table.

After dinner, Root goes to the kitchen and returns with a tray with cups of water, a knife, and the peyote in a white clay bowl. She puts the tray beside me on the table and begins to cut the cacti into disks.

Clear liquid on the blade. She's working steadily, indelicately. Varied thicknesses of disks. She says, "It's young peyote."

Bronner: "Not as strong. Root got this for you. Thank Root. What'd you think, I run the local desert nursery?"

"Are you going to use a midwife?" I ask Root.

"Midwives are dangerous. I'm going to the hospital."

"I did this," Bronner says to me and John, "in Arizona, maybe 1979. You're going to puke."

Ghost at the Loom

"I'll go outside," I say to Root. "Should I—"

"You won't puke." Root gives each of us a stack of disks and cup of water. "I'm not taking any. I'm just here to take care of who needs."

John puts two in his mouth and chews and says, "Tastes like vulture guano," and begins to perform an elaborate choking sound, but Bronner interrupts this: "No. Think about some time you weren't with anyone."

John: "Do you mean romantically?"

"Don't horseshit me. I mean relax. With anyone, anyone."

The fibrous disks are in my mouth, a flavor like tequila gone green and vile. Now John is reading something written on the metal of the crossbow butt. "What country was this manufactured in?"

"Denmark," I say.

John: "That's your *interpretation*. I say China."

Bronner: "Made in USA, horseshitters. Hey, Root, bring some pillows from my room. Guess we sleep with our heads on the table. I'm not doing anything. You know? Who knows any Navajo songs anyway? Those songs don't make much sense. We're just some people doing drugs."

Root brings each of us a small brown pillow. "Take a nap. It takes a long time."

Heads on pillows on the table. I know, this gets me no closer, but Leya, constant commonworld's too much for me, and this at least will break that for a few hours.

Bronner's quiet voice: "How did your family come into this country, what's that story?"

"Well..." says Minus.

Minus holds a cat up, making it bipedal, on the table, facing him. Root leans against the hung skin, watching us. *What is that smell?* Very close to my nose, as if a greenish plume curls upward from my mouth, except my mouth is closed. It's not the smell of cut peyote, that's distinct.

Tea...like woody tea.

Minus to the cat on the table: "Would you do me the honor?"

Minus stands, upending his chair. He picks it up and holds it for a moment above four spots of shadow on the floor, the legs like prongs of a giant electric plug. "Am I a stranger here? Am I not welcome? Fine with me, I'll go outside." He plugs it in, strides to the door, opens it, looks through, looks back at me, exits, and the door stays open.

I say, "I should get him."

Bronner: "Go."

I stand too fast. The room takes on the texture of rough paper, torn at the edges, but I'm steady, not hallucinating.

Standing in the gravel next to Bronner's pickup, John says, "Hello, friend."

"I am your friend."

Ghost at the Loom

"What's that?" He points at a metal bin beside the house. "Oh, never mind, I guess it's just an ammo dump."

"If you know better what to do for me than I do, what's my plan?"

"What I've been telling you for months. The puddlejump. I'm talking astrolabes. You think I am not serious. Is that what's going on here? Puddlejump. I've already done the whole Caribbean, it's cake, it's just malarial. Is your passport okay? Jesus, hey, is your passport acceptable? Last time I saw it in Europe it looked like a fake, all water-damaged, like you steamed the thing and slipped your picture in, but seriously, we need to dip our toes in the PGGG, that's Pacific Giant Garbage Gyre. Because the Yacht of Da, the new one, is in Baja. I mean, what are you doing out here with these people?"

Rougher paper out here, charcoal shading, hillocks, far trees, and white spots of confusion, like drops of— how can I explain this?—drops of hot white noise are falling, leaving spots of summer, not-yet-arrived, coin-sized spots of portent, on the gravel drive.

"It's so subtle."

"Yes," he says, "but no."

"I know," I say. "I have to get something out of my mother's house."

"Your passport, right?"

"And if I go there who knows when and in what hat I'll come back out, so what's my plan?"

"What hat."

"What mood, I mean."

Minus points at a bird or bat, barely visible, passing overhead. "What's that?"

I don't feel like talking.

We are two signposts. His tilts toward mine. "Your plan," says the Minus post, "is I come, too, and I distract your ma while you sneak in across the rear event horizon and pilfer the stash."

"Good plan," says my post.

Then the posts switch places too many times, like in a shell game; then they're still, and after a long time standing tilted in the beginning of nighttime, a post says, "It is possible to harvest crops from a compost of nothing but rotted books."

"This guano's too subtle for that," says the other.

"One might, however, try."

This wood-walled kitchen compresses my head. Meat, onion, brown scents. My head is brother to this onion in my hand.

"I need to have," says Bronner, "better luck this year." He stands beneath a hanging pot, beside a wooden block stuffed with knives.

"I lost my girlfriend," I say. "She was from the Congo."

"I just need some luck," he says.

"You're okay," that's my voice, "rhythm beats luck, rock beats paper. Hand me that?"

Ghost at the Loom

"Are you going to puke?"

Lodestar, lodestar—a taste in my septum, whiff of seasalt, physical pleasure. "Hand me that pot?"

He unhooks it, hesitates.

"Hand me, hand me, hand me that pot."

A lamp projects a yellow cone between us, through which Bronner moves the pot into my hands.

"I have to do, you know, to do." I hit the pot. Left fist once. A low iron knell. Again.

"Too loud," he says, with an ugly, forgiving smile.

"I'll complicate it, make it better," gripping the pot between my knees: *the shipwreck shipwreck echo answer hat or drum, hat, hat, hat! or drum, or drum, wreck's echo, wreck's deck's echo* beating with palms, fingers, heels of my hands, the rhythms echoing on cabinets and walls. I jam the signal, jamming beats between echo's echoes. The shadow of a tiny girl, faint at the fringe of the lamplight, dances like a matchflame to my drumming, out of the light, returning, out: *drum ech, drum ech break, echt echo ech back, break to gether to, wreck to, ech begin, ech to beg into, break break the wreck back together to begin with* half a heartbeat, twos, fours—finding the factor twelve by threes, the polycycle, waltz of never mind.

John crawls into the kitchen. "Are youai in here... oonderneath? Heee?"

"Hear what I'm saying? Too unsteady." Bronner says to John, "Like when he was a boy." Bronner goes into the main room and picks up the crossbow from the table and returns. "He hits my pots together."

"One pot. With his hands," John says. "He's hitting with his hands, not pots against each other. Whoa, wait, what are you going—"

"Some face coming through the window." Bronner aims the unloaded crossbow.

"Eavesdropping?" I say, "Is it my brother?"

"Nobody," says Bronner.

I exit backward into my long skull, as if descending on an elevator cable, down through New York City, floors of Rome, accelerating past the most upsetting strata, seeing soon below what look like low magnitude stars, coming to rest at the mouth of the Copper Mine—the cable snaps, an exquisite sound, and leaves me here, asking you why have you gone out on Horse Hill without me.

Behind the house, I sit on dust.

"You want to touch it?"

My hands on Root's belly—something sickens me. It will be a goblin.

"I might puke."

"You won't." Behind her back, a strand of shadow saplings bend. She says, "I'm not an idiot."

"I didn't think you were."

"Don't you feel good?" This air is raspy, thin, and voice-distorting: maybe she can take my voice, I hers. "I don't feel good, but no, I do. I don't know. I don't go anywhere," she says and takes my hands off her belly, into her hands. She looks at my face for a while with a doctorly seriousness. "Hey."

Ghost at the Loom

"What."

"Want to kiss me like when we were little?" Root's lying. We never kissed. "Not to lead to anything," she says. "A little kiss. I don't care but, if you want. Might feel good."

She wants to hurt you? I don't know. She'll bite my lip. Somehow this flips on me: I bite my lip. She tastes me where I bit.

"That's all." She licks her nether lip.

"I don't feel safe," I say.

The redwood rainledge of the house juts over us. It is a quarter of the sky, designed to break off in this light, wet wind and fall on us.

"You look good," she says.

"I'd be an awful father. I move, I—"

"You're confused."

"That's right, but I relocate—"

"Shh. You got confused. You know, I haven't been for more than a year away from my dad, and he's old and sometimes a fucker." She blinks, this is my signal: I look left.

John the Cactus? There's a male face in a window, grinning out at us.

Root: "Hey. Where did you go?"

"To Italy," I'm chanting, "Amsterdam, Vienna, Spain—"

Territories, coins, avarice and beauty alloyed, and a vulpine grace, all this in her black makeup and long-boned face. Shadows of coins from Old Spain on her eyelids. It comes, the wild clarifying, like a flash rain over fields. I don't know why, I think she's tried suicide at some point in the years since we were children together... to go somewhere.

Rider'whatsthis, windowdoor? A blindside prism. I can't see it, but it spins beside me. Blindly, wildly clear: you aren't but are but aren't here.

Bysshe: *She stood beside him like a rainbow braided.*

So I bend a colorblind night bow and fire a braid of ones and zeroes at an eye out there in the trees, looking in at me here in my head.

"Hey," says Root, "you own a car?"

"John has," I say. "John has a boat."

"My son!" but quietly.

"Oh," I say, "Mr. Sonnenreich."

Indeed, it's Eli's shadow's hand that slides off the wall onto mine. We're in the hall, our hands on a small, waist-high table. At my fingertips, in a bowl with a piece of dried sage and a gas receipt, is a petrified egg like a quail's. A ringwise crack approximates the egg's equator.

Bronner's shadow paces on the main room's wall, the crossbow's shadow swinging with his stumping stride. In Karuk, he demands something. I know too little to say what.

"He won't shoot it," I tell Eli's shadow. "Are you crying?"

"Does that trouble you, my son?"

Ghost at the Loom

Coming out of the floor, Rider' whatsthat? It looks like a valve. The one we keep closed. It controls the tide. Eli can't see it. He's our father.

"Two and three," I say, but not aloud, "I mean the numbers, are they weightless?"

"No, my son, that's not a question really. Weight's a category incompatible with pure numbers."

"So two weighs as much as thirty thousand?"

"No. Not on a piece of paper. Thirty thousand weighs more. More ink."

"But," I say aloud, "I'm talking about pure numbers."

"I don't think so."

"But," I cup my hot hands on his head, "I know why you were crying."

"Do you?" Low tide. "You aren't sure she was my daughter."

"No. I think she is." I turn the table/valve, *it's broken, see,* and drum its rim and then its middle, and the bowl with the sage in it skitters and patterns *Vitruvian Julian Boolean anything weaves into anything you / on paper squares and cubes / except the archetypes don't weave they tangle this is how you die / too many animals inside / the sinking Coliseum ark of two by two / by three. But see, the totems dip each other by / the heels in eternity water* a vitreous tide, crashing across the table's sensorium surface, this image drum outside my head, this drum contains: an Apollo mission crew drunk on blue Eleutherian wine, so the mission crashes and so does a 1999-year-old mayfly, into a quilt with each square an animal, city, or civilization, a piece of the rhythm, a Scythian Hittite Pelasgian myth of the serpentine idea that will not bite its tail because it loves the girl who lives there; that snake crashes, stockbrokers jump hand in hand from Manhattan towers, and the girl bites off her tongue into the Apple of Pure Numbers rather than remain a girl eternally. "She does have your black hair," I say.

"I'm bald," he says.

"You're just this little egg on Bronner's table."

"I would like to blame your mother."

"Don't think about Leya." I pet the egg. "I release you from any sadness concerning your children."

"Maybe *you* can find out out here what is going on," John whispers by the pond. "Frankly, I know my position. Mine is solider than state physics. Have I told you yet my parable of the prostitute and the physicist?" He covers his mouth and hiccoughs daintily. "Sorry."

"Why?"

"Wigwam garlic pasta," palpating his chest. "Jesus, put your hand right here, I'm dying, can you feel my tachycardia? Feel."

I can't feel his heartbeat, the beat on the back of my head is too present. "John," I say, "you think I could be someone's father? Do you think I like women?"

"And my head's all sweaty. Women? They don't stand by all our immature behavior. Mostly, I'm responsible for that. You're just a windblown floweret, a poet. You live off the labors of people. You don't have *responsibility*."

Ghost at the Loom

"Responsibility."

"Look, what can you do about movements? You can't draw a straight line in a curved space. If certain people eat and metacogitate together, movements are inevitable, and it's just bankrupt if you don't include some women in the fucking Movement."

"My mother decides what I do," I say. "Before my mother, Paro did. Paro tricked me. Someone did. Before Paro, my mother did."

He isn't listening, holding his hands to the sides of his head and observing his feet, which shuffle one and two and one and two as if he needs to urinate. "I mean, Jesus, what should we call ourselves? How 'bout the Fartoolatists? Don't be chauvinistic. Women are important. They invented long division, astrolabias, the wheel, the Internet, gunpowder, birth control pills. You should be into women."

A wind rushes through us. A blankness falls between us like a sheet of paper.

"What?" he says.

"I'm Rider Sonnenreich," I say, "dead on the beach, drowned. You've heard of me, I know you have."

A blue-black wind rushes through us, and John zips his leather jacket. "Heard of—no, look here, in any revolution it's just not enough to alter your environment to fit your wants, you need a basic lesson here, you have to alter, just as much, the *quality* and the direction of your wants, or else you lose your new utopia to erstwhile allies. French Rev, Late Art, not complete reversion but, you know, self-hating states of utopian anti-utopianism, dictatorship of the people, the virtual dollars and virtual people, anti-art, anti-aristocrats. You have to be the rarest revolutionary type, a lover of fucking fuck arms hanging out of sockets and aborted fetus in the road and violence against tyranny, of course, but then, you have to also be the type who, soon as the tyrants are headless, really loves aristocratic Pax Romana."

"No."

"The nineteenth century was reducible. We can't be in it! Whoa, this psychedelic is exactly like my normal mind!"

The Chinese on his buckle can't be relevant. The G8 summit can't be relevant. I've allowed these into my letter to you?! Please, don't let the center unravel. I zip my leather jacket.

"It's a moral failure, monstrous, not to live in one's own time," says John.

"Mmiaok."

"What?"

"M'okay with failure."

"Yes, but Sonnenreich, I tell a better story. I can even tell a better *olden tale*, if that's what the market demands, and my tales are more, what would you call them, honest?"

"No. I'll play whatever game you want. It doesn't matter if you're not my sister."

"Jesus, you don't say that. Not on drugs! You don't just say that kind of thing. There has to be a benevolent dictator, me. You need to be meek and inherit, okay?"

Each shadow has a weaker negative. What easily could be a cardboard cutout of a man and woman, leaned against the hood of Bronner's truck, is thinning into whiteness, pillars, cat's eyes, hairline fractures in the media of night.

John: "Okay, I'm ready, very sweaty. Who goes first?"

"I'll play whatever game you want," I say. "I have immunity to you."

His shoulders ripple backward. Ink floats on his shoulders. "Okay. I go first," he says. "I call this game Ye Olde Olden Tale Tennis. Start. I started my career as, um, a bitter almond poison manufacturer who did exist inside a wee shack on the Styx. I lived there—on the shore, and you can't see the other side. It was a summer eve, but summer here is as brown as my nose and stinks of Egypt, um, your serve."

It takes a moment for my mental mouth (which makes itself into an O and floats like smoke) to turn into my physical mouth, but then it says: "The poisoner, he crept out of his shack into the Hades sunset, which resembled a low-burning match in a daguerreotype, and gripped the handle of the valve that—"

"Yes! My fundamental problem was experience." The shapes his lips make do not match his words. "How could I dredge the muck of Styx and text, what could I *eke* in Hades, when I'd known—when all I'd known was fuck—and what about cosmology? And what about extreme varieties of coitus?" Minus gestures at me with an open palm.

"And so," I say, "he left behind his bitter laboratory, walking east, across the carbon-papery plateaus and dales below the world. He would have three trials on his journey, because that's how it is in folktales. He collected tales from travelers, by foot, by gondola, old-fashioned bicycle, and often stopped to rest and share——"

"——a cake of lemon soap! To remove the stink, or a limey tart, for the odd gastronomer, who usually came by gondola, because his gut and fundament were weighty, and then there was his manservant, Ed, who doubled as his gondolier and tripled as his bitch! Who never touched a morsel of the tart or took sugar in his almond roast, the gondolier, a gaunt man, prone to whispering about his lack of sense of self, and otherwise devoid of attributes!" Mock horror skews his mouth. His teeth are darkly yellowed at the crowns. "You pompous! What, you would kill your own brother? Are we at war?" He grabs my shoulder.

I thought it was theatre, but he said war, so I begin to see it so. My serve: "The first trial was to find the compass with its needle always pointed toward what you've been looking for, but then to find that compass he would need the compass with its needle pointed toward that compass, and he only longed for——"

"——brothels, brothels, filth, and codfish bones. Anything he found had been found. Nay," John snorts, "he was no Vinland lander, but a true fraud, but a total——"

Ghost at the Loom

"—second trial was written on an obelisk beside a fountain in the second capital of Pluto, where America is not even a word, the old capital having fallen to the Hittites. His instruction was to gather every piece of paper in the city that was ripped or partly burned and stitch them all into a—"

"—no, because I never finished trial number two or found trial three because of what happened en route. No," he spits, "there weren't any trials, just an old fat bald tourist and an almond cake. I tried to derail the whole thing, stop the bomb from blowing up the train, but, en route, I was caught up in a serious Don Juanic odyssey. You like that? It was fucked up! What do you know? You're inaccurate. You should have done your research. I went willy nilly, all in myriad missionary modes, the end of the line was a dark blue queen, she had a reputation for violence, hate crimes, there she was on all fours, or did she have six, or eight? Like an obelisk I—what a coup, that a river-dwelling crofter should transfix her tiny sapphire anus, when it was the godhead she'd expected, blasting in her holy deadly anti-womb!" He jerks his right hand out into the dark. His windy eyes are paranormal with confusion. He jerks his hand back, jams it in his pocket, doubles over.

I pace around him jauntily. After a minute, he still is still.

I become impatient. "What's this?"

"Don't."

"What?"

"Look at me."

I make a noise to hear a noise other than wind, some deep strange kin of whippoorwills. Still doubled, hand in pocket, Minus lopes off through the ink.

"WHAT ARE YOU DOING?" I say through the window.

"Getting money," Bronner says. He's on his laptop, out on the deck.

"How do you get that?"

"Hey, believe everything I say. I knew your mother before she was crazy. Why don't you go for a run. You'll get some longer muscles in your legs."

John's gone to Miami to make arrangements with his father. He's promised he'll meet me outside Mama's house in one week, then we'll go in, and he'll distract Mama while I break you out!

The lid of the barbeque on Bronner's deck creaks in the wind about once per second, as if to the pulse of a heart, not mine, a brainheartshape in the dark when I closed my eyes (when he was saying Mama's crazy) looking west through my skin at a phosphene blotch, orange-green, where the sun had been.

"I will leave you alone, I think," I say.

"Go fix your legs."

Shadows and echoes are related. What is this family? Who else is in it? I thought I saw you yesterday, a shadow-simulacrum in the dark blue air behind a tree. I nearly daily walk or run from Bronner's house to within far sight of the sea. Simulacrum is a place, not you. I left you at home with Mama. I left you in my sleep. It's a place in which absence is sovereign, and I sometimes talk to myself, stepping past a blue rim of a shadow. I say, "Simulacrum is the capital of an ill-defined imperium behind a pine tree in the coastal hills of California."

I am too protected by this slowness. Slowness in the house and hills and weather systems. I feel it again in the one white spot on the back of a tick on a dark brown stone. I run slowly. Consciousness becomes an exercise. When I write to you, I am distracted, then made sleepy, by these details, avatars of slowness: quarter-second graphite scratch, the long third note from a three-note bird, Morse code, wind pollen, SOS.

I have apophenia. John says I do. Something nearly unthinkably remote is trying to communicate.

It isn't difficult, when I look at the sea, to tell myself the Earth is flat, the gold tail of the cobra I gave Mama is transmutable to lead, and you are my sister, my living blood...but you're one white note on the high end of the piano hit too many times.

I like the saturated black-beyond-green of the redwood hills to the east and north when the sun's just down. Or, sometimes, when the sun's on the horizon, level with my averted eyes, my sunglasses catch a glimmer

Ghost at the Loom

of a glimmer, like an angel with the wing- and lifespan of a mayfly, in the corner of one lens.

Then, at night, when I write to you—the inhuman thread extends, when I read old dead rhymes, more and more slowly—near two a.m. comes an hour of idiot belief. We're almost there. I will glimmer again.

"Oil runs out," says Bronner, "no more military, no more companies. People who know how to live off land they live on will be okay. Other people, I don't know."

I listen carefully. We're eating Chinese takeout Bronner's brought in from the nearest town. Indeed, even I, accused of isolation and moral illiteracy, have been, of late, concerned with revolution:

> Science and her sister Poesy shall clothe in light
> the fields and cities of the free! Victory to the
> prostrate nations! Bear witness Night, and ye mute
> Constellations who gaze on us from your crystalline
> cars! Thoughts have gone forth whose powers can
> sleep no more! Victory! Victory!

Run, Bronner says. I do, in the shallon and fescue. I just left again. Root, in a window, watched as I did. My knees are getting limber. There's a cavity inside the day, and I have learned to run and jump across it. Sometimes I drag a hand across my forehead, and that sensation changes through the wind to buzzing between skull and skin, a sub-sub-glimmering bliss, and it stays for a few hills.

Straight as I can keep a path, I run west and turn
back and can't be lost, because I run back directly away
from the sun or the last light if the run was long. I run
blank-minded until the drifting thinking starts...of you,
the names and shapes of trees, what I might like to eat,
of what's inside you growing, of my waning, futile study
of the clues in Shelley, you, an email from Paro or two
I don't return. I'm tired when I return to Bronner's
house, but still, I like to "lucubrate my fill," as the good
lord wrote.

I know by rote *Queen Mab* and breathe the syllables
and match my running feet to *Mab*'s feet:

> *Celestial coursers paw the unyielding air;*
> *Their filmy pennons at her word they furl,*
> *And stop obedient to the reins of light;*
> *These the Queen of Spells drew in;*
> *She spread a charm around the spot...*

•

THREE WANDS OF WHITE wood. They stood in the sand.
Two boats rode onto the beach, and along with a party
of Pisan soldiers, Trelawny disembarked, carrying on his
shoulder the legs of an iron tripod furnace.

To the commandant, he said, "These were my
designators, after I found the poet, though I don't
remember planting one so distant from the others."

Soldiers gathered spades and mattocks from the
boats. To the north and south, small against the
Apennines, were unmanned watchtowers on the shore.

Ghost at the Loom

Noel Byron arrived in a carriage, escorted by dragoons and mounted quarantine officers.

Byron used his arms to launch himself out of the carriage, right leg slightly buckling as he landed running, stopping at Trelawny, heaving back his shoulders with theatrical hauteur and stomping one foot forward. Trelawny had seen this maneuver before, which Byron used to disguise his limp. And yet, behind the studied grief, a sort of Venetian half-mask grief, on Byron's face, was an uncomplicated sadness.

"What's this implement?" said Byron.

"To burn Shelley."

"Poor Shelley!" cried the limping lord. Gorgona, Capraji, and Elba were there in the bright noon sea, within swimmable distance it seemed.

Trelawny had first found the corpse of Edward Williams, who had sailed with Shelley into fog, in a ship designed by Byron, who'd demanded it be built according to his sketch, despite the shipwright's protests. Washed ashore miles north from Shelley, Williams had been shoeless in torn clothing, having tried to swim, while Shelley had died in shoes, undamaged clothing, and a wool coat. In a pocket of the coat, Trelawny found a ruined book of Keats's poems, and folded in this letter to you, Leya, I have found this letter:

My dear friend,

I reply, from a distant country, after an absence whose days have seemed decades, to the latest of your efforts

to subtract a fact from a dream of equal weight and yet leave a remainder of which we may make any use.

Without success, your efforts move me. They impersonate my own apprehensions of the beautiful and the just. I can also perceive in them the defects incidental to youth and impatience. These are virtues, too. What must you do?

I offer this much: that to stand in confrontation with the supernatural, to stand, not kneel, is not an act of hubris, for the supernatural is at once immense and nonexistent, both greater and less than a human, who may, if he so stands, know it far more meaningful to petition what was never there than what he has been told must be. It is not humility, but courage compounded, to petition the dark with full knowledge of what it does not contain.

All happiness attend you!
Your affectionate friend,
P. Bysshe Shelley

A soldier's spade cracked into tougher substance.

"I am overcome," said Byron. "It's a gross symbol. Poor Shelley, I am overcome. Who else will swim?" No one said they would, and he removed his coat and loped to the sea.

Ghost at the Loom

The corpse was indigo and mottled. It had Bandy arms and legs, a swollen gut. A dragoon and Trelawny assembled the furnace and lifted the corpse and packed it into the furnace with laths of resinous pine that soon burned green and gold and hissed as Byron turned in the sea to return.

Trelawny tossed a pouch of frankincense and salt, then poured a skin of wine and then a skin of oil, over the length of the corpse. He stepped back from the heat, and Byron limped out of the sea.

The corpse had split from wishbone to navel. The ribcage was open, baring to the fire and air the gray-red heart, which still held blood and did not quickly burn. The forepart of the skull broke where the spade had cracked it, and it fell into the embers. In the open skull, the brain's waters boiled.

"I should have liked to keep his skull," said Byron.

"You'd have used it as a drinking cup," Trelawny said.

"If ever I did, it would have been in honor. I defy you to say otherwise."

While I, Laon, led by mutes, ascend my bier of fire. The legs were ash. The lower skull had blackened.

Byron pointed, seawater thinly pouring from his cuff. "See, though, his heart is whole." It seared and bubbled, and the soldiers stood all at a distance with their backs to the pyre out of respect.

"For Mary, then, not you." Trelawny reached into the ribcage with the wineskin wrapped around his hand

and (had the soldiers witnessed this, they would have quarantined him) wrapped the smoking heart in the wineskin and oilskin.

Soldiers slung metal poles under the furnace, lifted it, and cooled it in the sea. A steam plume shot six heights of men above the surf. It formed a loose shape like a robe with wandering sleeves, then scattered.

Shelley, the night before sailing, had said, "If I die tomorrow, I shall have lived to be older than my father. I am ninety years of age."

◇◇◇◇◇◇◇◇◇◇◇◇

Mama's in the kitchen, cooking corncobs, cutting skin from salmon. Everything here is "normal." I guess because someone outside us is inside the house, the rarest event. Your room is closed, but not with you in it. You're right here talking to Mama about when the two of you yesterday photographed Eyeball in a trashbag in the backyard. Poor Eyeball, poisoned by Mama with who knows what household concoction.

"I'm salty," says John. "Don't you even begin to be scared. Do you have a map of the Pacific?"

"Atlas, somewhere."

"You're a farmer."

Such a simple sorrow, the death of a dog. I'm overfull of it, a sorrow too simple to need to describe.

The corn water boils.

"You're a farmer, Dagon."

"Sure. What should I do?"

"Dagon," he whispers.

"I know, John, I don't know anything."

"I'm a sailor. Just two years ago myself and Jacob Minus, Esq., cabin-cruised Miami to Sao Paolo, not a single altercation."

"I have to call Paro tonight if you'll let me. She has some drums of mine. I'll have to send some money to my mother, and I'll need my drums to pay for food."

"I have your drugs—I mean I pay for your food. Shut up, shut up. Don't call anyone. Call me. Go ahead, call my phone. I'm 'Paro.' That's just what you call me, your old pet name for me. Jesus, be truthful, you infant. You love women like men do. You're merely bored, a decadent. It's my job to organize your entertainments, and we're going to cross the whole Pacific. We'll be like your English friends, but longer distances. You can't say no to that, because I'm salty."

Mama's at the table. "Do you want to pick the music for dinner?"

"Leya picks." I nod at Mama, who looks at me carefully, full of something like convictions that, if said aloud, will cease to be convictions. Then, full of equally careful adjustments, she's looking at John. She nods and goes back to the stove.

"What the *fuck!*" he whispers. "That was deeply pathological, the two of you."

You're at the piano now, visible here from the table, not playing yet, posed, as if for a painter, but something is wrong. I've tried to fit too much into this letter. It will rip apart. Your form is too frail to contain all that I must have wanted you to, and now time's passing quickly, I'm eating and talking and turning out lights, and what is this sense (it comes and goes with threads of frost in the spooked nerves in my back and neck) that I must

Ghost at the Loom

go to Cairo *right now*, or Samarkand, or Lima, anywhere neglected in the readings/travels you've unsayingly assigned since I left California the first time, that I must somehow lie down in the central artery of all unknown cities collapsing together on Earth, lie down on my back and sleep and wake up to see No One beside me there with your face.

I'm near the paper wall again. Please, Leya, ask Mama to wait right here. I have to follow the wall away from too-vivid words I don't write here. In a negative landscape: a fold or dune, a livid smear, a curve of beach or sandstone road, and the sea pure white and vertical, a static tidal wave, no gatelike rips in it, words all over it. Oblivion is the thinnest place, between the words and wall.

Home, in my childhood bed, John asleep in the fire-and-piano room, and when you wake me, it's by reaching into the blankets and pulling my smallest toe. You're there at the foot of the bed, enunciating oddly, "I will go to Baja Mexico with you."

"I know. My plan was to take you. John set it all up. You're why I came home."

Then back onto a hypnagogic street of outdoor cafés, peopled with riderless black bicycles.

JOHN SELECTS THE ONLY female cab driver outside the Cabo San Lucas airport. She looks like a doctor (other than you, me, and Mama, *everyone* looks like a doctor, don't they?—I don't know what I mean by this, but subtly it's upsetting) and holds the door open for us. Sometimes, when I'm reading, I intake no meaning, only rhythm, then I recognize these rhythms later, in another poem, in car noise, drumming, speech. You don't like riding in the cab between me and John. I don't think you like John. I'm sorry, it is his boat.

We're at the seaport. "Anything on water's safer than your motorcycle," John is saying. "Counterarguments, concerns?"

"Is there a first-aid kit onboard?"

"Of course," he says.

"Thermometer?"

"Why not."

Then after much sauntering and inquiry, he locates the correct marina gate, at which the guards explain the coming weather or the price of fuel or harpoon guns; who knows, their English is as good as our college Latin. Our bastard Latin-Spanish must sound like the speech of idiots or atavistic priests to them. I show them my passport. John shows them his sunglasses. One of them keeps John's sunglasses. They agree the boat belongs to John's father. Now the gate is open. John presents a twenty US dollar bribe, which they accept, offended.

"That was out of sequence," I say on the pier.

"Seems like," rubbing between his hands one of the disposable towelettes he carries in his wallet (he hates touching cash), "unless I paid for not the gate but something you don't know about. Which is it? You tell me."

My boots and his shoes and your sandals on flinders of fish crates, gull feathers, hemp strands, and the shipworm-eaten wood of the pier, built by slaves of missionaries, a placard on a post beside you says in Spanish. Wind sucks up and down with the up-and-down of raggedly lived-in and unused expensive craft. It's like the fecal breath of a huge, diseased animal sleeping to death in the water.

John rudely points. "Look at that!"

A man and woman in the window of a peeling 1950s yacht kiss without urgency, half-seated on a cabin table, his arm around her hip.

"That's good," I say.

"To kiss one's wife is good. Yes. Let's." He leans.

"I'm not your wife," I remind, and so he leans away and smiles at me, then walks ahead.

They're like butterfly knives, these skimming gull shadows, flipping and folding across your face and chest and the pier. In my image drum, a huge, wood-colored horse stands at the far end of the pier. It lifts its head— it's been drinking the sea—and turns and approaches us, trotting on shadowy shanks. It stops a yacht's length away and lifts a forehoof. This is nothing, not a gesture, no communication. Speechless animals are easier to know than humans. Dogs and birds and horses do not think in symbols. Snout pointed skyward, heraldic, it barks, herds of gull shadows crying/flying from the void revealed by parted topaz teeth. Shadows flip, fold, and bloom on the wood of the pier and the sides of ships and folded sails.

"Flowers," I say, "they'll deliver flowers. You gave them twenty dollars for flowers, John. That's my guess."

"There," he says, "right there she is, the titian and ecru, middle-classically decorated. *That's* appeal, but wouldn't it be better if we had a cargo of dear friends? I should have thought of that before and made some friends."

John is sneaky. We could try to stop whatever he's doing (he's doing something to us, do you feel it?), except how? Don't get onto the boat, flee penniless through Mexico?

"What's out of sequence? This? Rider*'this?*" This is your voice behind me.

John has jumped aboard and is lowering the U.S. and Israeli flags his father flies.

"Leya, how—"

"Lift my bag." Since when do you interrupt me? I don't mind, but you startled me.

Ghost at the Loom

John's unlocking the door to below deck. "I'll locate the wine cache."

"Why is your bag so heavy?" I ask you.

"You put books from Amsterdam in it." You're pointing at the ship. "He's out of sight."

"It's fine. He only went below."

I step aboard and lift you and the bags aboard.

"Six beds!" This comes through a rubber-ringed hole in the deck, nickel-sized, by your foot.

I say, "Can you be certain you won't be upset by open ocean?"

"No."

"You won't?"

"I know about it. You have Eyeball...'s in your backpack."

"Did you see me put the jar in there?"

I keep returning in my head to Mama's wordless (but she knew we'd do this without her at last) misery during the hours leading up to our leaving, Mama sitting in your place at the piano, not playing, wearing ostentatious earrings I have never seen before, plastic or amber the color of redwood heartwood. Finally she spoke, but only: "I can't talk. I'm mute from now on."

"Did you just say *mute*?" I said to Mama.

Stop. I can't begin to consider what's between me and Mama until I am done with this letter to you.

On the boat, you say, "I looked through your back, Rider'hider."

"Did you?" But I've hidden nothing in my backpack. This book's in my jacket.

"Taste her ash."

"You tasted dog ash? Is it good?"

"Not really. I like tea and edamame. Did you bring some food for me?"

"You mean...food?"

John bounds onto the deck. "This is the curve's knee, Jesus. I am giddy as the president." He gapes at me packing a honey jar full of ash into your bag. "Now what's this business?"

"We were talking about our dead dog."

"Were we?"

"John," I explain, "when he was a child, cooked his poodle and tried a bite."

"It had been slain already, not by me," he clarifies.

Do I show pain when you squint at me? Sometimes it's like I'm no more than a figure in a crowded painting, a freak egg-with-legs in a Bosch. You blink, then walk to the stern, which faces the ocean.

"Structurally, logically, axiomatically," John continues; we seem to have missed the transition from dead dogs to this.

I am watching your small back. "What?"

John: "The moment at which the egg cell descends."

"I don't know. No opinion."

"No, not your style, I know, I know."

No land on any horizon, no seasickness. I've dragged a mattress to the bow for you. Confusion into clarity

Ghost at the Loom

into confusion: in and out of moments in which my awareness seems to hover to one side of us. The ocean, this drumskin tabula rasa sensorium surface, this worldmindmindworld, the tension of it drums my hands on the rail.

"I'm telling him," you say, "about a ship."

"Tell who? Not John."

"Not John. One of them. It goes on the water the water is made of."

"One of whom? This isn't any city, see, just water, so you don't mind if I ask more than one question here."

"It doesn't matter now how many."

"One of whom and what's the water made of?" I don't like my tone. I sound like Mama, but less confident.

"It's like an inside out."

"What's that?"

"When the water gets black with a blacker hole where the sun, it has stars in it. The ocean has stars goodbye."

"Oh...bye, Leya."

"Rider'I was telling him about the ship that won't go if they stop playing, sometimes just the trio, sometimes the orchestra to make the ship fast, and sometimes everyone sleeps but one, the cellolin, plays all night. They don't want wind at all. They're not bad people on there."

Reading, scratching notes, sketching shapes of the rhythms the clouds make...I'm almost asleep on your mattress. At some point, you've lifted my head to your lap. Your profile, seen from below, has a ship-like shape—to cut the wind, the velocity of which has been increasing. Looking past your stomach, flat, up past your chest and upborne hair, into curling cumuli, and yet, sometimes, when I look at you across the yacht, your stomach isn't flat.

You are my sister. Nothing is more delicate and harrowing than this. Human laws declare you a woman. Leya, my missing blood. A man with a beloved sister can't be a desperado. You are me, but less carved by a frightening culture—me, but rendered from chaos more graceful than mine. You are singing to me in my sleep, the song you've been singing since we left Mexico.

Six days west. "With sails," I say, "we could ride this zephyr to Asia."

"My dearest friend," says John, "east winds blow west."

"I didn't know that."

We are at the helm controls.

"Anyone knows that."

"I didn't."

"That's okay. We dodge the storms with this." A weather application on his satellite-linked laptop.

"How well does it work?"

"The Internet out here? It's spottier than ladybugs, but it will do," he says. "They've just invented it. It goes like this. First the military gets these contraptions, then the Minuses, then everybody else."

Ghost at the Loom

"Nobody," I say, "can consistently dodge storms."

"Oh no? Nobody? I'm a weather cowboy. How do you think I pay for you to take such lovely trips? The market is the weather. Look, don't I make situations for you, don't I improve you? I need you to fathom, at least, that there are, in a life, hours, sometimes whole days, when a local maximum arrives, of consciousness I mean, or not arrives but seems to constantly have just arrived. Now sometimes this happens in more than one life in the same place same time. Playwrights, certain filmmakers have tried to frame that, you know, arrest, arrest—the moment of group revelation—duration, cut-glass Duration, immediate *this*. They look at each other. You know what I'm telling you?"

Mockery and laughter maybe don't appeal to him at sea. He reads and navigates. He dodges surges on the Internet. How can the jester jest when his court is alien and drifting toward the dark?

"Who gave your baby to you, Leya?" Am I saying this aloud?

I keep thinking you've just been saying something frantically important, but if so, it happened in an anti-mnemonic moment. Picking at blanks in these ebb-states, *I am here with you* I say, but not aloud, and aren't we suffering the opposite of John's Duration? It's a slipping out to sea of pieces of us talking, blanks, the frames, like negatives, in which I see you *right here*, bits of flying paper, you (your lips are moving), also fierce protector-brother energies that slip out of my blanks-in-

place-of-hands reaching to hug you, because it's windy—
or because you've just now told me something frantically
important? But to look at an eclipse you have to use a
camera obscura. I can only hear you indirectly.

"What did you tell Mama?"

"You can tell her for me," sipping tea, a strand of
your hair in the cup.

"Am I *here* with you? Are you there, I mean?" I'm
nearly saying this aloud.

"You are little," petting my face, "good, good."

Or is this, too, what we are undergoing here,
Duration, just a very cryptic kind?

Then no more wind. Stonelike flats, apatite. A sea the
pastel green of hospital walls. My language-flooded mind
hunts Roman characters in whorls of foam and cloud, hears
broken strands of English, Karuk, Dutch, Italian in birdcries
and immethodical noise of water on the hull at night.

"Did you pour out my carbamazepine?"

John: "I thought you said you didn't use it anymore.
I thought it was for 'just in case.'"

"You threw it in the ocean?"

"I touched it not, my friend."

"Where is it, then?"

"I said, I'm not to blame. Perhaps you have been
regularly taking it."

The papery emotion folds and rips along my brain's
equator—I am yelling in his face, "We never went to
Copenhagen!"

Ghost at the Loom

"Did we not?"

I run across the deck and down the stairs. You're on my bunk. You're standing by the tiny cabin closet. Now you're fetal on the floor. I can't see motion place to place. You're just these photographs. *How old are you?* How old are you?

"Where are my pills?" I say. "Where are my pills, where are my pills?" and the wing plunges in from wherever it waits and beats on the back of my head with a sound like sobbing.

You're holding your hand across your mouth. Your belly is round, flat, round.

"How many did you eat—them all?" I yell into your ear, "them all?" The wall is flipping, folding, ripping, yelling: "I can hear me yelling, Leya! Writing to you, Leya, make yourself throw up!" In the past present, hearing me asking you, "Where are my pills and the wing plunges in?"

"Rider'I don't want a baby."

So, though I'm not ready (in this panic, there is no light, no sound, something delicate is being bludgeoned with a mass like a ten-ton idiot brain, and something delicate is made of filaments of stories I don't tell, symbols and symmetries I can't tie into place; I don't feel horror or exactly guilt, though it's I who am bludgeoning, over and over), the overdetermined event has arrived on schedule. Reach a certain age and the structure of time collapses, back to the nearest metastable point, back before we were grown, or before we were born, I don't know; all the myths of He Who Loses Her are crashing onto me and catapulting ignes fatui down the path of your unsaid request, this Eurydicean call for my life, my short life summed up as a rescue mission, certain to fail.

A SWINGING BOOM OF LIGHT across the sea in a shallow arc struck a bipedal form dressed in black strings, with a cipher, Ø, in place of a head. It stretched and cracked its fingers, back, and wrists—knots and coin-shaped beads on the strings knocked together, and from no direction, from the abstract background, came a noise like bent wind chimes, like the background noise of mental disorganization—and with its long-toed feet, as black as the sky, it braced against the inner walls of a canoe/scythe (Scythian canoe?) for balance.

The sharp prow curved higher than the hood of the woman in the stern, who faced away, out toward the sea. She held a scull of a slaggish, melted, re-hardened material. She held it absolutely still, the canoe motionless. No moon, no tide. A tailored, hooded coat revealed her narrowness, her hiplessness. She sat straightbacked in her backward cockpit, surrounded by instruments. It was like the cockpit of an old biplane, except that every instrument was an identical altimeter at zero.

Bandy'cipher stepped uncertainly toward her. Bones or something bonelike clicked and cracked inside its knees. It splayed its boyish toes in the bilge. The sea was full of nebulae and forfeit stars *while I, Ø, led by mutes—hello?*

Dis knot make noise.

Shall rob thee of the face thou wearest—Bandy'cipher placed its fingers on the shoulder of her coat. It hurt. It looked at its fingers. Dozens of tiny cuts. A belted, robelike coat of interwoven braids of dark plant fiber. It stared at the coat from an inch away. A maggot or a horse's eyelash hooked out of the fiber.

"Turn, please," said the Bandy'cipher.

She refused or couldn't *make yourself throw up*—*for I now, gone beside thee, thaw.* The stern was low and pointed out to sea.

—it was language in the water, jetsam, entrails of aborted verses, wavering a hand's length under, impossible to translate well from Water into English, but the Bandy'cipher tried:

> *I, Ø, tried. Dis hole nocturne*
> *shall rob thee of the facts thou*
> *warpest. Unreturn, for I now,*
> *gone insane beside thee, thaw*
> *in thy brainwater, burn in thy urn.*

These languages that compose abandoned worlds are supple, alterable at the level of the grain or droplet, letter, mark. The cipher pulled her shoulders gently. She refused or couldn't move. The cipher said, "Hello, return?" and turned her by the shoulders roughly toward the lighthouse on the shore that, after further study, was a lattice tower that, after further study, was an obelisk with the obsolete function of warding away low-flying craft (no flights come here anymore), and the scythe turned as her shoulders turned, so the stern's path in the sea described a quarter-circle. Then the prow moved in a quarter-circle to correct this, because, according to the laws of psychosis, faceless women in canoes must always face out to sea.

The cipher pulled her harder, and the scythnoe turned a half-circle, scattering the language, which immediately recomposed (but had been warped and shaken into looser composition) as the water stilled:

I Ø
led by mutes
disrobe thee
of the place thou
writ in what
for you'l now
gone in thy brain
thaw in thy bury
me here burn
in Ø

How long did the cipher stare over the side? This language, was it necessary? Presumably it could be warped by hand or keel countless times, making less and less sense, or more, but either way, why stay and play at such a narrow art, mere entrails in the water. Mere no one had written it.

The air traffic control tower had a needle spire, and in the needle's eye, an industrial torch, a gold S with a line through it, burned without flickering, and the beam roved on the sea, the city, the delta, the sea, and as the cipher pulled and pulled the silent woman's shoulders, the scythnoe scissored an inch at a time toward shore. *I'm going to put my finger in your throat, okay?*

"What is this, wheat?" the cipher said, bending to bite with its front two teeth at the nape of her hood, "this fiber, nn—amaranth, moly, carbon paper?"

Something bumped the bottom of the craft. The cipher, leaning overboard, observed the underwater slope up to the beach was full of office chairs or maybe thrones. Half in sand, warped gold, highbacked, cameoed, kelp and plush tatters, extension cords snaking out of the legs—powerstrips, converters, batteries, bits, the last, infinitesimal sparks, abwatts: a cipher is sensitive enough to feel these in its spine.

"No one taught you to talk," said the cipher and walked ashore and up the beach toward the delta.

Volcanic fallout, old but warm, composed the bed in which the marble pebbles of the beach, with dog's- and snake's and cat's-eye slashes on them, nictitated in the passing beam. The cipher moved toward the delta, the control tower, and the city with its high walls and renegade populace.

The populace, they've toppled all the statues. One can smell it from the beach—they're burning libraries and symphony halls—the scent of lost data, with notes of violinsmoke and pianosmoke. It is the hour after the hour of the renegade who, having waited for the wind to be behind him, sprints onto the worldstage and flings a goblet of poison over the

Ghost at the Loom

astonished royal family. One drop on the tip of the nose worms its way to the brain.

The only lightsource other than the tower and the deepsky objects in the ocean was a cookfire by the river's edge, and entering the light of it, the cipher said, "Hello."

Most of the figure's face was gone. The remainder was sketched by an amateur. "I'm cooking eels in here." It poked at a pot with a long fork.

"Did they take her past you here?" the cipher asked.

"Not she in the——"

"No," looking back at the woman's back (she floated at the waterline), "the other one, my sister."

"Other one, two, four. No one taught me numbers here. I'm cooking eels."

"Fuck," the cipher said in despair and frustration.

"Yes yes," the cooker said, "my heart aches, a drowsy numbness pains my sense."

The cipher pointed at the city. "Is she there?"

"Something like...something like..."

"Whatthinglike!" except the cipher's cry was broken down into its sub-syllabic particles and scattered, made inaudible, by a low grind, like a generator's, from behind the distant walls.

The cooker of eels: "Something like...we've tested every recipe and have selected some of those that have eels in them in some form or other, with Bordeaux and hemlock for instance, for eels are now at their best and are to be considered foremost among remedies for the *tic douloureux*."

"What about for *swollen belly?*"

"Help me stack some people," said the cooker and stooped and took a stone shaped like an Oxford English Dictionary from the fire and drifted twenty paces to the riverbank to stack the stone atop three larger stones. Then the cooker returned and repeated the action.

The cipher, lacking any manifest alternative, began to help. In its long-fingered hands, each stone was as light as hair.

With a sky without heavenly bodies, time must be measured by rotations of the control tower's beam. This was a time of work, of hope and reconstruction.

Cairns along the river turned to ziggurats, the cipher and the cooker slept under the sky, and as the wind velocity increased, they spoke of "compassion, ardor, equity, brotherhood," etc., on and on, and on all complex surfaces, for example the inner whorls of their fingerprints on the stones of the ziggurats, it seemed a sort of *Epistles to the No Ones* had been written, but, upon further study, it was merely nothing.

Wandering upriver, after many full rotations of the beam, the cipher came to a landing with scrapes from keels on flat, brain-colored stone. Steel bolts, around the bases of which fathom-lines were tied, impaled the stone along the water. *Each of these lines is a thought.* The cipher knelt and took one in its hand and pulled hand over hand, generating parabolic ripples, coiling the line around its arm, until the thought came up that

Ghost at the Loom

it was time to cross the river, and the line's end gyrated in the wind.

"Ferry me?"

"For a rhyme," said a beautiful, bull-torsoed man with a precisian's underfed face, "for with aught else will our souls interknit."

"I don't think Ø has a 'soul,'" the cipher tried. "Ø has no...core shifts thought else will ptower gold enburn it?"

"Not abysmal, not impressive," said the man, and threw a blank across the water to the shore.

The cipher hopped across, pulling the bplank in behind it, laying it across the gondola, a bench, and while the man sang microtonally and sculled, the cipher watched over the side: below the ripples, hands, some with light-catching rings, some dancing in Carnatic style, male and female, passed as fish. Knotted strings from the cipher's sleeve trailed in the water. Along its long spine, it felt the delta current changing, flowing through a potential difference—the cipher reported: "Captain, I measure 1.6181999 abwysts."

"That ought to be enough to get us to the other shore."

"What ship is this?"

"The *Childe Variable*," said the captain proudly. "Once she even had a set of sails, but those all tattered into nothing," and the wind increased, and the papery mind of the cipher was blown to the back of its skull, the stern of the ship, the end of a small, irrecoverable world.

"Did someone get hurt?" The wind had slowed. The cipher's mind returned. "I heard someone crying," it said to the captain.

"Fair night, creature. Is it not?"

"I guess it is. I guess it is an okay night for being on a boat." The cipher was ill. Between the delta and the sea, some wakes and sleeps ago, it had drunk from a stagnant pond with a film of salted ash.

"Trust nothing you digest," professed the *Childe*'s captain. "Trust *me*. I knew one like you, who to this city came some months ago." His scull was gone. He leaned on a long caduceus, a crutch. "Observe the wildness at the center of the river. It will spirit a weak swimmer to sea, to drown, or if his belly is swollen with wind, to cast up after Aneternity on the Shores o' Foblivion!"

"Need to throw up," said the cipher.

1, 1, 2 and 3, or Ø, 1, 1, 2 or 3 and forth, the captain stomped a pattern on the deck. The cipher tried to match the captain's pattern, but the beats that were the ands and ors did not compute, and something cradled next to logic broke. *First-aid kits don't have stomach pumps!* The ship sped toward the city.

"Once again upon the water!" yelled the captain as they passed the river's middle, spume spraying at the prow. "The current bound beneath, a steed that knows its rider! Welcome to the roar!"

I allowed the captain a brotherly kiss goodbye and waded through the shallows to the shore and tried not to look at

Ghost at the Loom

or listen to a homeless creature crouched there, rocking in a heap of rainbow paper garbage, mumbling, "Riggid, ragged, rawntawn, don't look at me, me riggid rig—be safe in di ode drumhead, rig rag headdrum—" on and on, and in the wind behind my head, I felt the future-presence of the wing, beating to the ragbeat of the riggid rawn.

I ran through a meadow of petrified flowers, then onto a slope of flowerless stone. The obelisk beam, where it pooled on the jags and spindles of the igneous terrain, sometimes would remain a long time, arguing a deeper image, the light as-if-digging, surgically opening the hillside (*like a volcano's meteor-breathing chasm, whence the oracular vapour is hurled up which lonely men drink wandering in their youth*, as Bysshe once wrote in tiny script across my doppelgänger's forehead in the mirror in a bad dream), opening a tunnel ringed with asphodelphs and irises, but when I tried to dip my toe into it, it was closed.

I crossed the glacis toward the city walls. Embedded in hardened pools of slag and in the wrinkled gray clay of the glacis were meteoric nickel-iron pentagrams. Some impaled the path by one or two points. Others were fitted with wires and diodes. Some acquired a sixth point when kicked. I picked one up and noticed fine etchings of breasts and genitals on the metal. So this was the elephant graveyard where symbols no longer symbolic came to die.

I was at the wall. If the sea was west, a muted jazz trumpet in the east blew. Then a deeper, rounder horn sounded from a nearer east, atop the wall, which I had touched, a wall of interlocking ingots of a dark, unnameable material. I followed these toward the sea. *I'm very clear right now why are you crying Rider'why so little you forgot to write a hundred more pages of we were little*—here the curving wall extended from the sand into the water.

At the waterline, a man in elegant black clothes removed his canted hat. "Home."

"Home?"

He nodded. "I am horribly upset, but find it difficult to show you." The towerlight struck him. "And, proud sufferer, who are you?"

"I fucked it all up."

"I think," he placed a hand on me, "these strong words may never pass away. If I had known we would attack the very Art designed to free us..." the hand on my chest was fragile, the voice full of self-doubt and pain, "for it seems Liberty and Time have broken Beauty on the rack of threads, brother, but I *will* let you into the belly," stepping aside, "for it doesn't matter now."

A door in the wall opened across the motionless water. I pulled the latch and stepped through.

"Except," said the horribly upset man, "have you no desire to speak of History awhile?"

"I'm sorry, but I don't have time," I said and again stepped through.

Ghost at the Loom

"And yet the true poetry of Rhome lived in its institutions. Should I let you into the hospital then?"

At his side, I stood outside the city still. "I'm looking for my sister."

"Hwat?"

"My ragged drumhead. My *mnemomnos*. Do you understand?" I said.

"I understand you still harbor a mote of hompe, which I have not."

I stepped through, this time with success, onto a road along a harbor. Ships were aflame. A white van lay on its side in the road. From the water rose a stench of silver nitride, and in the firelight, barrels and boxes marked TEA and HERE LIES ONE floated amid buoys and canoes. In the artificial harbor's opening, between the ringwall's head and tail, silhouettes of battleships could be discerned. A cannonball shattered a pier, and I stood awhile after in a quietness of slow fire, sea on hulls, and faraway horns.

A flash lit up a fleet of hundreds, arrayed into the ocean's distance, and another ball destroyed another pier. A tiny ship came unmoored. The road, too, showed evidence of bombardment: between my feet, between two cobbles, was a patch of starless void. I poked a toe into it and the toe came out anaesthetized. On my knees, I examined whether a whole head might fit through the gap in the road, but certain acts can't be committed with an audience, and an old man leaned against a warehouse, so I stood and limped to him.

316

"Back up," he said. "I dislike your color."

A nearby house collapsed into a pyre of reeds. A ball rolled from the pyre and stopped beside us. It had lines and craters and appeared to be a global map.

"Of Tug Foot?" I inquired.

"Plutomars," the man corrected.

A ship's mast blasted apart, and the deck caught fire. It sounds violent, but it was all gentle, not a war, a pantomime, a quiet place. I stepped into the shadow of the warehouse.

"Hey, these warehouses are no protection. Go get underground." He removed a weapon from his vest and began to load it with copper spheres from his pockets. For a moment, he studied my head and torso and lowered his eyelids and then held out some spheres in his palm for me to study, on each an engraved symbol: J, Æ, Z, ™, Δ, Ω, &, and some Chinese ideograms.

"They're slow," I said. "They could have bombed the city into ash into the sky by now."

"Yes," said the man, "the war of leisure."

"So I have a lot of time to find her?"

"No. I didn't say that." With his thumb, he spun the miniature cartwheel on his gun.

"But you *are* here to guard the port? You can keep them from landing a little while longer?" But he didn't seem to hear me, so I made my mouth smaller. "Who are dey den? Me thought di revolution was over."

Quietly, a gondola exploded, and he clapped the weapon on his palm. "Who are they? Who are you? A little boy?"

Ghost at the Loom

"Which way go den?"

"I don't like your arrogant tone." The hook of his thumb pointed down, behind his back. "Follow this vein. It's silver oil. Her uterus is down that hill."

Quicksilver globules scurried from between two warehouses and down an alley with no doors or windows.

"Thanks, thanks," I said. "It isn't oil, it's mercury. Here, you can have this." I gave him my anaesthetized toe, which had fallen off, and he loaded it into the wheel.

Following the vein, the alley spread into a street. The harbor blasts diminished. If the sea was west, a boil of metallic arrhythms increased in the east, and it sounded like *you don't get it, she swallowed her* horns, torsion, battering, and whining giant hinges.

It was all quiet though. Something unseen brushed my legs and hurried back the way I'd come, a dog judging by the sound of toeclaws clicking on cobbles. I heard horses, too. I was on one of the great avenues, looking for a hiding place.

I was a shadow in a phonebooth when a file of cavalry articulated millipedelike past, trampling the vein, which reformed, and I noticed a line of red glass (above which was a helpful blue graffito: 108°) had been wrought, perpendicular to the vein, into the avenue outside the booth.

Of course I picked up the phone. "Hello?"

A confused voice: "If, in swollowed riggid ragged tongue, the serpent that constricts all glimmage drummers with its length, you can't go home, till Hope creates from its own wreck the thing it contemplates, be 1, 1, 2 or 3, for 1—" *For I now, gone.*

I hung it up and picked it up. "I'm here."

A smaller, worried voice: "Are you the messenger?"

"I think so, yes."

"Then where is your horse?"

At the city center, all streets opened to a sloping plaza, circular with painted stones: a sixteen-point compass without a needle, the control tower being outside the city. At the plaza's center was a tent of dirty paper, and the vein of mercury, which split the compass's west-symbol into a pair of vees, ran in through a rip in the side of the tent.

This tent, I knew, was an attempt to rig a shelter from thousands of cuttings and tearings of typeset and handwritten pages. It took me a long time to enter. I knew what such an action was supposed to mean and therefore didn't mean at all, and so I stood there in the belly/cortex/city center, no one watching, no one in the balconies and loges on the perimeter buildings, no text on the tent's exterior; the text-sides all faced inward. I wanted to cheat, to read the letters through the tent like through an envelope held up to the sun, but suns were obsolete.

At last, like a Jew in a graveyard, I picked up a stone, off which some mercury beaded and fell, and put it on the tent, which sagged in that spot. Even this gesture felt

Ghost at the Loom

false, unworthy, so I simply went in through the rip and sat and held my head and then my ribs.

The need for a grand metaphorical climax pulsed so desperately in here that the brim of the well the mercury ran into was a beating, pulled-thin heart, fastened in a ring.

You you, it beat, *you you, you you—*

No tell, bermemb, bermemberem, no tell—

It beat until the past pulled thin into a ring into the present and I dive into the navel of the city, heart twined garlandwise around my skull—it flies off as I fall, the tubular walls clenching and unclenching, down to a dry dark summer place, a dry metal smell...

I've been down here a long time in a peace of no more riddle, no more cipher. Sitting very still, my back against the rusty ribcage of an old piano at the back of a runoff pipe built into the hill. Until, in the circular view of the valley, a man is visible. He goes on foot and radiates, in equal parts, guardianship and hopelessness. He plays a little drum, and children follow him. The line of children stretches out of view.

◇◇◇◇◇◇◇◇◇◇◇◇

WHAT DOES ONE DO when the question's already at rest, when the minds ceased to wander, picking up stones and flowers, before we were born? Could I, in some earlier time, have been a handshaking, bearhugging, lovemaking man, a companion of red-blooded women and men? Outrageous to wonder if I might become one now? I would not overstep. I would start with a handshake. Who decides if I'm to be provisionally accepted?

Windlessness is not a problem when you run on batteries and fossil fuel. I gather up my blank mind here and there from the deck and *go to sleep, I say, been out here long enough.*

If it's taken me longer than others to get out from under the twentieth century's (here, ideally, an adjective goes, but none fits, except maybe a hole in the page or a thousand pairs of opposites, each word written over the next, until the total is an inky core with spidery edges from longer words) fullness and emptiness, it's because I tried the door to the nineteenth first, or if that's too neat, too grandiose, because I kept trying the door to your room that's been closed since I remember.

I feel as if kicked in the back, headfirst through a back door that nevertheless leads out to the front of the house, or the front of the ship, or wherever I live without you, without Mama.

But I'm not alone on the ship. It seems there still is John. Despite all antic speed and flippancy, despite Anxiety, there is a great easiness in him, a casually won adulthood, almost as if you had left him, too, but decades ago, before he was born, and so it didn't hurt and doesn't now. He steers without a tiller, with a laptop wired to the helm controls.

—your brother

◇◇◇◇◇◇◇◇◇◇◇◇

My dear Trelidori [sic],

I've typed and redacted poor R's epic poem such that it now reads as a gentleman's memoir in prose. I've altered only surnames (I hope you like them) and only those not fiddled with already by the poet. Because, you know, some of us have names to protect, and I plan to publish something of my own, tremendous, soon.

It was all butchered into pieces with I think ideas for alternative enjambments, ///, which I've removed, except from certain rhymey bits. You'll see I've also left some bits in verse to vindicate my editorial choice of prose. Maps, unintelligible diagrams, deliberately blank pages, doodles, etc., having no artistic merit, have been cut, along with several marathons of readable but crossed out lines. For reader-friendliness, I've put into italics what are clearly thoughts, despite my distaste for "stream of consciousness."

Okay, I confirm the events he depicts. I was witness to those involving the canard I call Minus. As for those I did not witness, I aver the madman he calls Sonnenreich is not a liar, for he does not know how lying works. My proof? Look how helpless he is when constrained to spin fictions, to wit, the screwy bit about his mother in Montana or the hackneyed fooled-you-it's-a-dream of vomit in the shower in old Amsterdam, although I guess it wasn't fiction per se when he channeled Shelley et alii, for (I'm going off the one time I had wine and dainties with them) he portrayed fairly well their thoughts and mannerisms and was not unfaithful or confused when forced to "lie" about them as they would have "lied" about themselves. He must have known his "sister" had a quail-egg of a tumor or what you *will*. Why else chaperone her all around the Earth? That's what you do with dying young people, whether or not they are objectively——well, you know. Whoa, I mean, where is her passport? That obliterated my helpful suggestion we have her cremated in Honolulu. He is not a *liar*. I know the bulk of it was written when he was not yet wholebrainedly mad!

The very style of this letter proves how well he portrayed me, especially at the teepee in the Mendocino coastal hills, where we ate peyote, a fraudulent entheogen, hardly a pixie's tit or nostril to be noticed, nope, and no euphoria for the poor.

You'll relish making certain the attached manuscript is published (via your stupendous connections to the bourgeois presses). Give my love and middle finger to the English, Jews, Scotch, French, Americans, bards, elders, reviewers, theorestheticians, and resentimentalists. And lastly this: however tempting, best to not include this letter as an endnote, as I've always had such difficulty communicating sadness. I defend myself, but this defense of poetry needs no defending.

In the hope of your successes and my own, I remain most sincerely yours. Believe me,

John Minus [sic]

Sumbawa Besar, Indonesia, July, 1822